"You have pl[aced me in an] impossible position. I cannot turn you in without risking being found guilty by association, but neither can I in all conscience simply abandon you."

Rafe was not a man given to chivalry. He was not a man much given to impulsive action either, but Henrietta Markham's endearing courage, her genuine horror at the accusations leveled against her, and the very real dangers which she faced, roused him now to both. Whether he wanted to be or not, he was involved in this farce.

"I have no choice. I'll help you," he said, nodding to himself. It was the only way.

"Help me to do what?"

"Whatever it takes to clear your name."

"I am perfectly capable of doing that myself," Henrietta said indignantly—and quite contrarily, because for a moment there, when he had offered, her heart had leapt in relief.

* * *

Rake with a Frozen Heart
Harlequin® Historical #1088—May 2012

Praise for Marguerite Kaye

"Kaye delights readers with a heated seduction
and fiery games that burn up the pages when
her heroine takes *The Captain's Wicked Wager.*"
—*RT Book Reviews*

"A spellbinding Regency romance with a difference,
The Governess and the Sheikh is another winner
for Marguerite Kaye!"
—*Cataromance.com*

"Kaye closes her brilliant Princes of the Desert trilogy,
in which Regency Roses meet and fall in love
with desert sheikhs. Book three is irresistible,
with its fantastical kingdom, all-powerful prince and
the allure of the forbidden. Sensual, ravishing and funny.
A must for all lovers of sheikh romance."
—*RT Book Reviews* on *The Governess and the Sheikh*

MARGUERITE KAYE

Rake
WITH A FROZEN HEART

3 1336 09890 7836

TORONTO NEW YORK LONDON
AMSTERDAM PARIS SYDNEY HAMBURG
STOCKHOLM ATHENS TOKYO MILAN MADRID
PRAGUE WARSAW BUDAPEST AUCKLAND

Recycling programs
for this product may
not exist in your area.

ISBN-13: 978-0-373-29688-0

RAKE WITH A FROZEN HEART

Copyright © 2012 by Marguerite Kaye

MARGUERITE KAYE

Born and educated in Scotland, Marguerite Kaye originally qualified as a lawyer but chose not to practice. Instead, she carved out a career in I.T. and studied history part-time, gaining a first-class honors and a master's degree. A few decades after winning a children's national poetry competition, she decided to pursue her lifelong ambition to write, and submitted her first historical romance to Harlequin Mills & Boon. They accepted it, and she's been writing ever since.

You can contact Marguerite through her website at www.margueritekaye.com.

Chapter One

Sussex—May 1824

The early morning mist was just beginning to clear as he turned Thor, his magnificent black stallion, towards home, taking the shortcut through the long yew-tree walk that bordered the formal gardens of Woodfield Manor. The bright sunlight of an early English summer shafted down through the tall trees, causing the dew on the grass to sparkle as if strewn with a myriad of tiny diamonds. The earthy scent of freshly disturbed soil and roots churned up by Thor's prancing hooves mingled with the heady perfume of the honeysuckle, which roamed untrained around the trunks of the stately yews. It was a perfect morning, the prelude to what would undoubtedly be a beautiful day.

The Right Honourable Rafe St Alban, Earl of Pentland, Baron of Gyle and master of all he surveyed was, however, completely oblivious to the glories of nature, which assailed him from all sides. Mentally drained after another sleepless night, physically exhausted after his strenuous early morning gallop, his only interest was in falling into the welcoming arms of Morpheus.

Reining his horse in, Rafe dismounted to unlatch the wrought-iron gates, which opened on to the gravelled side path leading directly to his stables. The tall, perfectly proportioned man and the huge ebony horse made a striking pair, each in their own way glorious examples of blue-blooded pedigree, perfect specimens of toned and honed muscle and sinew at the peak of physical perfection. Rafe's skin glowed with a healthy lustre. His raven-black hair shone in the sunlight, the severe lines of his Stanhope crop emphasising his faultless profile, the angle of his cheekbones highlighted by the flush of exertion from the break-neck gallop across the downs. The bluish hue of stubble only served to accentuate a strong jaw and very white teeth.

Byronic, is how one infatuated young lady had breathlessly described him, a compliment that Rafe dismissed with his customary crack of sardonic laughter. Though his handsome countenance and fabulous wealth made him one of society's most eligible bachelors, even the most determined ladies on the catch wilted under his aloof stare and acerbic wit—which suited Rafe very well, since he had no interest at all in leg-shackling himself for a second time. He'd had enough of marriage to last him a lifetime. Several lifetimes, in fact.

'Nearly home now, old friend,' he murmured, patting the horse's sweating flank. Thor tossed his massive head, expelling a cloud of warm air from his nostrils, as anxious as his owner for the warmth of his sleeping quarters. Deciding to walk the short distance to the house rather than remount, Rafe shrugged off his riding coat and slung it casually over his shoulder. Having no expectations of meeting anyone this early, he had come out wearing neither hat, waistcoat nor neckcloth. The clean white folds of his linen shirt clung to the perspiration on his back, the open neck at the front revealing a sprinkling of hair on a muscled chest.

The gate swung soundlessly back on its well-oiled springs and Rafe urged his horse forwards, but Thor pawed at the grass and snorted. In no mood for playfulness, Rafe tugged on the reins again, more sharply this time, but the stallion refused to move, giving a high whinny.

'What's spooked you?' Scanning their immediate surrounds in the expectation of seeing a rabbit or a fox peering out from the deep ditch that ran parallel to the path, instead he saw a shoe. A lady's shoe. A small leather pump, slightly scuffed at the toe, attached to a very shapely ankle clad in eminently practical wool. With a muffled exclamation, which expressed more annoyance than concern, Rafe looped his horse's reins round the gatepost and strode over to peer into the ditch.

Lying lengthways on her back, and either dead or deeply unconscious, was the body of a young woman. She was clad in a serviceable round gown of brown worsted, buttoned high at the neck. She wore no hat or pelisse, and her chestnut hair had unravelled from its pins to fan out behind her, where the ditchwater had soaked it, turning its curling ends almost black, like a dark halo. The face revealed, when Rafe cautiously brushed back the obscuring reeds, was stripped of colour, marble-white and ghostly. With her arms folded protectively over her bosom, the overall impression she gave was of a prosaically dressed effigy, the image marred only by the awkward angle of the little foot that had first betrayed her presence.

Casting his coat aside, Rafe knelt down at the edge of the ditch, noting with irritation the water seep into his riding breeches. He could detect no movement, not even a flicker from beneath the closed lids. Leaning over further, he tentatively lowered his head to place his ear close to her face. A faint whisper of breath on his cheek betrayed the first glimmer of life. Grasping one slim wrist, he was relieved to find a pulse beating, faintly but steadily. Where had she come from? More importantly, what the *hell* was she doing lying in his ditch?

Rafe got to his feet again, absently noticing the green patches on his breeches, which would have his valet tutting in dismay, and pondered his options. The easiest course would be to leave her here, return to the house and send a couple of the stable hands to recover her. He eyed the recumbent form appraisingly, his frown accentuating the upward slant of his brows. No, whatever she was doing here, he could not in conscience walk away from her. She looked like Ophelia. Something about the angle of that little foot of hers made her seem horribly vulnerable. And she was but a slight thing, after all, hardly worth the trouble of summoning two men when he had his horse. Resignedly, Rafe set about removing her from her temporary resting place.

'That will be all, thank you, Mrs Peters. I'll call if I need any further assistance.'

The words, so faint they seemed to be coming from the end of a long tunnel, penetrated the dense fog engulfing Henrietta's mind. She moaned. It felt as if someone was squeezing her skull with some medieval instrument of torture. She tried to raise her hand to her forehead, but her arm would not comply, lying heavy on her chest as if weighted down. White-hot sparks of stabbing pain forced her eyelids open, but the swirling collage of colour that she then encountered made her close them again immediately. Now her head felt as if it were being pounded by a blacksmith's hammer. The painful throbbing was unbearable.

A welcome coolness descended on her brow and the pain abated somewhat. Lavender, she could smell lavender. This time when she tried to move, her arm cooperated. Clutching the compress, Henrietta opened her eyes again. The world tilted and the room swam before her. She scrunched her eyes closed, then, breathing deeply and counting to five, resolutely opened them, ignoring the siren call of black, comforting unconsciousness.

Starched sheets. Feather pillows. A warming pan at her feet. Damask hangings overhead. She was in bed, but in a bedchamber that was completely foreign to her. A bright fire burned in a modern grate and light streamed in through a small gap in the curtains which had been drawn across the windows. The room was furnished in the first style of elegance, with pale-yellow tempered walls and darker-gold window hangings. A lurching wave of nausea swept over her. She *could* not be sick in such pristine surroundings. With a truly heroic effort of will, Henrietta swallowed hard and forced herself upright.

'You're awake.'

She started. The voice had a rich, deep timbre. A seductive quality. It was unequivocally male. Obscured by the bed curtain, she had not noticed his presence. Shrinking back against the pillows, Henrietta pulled the covers high up to her neck, realising as she did so that she was clad only in her undergarments. The compress dropped from her head on to the silk coverlet. It would stain, she thought rather distractedly. 'Don't come any closer or I'll scream.'

'Do your worst,' the man replied laconically, 'for all you know I may already have done mine.'

'Oh!' His tone was amused, rather than threatening. Completely disconcerted, Henrietta blinked owlishly. Then, as her vision cleared, she gulped. Standing in front of her was quite the most beautiful man she had ever seen. Tall, dark and really quite indecently handsome, he was a veritable Adonis. Ink-dark hair ruthlessly cropped revealed a bone structure flawless in its symmetry. Winged brows. Hooded eyes that were a curious shade of blue—or was it grey? Like the sky on a stormy night. He was in shirt sleeves and had not shaved, but this slightly dishevelled state served only to emphasise his physical perfection. She knew she was staring, but she could not tear her eyes away. 'Who are you? What on earth are you doing here in this—this bedchamber? With me?'

Rafe allowed his gaze to drift over the damsel in distress. She was clutching at the sheet as if it were her last defence, looking at his coatless body as if he were half-naked, her thoughts written large on her face.

He could not resist toying with her. 'I can't imagine. Can you?'

Henrietta gulped. The obvious answer was shockingly appealing. She was in her underwear. He looked as if he had not finished dressing. Or undressing? Did he mean it? Had they—had *he*? A *frisson*, a shiver of heat, made her close her eyes. No! She would have remembered *that*! Not that she had much idea what *that* was precisely, but she was certain that she would have remembered it. He was unforgettable.

So he was teasing her, then? *Wasn't he?* She slanted him a look from under her lashes. Her gaze clashed with his and she looked hurriedly away. No. Greek gods did not descend from the heavens to seduce slightly plump young ladies with hair hanging down their backs like rats tails and smelling—Henrietta sniffed cautiously— yes, there was no getting away from it, smelling slightly of ditch water. Absolutely not. Even if they did imply…

As his gaze drifted deliberately down to where the sheet was tucked under her chin, Henrietta felt heat flood her cheeks. A quirk of his eyebrow and his eyes met hers. Her blush deepened. She felt as if she had just failed some unspoken test and couldn't help wishing that she hadn't. She tilted her chin defiantly. 'Who are you?'

He raised an eyebrow. 'Shouldn't I be asking you that question? You are, after all, a guest, albeit an uninvited one, in my home.'

'Your home?'

'Precisely. My home. My bedchamber. My bed.' Rafe waited, but to his surprise the young lady seemed to have done, for the moment, with acting the shrinking violet. 'You are in Woodfield Manor,' he conceded.

'Woodfield Manor!' It was the large estate that bordered her employer's. The large estate owned by— 'Good grief, are you the earl?'

'Indeed. Rafe St Alban, the Earl of Pentland, at your service.' Rafe made a sketchy bow.

The earl! She was in a bedchamber with the notorious earl, and she could quite see, could see very, very clearly, just exactly why his reputation was so scandalous. Henrietta clung to the bedclothes like a raft, fighting the impulse to pull them completely over her head and burrow deep down in the luxurious softness of the feather bed. 'I am pleased to make your acquaintance, my lord. I am Henrietta Markham.' The absurdity of the situation struck her suddenly. She felt an inappropriate desire to laugh. 'Are you sure you're the earl, only—no, of course if you say you are, you must be.'

Rafe's mouth twitched. 'I'm fairly sure who I am. What makes you think I might not be?'

'Nothing. Only—well, I did not expect—your reputation, you know…' Henrietta felt her face colouring.

'What reputation would that be?' He knew perfectly well, of course, but it would be amusing to see just how, exactly, she would phrase it. There was something about her that made him want to shock. To disconcert. Perhaps it was her eyes, wide-spaced and clear-gazing, the colour of cinnamon. Or was it coffee? No, that wasn't right, either—chocolate, perhaps?

Rafe settled himself casually on the edge of the bed. Henrietta Markham's eyes widened, but she didn't shrink away as he'd expected. There was just enough space between them to seem at the same time too much and not enough. He could see her breasts rising and falling more rapidly beneath the sheet.

She wasn't what received wisdom would call beautiful. She lacked inches, for one thing, and could not by any stretch of the imagination be described as willowy. Though her skin was flawless, her mouth was too generous, her eyebrows too straight and her nose not straight enough. Yet now that some colour had returned to her cheeks and she no longer resembled a marble effigy, she was—no, definitely not beautiful, but rather disturbingly attractive. 'What, Miss Markham, at a loss for words?'

Henrietta licked her lips. She felt like a mouse being toyed with by a cat. No, not a cat. Something much more dangerous. He crossed one leg over the other. Long legs. If she were sitting where he was on the edge of the bed, her feet would not touch the ground. She was not used to sitting so close to a man. Had not ever—in bed—on bed—whatever! She had not. It was— She couldn't breathe. She was not frightened exactly, but she was intimidated. Was that his intention? Henrietta sat up straighter, resisting the impulse to scuttle over to the other side of the bed, confused by the contrary impulse to shuffle closer. Dangerously close. She decided she would not allow him the upper hand. 'You must know perfectly well that you are notorious,' she said, her voice sounding near enough steady for her to be quite pleased.

'Notorious for what, precisely?'

'Well, they say that—' Henrietta broke off, rather unusually at a loss for words. There were grass stains on the knees of his breeches. She caught herself staring at them, wondering precisely how they had come to be there and whether they were anything to do with her. Realising he had noted her blatant gaze, she blushed yet again, pressing on. 'Not to put too fine a point on it, they say that you are—only I am sure it is nonsense, because you can't possibly be as bad as—and in any case, you don't look at all like I imagined one would look like,' she said, becoming quite flustered.

'I don't look like *what* one what would look like?' Rafe said, fighting the urge to laugh.

Henrietta swallowed. She didn't like the way he was looking at her. As if he might smile. As if he might not. Appraising, that was the word. If it was a word. Once again, she worried about being found lacking. Once again, she chided herself for such a pathetic response, but he was so overwhelmingly male, sitting far too close to her on the bed, so close that her skin tingled with awareness of his presence, forcing her to fight the urge to push him away. Or was that just an excuse to be able to touch him? That crop of raven-black hair. It looked like it would be silky-soft to the touch. Unlike the stubble on his cheek, which would be rough. 'A rake,' she blurted out, now thoroughly confused by her own reactions.

The word jarred. Rafe got to his feet. 'I beg your pardon?'

Henrietta blinked up, missing the warmth of his presence, at the same time relieved that he had moved, for his expression had altered subtly. Colder. More distant, as if he had placed a wall between them. Too late, she realised that calling someone a rake to their face, even if they *were* a rake, wasn't perhaps the most tactful thing to say. She squirmed.

'Pray enlighten me, Miss Markham—what exactly does a rake look like?'

'Well, I don't know *exactly*, though I would say someone not nearly so good-looking for a start,' Henrietta replied, saying the first thing that popped into her head in her anxiety to make up for her lapse of manners. 'Older, too,' she continued, unable to bear the resultant silence, 'and probably more immoral looking. Debauched. Though to be honest, I'm not entirely sure what debauchery looks like, save that you don't. Look debauched, I mean,' she concluded, her voice trailing off as she realised that, far from appeasing him, the earl was looking decidedly affronted. Both his brows were drawn together now, giving him a really rather formidable expression.

'You seem quite the expert, Miss Markham,' Rafe said sardonically. 'Do you speak from personal experience?'

He had propped his shoulders up against the bed-post. They were very broad. Powerful. She wondered if perhaps he boxed. If he did, he must be good, for his face showed no marks. *Her* face was level with his chest now. Which also looked powerful, under his shirt. He had a very flat stomach. She hadn't really thought about it before, but men were built so very differently from women. Solid. Hard-edged. At least this man was.

Henrietta chewed on her bottom lip and tried hard not to be daunted. She wouldn't talk to his chest, but she had to crane her neck to meet his eyes. Slate-grey now, not blue. She swallowed again, trying to remember what it was he'd asked her. Rakes. 'Personal experience. Yes. I mean, no, I haven't previously met any rakes personally, at least not to my knowledge, but Mama said—my mother told me that…' Once again, Henrietta trailed into silence, realising that Mama would prefer not to have her past held up for inspection. 'I have seen the evidence of their activities for myself,' she said instead. Her voice sounded horribly defensive, but little wonder, given the way he was standing over her like an avenging angel. Henrietta bristled. 'In the Parish Poor House.'

The earl's expression was transformed in an instant, more devil than angel. 'If you are implying that I have littered the countryside with my illegitimate brats, then you are mightily misinformed,' he said icily.

Henrietta quailed. The truth was, she had heard no such thing of this particular rake, though, of course, just because she had not heard did not mean—but really, he looked far too angry to be lying. 'If you say so,' she said deprecatingly. 'I did not mean to imply…'

'None the less you did, Miss Markham. And I resent the implication.'

'Well, it was a natural enough assumption to make, given your reputation,' she retorted, placed firmly on the back foot, a position to which she was most unused.

'On the contrary. One should never make assumptions until one has a full grasp of all the facts.'

'What facts?'

'You are, as you point out, in my bed, in your underwear, yet you have been neither ravaged nor despoiled.'

'Haven't I? No, of course I haven't. I mean—do you mean that you're not a rake, then?'

'I am not, Miss Markham, in the habit of defending

my character to you, or anyone else for that matter,' Rafe said, no longer amused but furious. He might indeed be a rake, though he despised the term, but he was very far from being a libertine. The notion that he would wantonly sire children in pursuit of his own pleasure was a particular anathema to him. He prided himself on the fact that his rules of engagement were strict. His raking was confined to females who understood those rules, who expected nothing from him. His encounters were physical, not emotional. Innocents, even if they were wide-eyed and lying half-naked in his bed, were quite safe. Not that he was about to tell this particular innocent that.

Henrietta cowered against the pillow, taken aback by the shift in mood. If he was the rake common knowledge called him, then why should the earl take such umbrage? It was well known that all rakes were unprincipled, debauched, irresponsible....

But here her thoughts stuttered to a halt, having come full circle. He might be a rake, but he hadn't—though perhaps that was because he didn't find her attractive enough? A strangely deflating thought. And a ridiculous one! As if she should mind at all that a notorious rake thought so little of her that he hadn't tried to seduce her. Which reminded her. 'How did I come to be in your—I mean, this bed?' she asked, grasping at this interesting and unanswered question with some relief.

'I found you quite unconscious. I thought you were dead at first, and despite what you have been imagining, Miss Markham, I much prefer my conquests both *compos mentis* and willing. You can be reassured, I made no attempt to molest you. Had I done so, you would not have readily forgotten the experience. Something else I pride myself upon,' Rafe said sardonically.

Henrietta shivered. She had absolutely no doubt that he was entitled to boast of his prowess. His look told her he had once again read her thoughts. Once again she dropped her gaze, plucking at the scalloped edge of the sheet. 'Where *did* you find me?'

'In a ditch. I rescued you from it.'

This information was so surprising that Henrietta let fall the bedclothes shielding her modesty. 'Goodness! Really? Truly?' She sat up quickly, forgetting all about her aching head, then sank back on to the pillows with a little moan as the pain hit her. 'Where?' she asked weakly. 'I mean, where was this ditch?'

'In the grounds of my estate.'

'But how did I come to be there?'

'I rather hoped you could tell me that.'

'I don't know if I can.' Henrietta put her fingers carefully to the back of her head where a large lump was forming on her skull. 'Someone hit me.' She winced at the memory. 'Hard. Why would someone do that?'

'I have absolutely no idea,' Rafe replied. 'Perhaps whoever it was found your judgemental attitude tedious.' The hurt expression on her face didn't provide the usual sense of satisfaction he experienced when one of his well-aimed barbs struck home. On this occasion something more like guilt pricked him. She really was looking quite pale, too. Perhaps Mrs Peters was right, perhaps he should have summoned the local quack. 'Apart from the blow to the head, how are you feeling?'

The true answer was awful, but it was obvious from the falsely solicitous tone of his voice that awful was not the answer he wished to hear. 'I'm quite well,' Henrietta said, striving and failing to keep the edge out of her voice, 'at least I'm sure I will be directly. You need not concern yourself unduly.'

He had been ungracious, not something that would normally bother him, but her *not* pointing it out somehow did. Rather too quick with her opinions she most certainly was, but Henrietta Markham was not capricious. Her frankness, when it was not rude, was refreshing.

The memory of her curves pressed against him as he had lifted her from the ditch crept unbidden into his mind. Awareness took Rafe by surprise. It irked him that he remembered so clearly. Why should he? 'You may, of course, take as long as you require to recuperate,' he said. 'What I want to know right now is who hit you and, more importantly, why they abandoned you on my land.'

'What you really mean is, why didn't they pick somewhere less inconvenient to dump me?' Henrietta retorted. She gasped, pressed her hand over her mouth, but it was too late, the words were out.

Rafe laughed. He couldn't help it, she was amusing in a strange kind of way. His laugh sounded odd. He realised it was because he hadn't heard it for such a long time. 'Yes, you are quite right,' he said. 'I would have happily seen you abandoned at the very gates of Hades instead, but you are here now.'

He had a nice laugh. And though he might be ungracious, at least he was honest. She liked that. Henrietta smiled tentatively. 'I didn't mean to be quite so frank.'

'You are a dreadful liar, Miss Markham.'

'I know. I mean— Oh dear.'

'Hoist with your own petard, I think you would call that.'

The band of pain around Henrietta's head tightened, making her wince. '*Touché*, my lord. You want me gone, I am sure you have things to do. If I could just have a moment to collect myself, I will get dressed and be out of your way directly.'

She had turned quite pale. Rafe felt a twinge of compassion. As she had so clearly refrained from pointing out, it was not her fault she had landed on his doorstep, any more than it was his. 'There is no rush. Perhaps if you had something to eat, you might feel a little better. Then you may remember what happened to you.'

'I would not wish to put you out any more than I have already done,' Henrietta said unconvincingly.

Once again, he felt his mouth quirk. 'You are as poor a prevaricator as you are a liar. Come, the least I can do is give you breakfast before you go. Do you feel up to getting out of bed?'

He was not exactly smiling at her, but his expression had lost that hard edge, as if a smile might not be entirely beyond him. Also, she was ravenous. And he did deserve answers, if only she could come up with some. So Henrietta stoically told him that, yes, she would get out of bed, though the thought of it made her feel quite nauseous. He was already heading for the door. 'My lord, please, wait.'

'Yes?' She had dropped the sheet in her anxiety to call him back. Long tendrils of chestnut hair, curling wildly, trailed over her white shoulders. Her chemise was made of serviceable white cotton. He could plainly see the ripe swell of her breasts, unconfined by stays. Rafe reluctantly dragged his gaze away.

'My dress, where is it?' Realising that she had dropped the sheet, Henrietta clutched it up around her neck, telling herself stoutly there was nothing to be ashamed of to be found to be wearing a plain white-cotton chemise which, after all, was clean. Nevertheless, clean or no, she couldn't help wishing it hadn't been quite so plain. She wondered who had removed her gown.

'My housekeeper undressed you,' the earl replied in answer to her unasked question. 'Your dress was soaking wet and we did not wish you to catch a chill. I'll lend you something until it is dry.' He returned a few moments later with a large, and patently masculine, dressing gown, which he laid on the chair, informing her breakfast would be served in half an hour precisely, before striding purposefully out of the room.

Henrietta stared at the closed door She couldn't fathom him. Did he want her to stay or not? Did he find her amusing? Annoying? Attractive? Irksome? All or none? She had absolutely no idea.

She should not have mentioned his reputation. Though he hadn't exactly denied it, she could very easily see just how irresistible he could be, given that combination of looks and the indefinable something else he possessed which made her shiver. As if he was promising her something she knew she should not wish for. As if he and only he could fulfil that promise. She didn't understand it. Surely rakes were scoundrels? Rafe St Alban didn't look at all like a scoundrel. Rakes were

not *good* people, yet he must have some good in him—
had he not rescued her, a noble act?

She frowned. 'I suppose the point is that they must be
good at taking people in, else how could they succeed
in being a rake?' she said to herself. So was it a good
thing that he hadn't taken her in? She couldn't make up
her mind. The one thing she knew for certain was that
he was most eager to be rid of her. Henrietta tried not
to be mortified by that.

Perhaps he just wanted to know how she had come
to be on his estate in the first place? She'd like to know
that herself, she thought, touching a cautious finger to
the aching lump on her head. Last night. Last night.
What did she remember of last night?

That dratted pug dog of Lady Ipswich's had run off.
She'd entirely missed her dinner while looking for it,
no wonder she was so hungry now. Henrietta frowned,
screwing her eyes tightly shut, ignoring the dull ache
inside her skull as she mentally retraced her steps. Out
through the side door. The kitchen garden. Round to
the side of the house. Then…

The housebreaker! 'Oh, my goodness, the housebreaker!' Her mind cleared, like the ripples of a pool
stilling to reveal a sharp reflection. 'Good grief! Lady
Ipswich will be wondering what on earth has happened
to me.'

Gingerly, Henrietta inched out of the luxurious bed
and peered at the clock on the mantel. The numbers
were fuzzy. It was just after eight. She opened the curtains and blinked painfully out at the sun. Morning.
She had been gone all night. Her rescuer had clearly
been out and about very early. In fact, now she had a

chance to reflect upon it, he had had the look of a man who had not yet been to bed.

Raking, no doubt! But those shadows under his eyes spoke of a tiredness more profound than mere physical exhaustion. Rafe St Alban looked like a man who *could* not sleep. No wonder he was irritable, she thought, immediately feeling more charitable. Having to deal with a comatose stranger under such circumstances would have put anyone out of humour, especially if the aforementioned stranger looked like a—like a—what on earth *did* she look like?

There was a looking glass on top of the ornately inlaid chest of drawers in front of the window. Henrietta peered curiously into it. A streak of mud had caked on to her cheek, she was paler than normal and had a lump the size of an egg on her head, but apart from that she looked pretty much the same as always. Determinedly un-rosebuddish mouth. Eyebrows that simply refused to show even the tiniest inclination to arch. Too-curly brown hair in wild disorder. Brown eyes. And, currently in the hands of the aforementioned Mrs Peters, a brown dress.

She sighed heavily. It summed things up, really. Her whole life was various shades of brown. It was to her shame and discredit that no amount of telling herself, as Papa constantly reminded her, that there were many people in the world considerably worse off than her, made her feel any better about it. It was not that she was malcontent precisely, but she could not help thinking sometimes that there must be more to life. Though more of what, she had no idea.

'I suppose being thumped on the head, then being

left to die of exposure, to say nothing of being rescued by a devastatingly handsome earl, counts as a burst of genuine excitement,' she told her reflection. 'Even if he is a very reluctant knight errant with a very volatile temperament and an extremely dubious reputation.'

The clock on the mantel chimed the quarter-hour, making her jump. She could not possibly add keeping the earl from his breakfast to her other sins. Hastily, she slopped water from the jug on the nightstand into the prettily flowered china bowl and set about removing the worst of the mud from her face.

Almost precisely on time, Henrietta tripped into the breakfast parlour with her hair brushed and pinned, her body swathed in her host's elegant dressing gown of dark green brocade trimmed with gold frogging. Even with the cuffs turned back and the gown belted tightly at her waist, it enveloped her form completely, trailing behind her like a royal robe. The idea that the material that lay next to her skin had also lain next to his naked body was unsettling. She tried not to dwell on the thought, but it could not be said she was wholly successful.

She was nervous. Seeing the breakfast table set for just two made her even more nervous. She had never before had breakfast alone with a man, save for dear Papa, which didn't count. She had certainly never before had breakfast with a man while wearing his dressing gown. Feeling incredibly gauche and at the same time excruciatingly conscious of her body, clothed only in her underwear, handicapped by the voluminous folds of the dressing gown, Henrietta tripped into the room.

He didn't seem to notice her at first. He was staring into space, the most melancholy expression on his face. Darkly brooding. Formidable. Starkly handsome. Her pulses fluttered. He had shaved and changed. He was wearing a clean shirt and freshly tied cravat, a tightly fitting morning coat of dark blue, and buff-coloured pantaloons with polished boots. The whole ensemble made him look considerably more earl-like and consequently considerably more intimidating. Also, even more devastatingly attractive. Henrietta plastered a faltering smile to her face and dropped into a very far from elegant and certainly not, she was sure, deep enough curtsy. 'I must apologise, my lord, for being so remiss, I have not yet thanked you properly for rescuing me. I am very much obliged to you.'

Her voice dragged Rafe's thoughts back from the past, where he had once again been lingering. Be dammed to the precious title and the need for an heir! Who really cared, save his grandmother, if it was inherited by some obscure third cousin twice removed? If she only knew what it had cost him already, she would soon stop harping on about it. He gazed down at Henrietta, still smiling up at him uncertainly. Holding out his hand, he helped her back to her feet. 'I trust you feel a little better, Miss Markham. You certainly look very fetching in my robe. It is most becoming.'

'I'm perfectly all right, all things considered,' Henrietta said, grateful for his support as she got up from her curtsy, which had made her head swim. 'And as for the robe, it is very gallant of you to lie, but I know I must look a fright.'

'Frightfully nice, I'd say. And you must believe me,
for I am something of an expert in these matters.'

His haunted look had disappeared. He was smiling
now. Not a real smile, not one that reached his eyes, but
his mouth turned up at the corners. 'I think I've finally
remembered what happened,' Henrietta said.

'Yes?' Rafe shook his head, dispelling the ghosts that
seemed to have gathered there. 'It can wait. You look
as if you need food.'

'I *am* hungry—a dog made me miss my dinner.'

For the second time that morning, Rafe laughed
aloud. This time it sounded less rusty. 'Well, I am
happy to inform you that there are no dogs here to make
you miss your breakfast,' he said. The dressing gown
gave Henrietta Markham a winsome quality. It gaped at
the neck, showing far too much creamy bosom, which
she really ought to have had the decency to confine
in stays. She looked as if she had just tumbled from
his bed. Which in a way, she had. He realised he'd been
staring and looked away, slightly disconcerted by the
unexpected stirrings of arousal. Desire was usually
something he could conjure up or dispense with at will.

Helping her into a seat, he sat down opposite, keeping his eyes resolutely on the food in front of him. He
would feed her, find out where she had sprung from and
return her there forthwith. Then he would sleep. And
after that he must return to town. The meeting with his
grandmother could not be postponed indefinitely. An
immense malaise, grey and heavy as a November sky,
loomed over him at the thought.

So he would not think of it. He need not, not just yet,
while he had the convenient distraction of the really

quite endearing Henrietta Markham sitting opposite him, in his dressing gown, with her tale to tell. Rafe poured her some coffee and placed a generous helping of ham on to her plate along with a baked egg and some bread and butter, helping himself to a mound of beef and a tankard of ale. 'Eat, before you faint with hunger.'

'This looks delicious,' she said, gazing at her loaded plate with relish.

'It is just breakfast.'

'Well, I've never had such a nice breakfast,' Henrietta said chirpily, at the same time, thinking *be quiet*! She was not usually a female who wittered, yet she sounded uncommonly like one this morning. Nerves. Yet she was not usually one to allow nerves to affect her behaviour. Off balance. He disconcerted her, that's what it was. The situation. The dressing gown. The man. Definitely the man. This man, who was telling her, with a quizzical look that meant she'd either been muttering to herself or allowing her thoughts to be read quite clearly on her face, that it would be a nice cold breakfast unless she made a start on it.

She picked up her fork. Was he just teasing, or did he think she was an idiot? She sounded like an idiot. He had the ability to make her feel like one. Taking a bite of deliciously soft egg, she studied him covertly from under her lashes. The dark shadows were clearer now in the bright morning light that streamed through the windows. He had a strained look about his mouth. She ate some more egg and cut into a slice of York ham. He was edgy, too. Even when he smiled, it was as if he were simply going through the motions.

Clearly not happy, then. Why not, she wondered, when he had so much more than most? She longed to ask, but another glance at that countenance, and the question stuck in her throat. More than anything, Henrietta decided, what Rafe St Alban was, was opaque. She had no idea what he was thinking. It made her want, all the more, to know, yet still—quite unusually, for Henrietta had been encouraged from a very early age to speak her mind—she hesitated.

A tiny *frisson*, this time excitement mingled with fear, caused goose bumps to rise on the back of her neck. He was not just intimidating. He was intimidatingly attractive. What was it about him that made her feel like this? Fascinated and frightened and—as if she were a rabbit faced with a particularly tasty treat, though she knew full well it was bait. She was beginning to see Rafe St Alban's reputation might well be deserved, after all. If he set his mind to something, she would be difficult to resist.

She shivered again and told herself not to be so foolish. He would not set his mind on her! And even if he did, knowing the type of man he was, being fully aware of his lack of morals, she would have no difficulty at all in resisting him. Not that he had made any such attempt, nor was likely to.

More to the point, why was she wasting her time thinking about such things? She had much more important matters to attend to now that she remembered the shocking events of last night. Even before that, she must attend to her stomach, else she would be fainting away, and Henrietta, who prided herself on her pragmatism, would not allow herself such an indulgence. With resolution, she turned her attention more fully to her breakfast.

Chapter Two

When they had finished eating, Rafe stood up. 'Bring your coffee. We'll sit by the fire, it will be more comfortable there. Then you can tell me your tale.'

Awkwardly arranging the multitudinous folds of silk around her in the wing-backed chair, Henrietta did as instructed. Across from her, Rafe St Alban disposed his long limbs gracefully, crossing one booted foot over the other. She could see the muscles of his legs move underneath the tight-fitting material of his knitted pantaloons. Such unforgiving cloth would not show to advantage on a stouter man. Or a thinner one. Or one less well built.

'I'm a governess,' she announced, turning her mind to the thing most likely to distract her from unaccustomed thoughts of muscled thighs, 'to the children of Lady Ipswich, whose grounds march with yours.'

'They do, but we are not on calling terms.'

'Why not?'

'It is of no relevance.'

Anyone else would have been daunted by his tone,

but Henrietta's curiosity was aroused, which made her quite oblivious. 'But you are neighbours, surely you must—is it because she is a widow? Did you perhaps call when her husband was alive?'

'Lord Ipswich was more of an age with my father,' Rafe said curtly.

'He must have been quite a bit older than his wife, then. I didn't realise. I suppose I just assumed….'

'As you are wont to do,' Rafe said sardonically.

She looked at him expectantly. Her wide-eyed gaze was disconcerting. Her mouth was quite determined. Rafe sighed heavily, unused to dealing with such persistent questioning. 'His lordship passed away under what one might call somewhat dubious circumstances, and I decided not to continue the acquaintance with his widow.'

'Really?'

'Really,' Rafe said, wishing he had said nothing at all. The poor innocent obviously had no idea of her employer's colourful past and he had no intention of disclosing it to her. 'How came you to be in Helen Ipswich's employ?' he asked, in an attempt to divert her.

'There was a notice in *The Lady*. I happened to be looking for a position and Mama said that it all looked quite respectable, so I applied.'

'Your previous position was terminated?'

'Oh, no, this is my first experience as a governess, though not, I hope, my last,' Henrietta said with one of her confiding smiles. 'I am going to be a teacher, you see, and I wished to gain some practical experience before the school opened.' Her smile faded. 'Though from what Mama says in her latest letter, that will be quite some time away.'

'Your mother is opening a school?'

'Mama and Papa together—' Henrietta frowned '—at least, that is the plan, but I have to confess their plans have a habit of going awry. The school is to be in Ireland, a charitable project for the poor. Papa is a great philanthropist, you see.'

Henrietta waited expectantly, but Rafe St Alban did not seem to have a burning need to comment on Papa's calling. 'The problem is that while his intentions are always of the best, I'm afraid he is not very practical. He has more of a care for the soul than the body and cannot be brought to understand that, without sustenance and warmth, the poor have more pressing needs than their spiritual health, nor any interest in raising their minds to higher things. Like statues of St Francis. Or making a tapestry celebrating the life of St Anthony—he is the patron saint of the poor, you know. I told Papa that they would be better occupied making blankets,' Henrietta said darkly, too taken up with her remembered resentment to realise that she was once again rambling, 'but he did not take my suggestion kindly. Mama, of course, agreed with him. Mama believes that distracting the poor from their situation is the key, but honestly, how can one be distracted when one is starving, or worried that one is expecting another child when one cannot feed the other five already at home? The last thing one would want to do is stitch a figure of St Anthony voyaging to Portugal!'

'I don't expect many of the poor even know where Portugal is,' Rafe said pointedly. Papa and Mama

Markham sounded like the kind of do-gooders he despised.

'Precisely,' Henrietta said vehemently, 'and even if they did—are you laughing at me?'

'Would you mind if I were?'

'No. Only I didn't think what I was saying was particularly droll.'

'It was the way you were saying it. You are very earnest.'

'I have to be, else I will never be heard.'

'So, while Mama and Papa pray for souls, you make soup—is that right?'

'There is nothing wrong with being practical.'

'No, there is not. If only there was more soup and less sermons in the world....'

'My parents mean well.'

'I'm sure they do, but my point is that meaning well is not the same as doing well. I come across many such people and—'

'I was not aware you had a reputation for philanthropy.'

'No, as you pointed out,' Rafe said coldly, 'my reputation primarily concerns my raking. Now you will tell me that one precludes the other.'

'Well, doesn't it?' Henrietta demanded. Seeing his face tighten, she hesitated. 'What I mean is, being a rake presupposes one is immoral and—' She broke off as Rafe's expression froze. 'You know, I think perhaps I've strayed from the point a little. Are you saying that you *are* involved in charitable work?'

She was clearly sceptical. He told himself it didn't matter a damn what she thought. 'I am saying the world is not as black and white as either you or your parents seem to think.' His involvement with his own little project at St Nicholas's was extremely important to him, but he did not consider it to be charitable. With some difficulty, Rafe reined in his temper. What was it about this beguiling female that touched so many raw nerves? 'You were telling me about the school your parents want to set up.'

'Yes.' Henrietta eyed him uncertainly. 'Have I said something to offend you?'

'The school, Miss Markham.'

'Well, if—when—it opens I intend to be able to contribute in a practical sense by teaching lessons.' Practical lessons, she added to herself, remembering Mama's curriculum with a shudder.

'Lessons which you are trying out on Helen Ipswich's brats?'

'They are not brats,' Henrietta said indignantly. 'They are just high-spirited boys. I'm sure you were the same at their age, wanting to be out riding rather than attending to your studies, but—'

'At their age, my father was actively encouraging me to go out riding and ignore my lessons,' Rafe said drily. 'My tendency to bury my head in a book sorely disconcerted him.'

'Goodness, were you a scholar?'

'Another thing that you consider incompatible with being a rake, Miss Markham?'

He was looking amused again. She couldn't keep pace with his mood swings, but she couldn't help responding to his hint of a smile with one of her own. 'Well, to cut a long story short, which I'm sure you'll be most relieved to hear I intend to do, I like being a governess and I like the boys, even if their mama is a little—well—high-handed. Not that I really see that much of her, governesses clearly meriting scant attention. Anyway, I'm sure there are worse employers, and the boys do like me, and if—*when*—the school is opened, I am sure the experience will stand me in good stead. It is due to do so in three months or so, by which time my current charges are destined for boarding school, anyway, so hopefully they won't miss me too much. Not anything like as much as I shall miss them.'

'There, we must agree. Small boys, in my experience, are remarkably fickle in their loyalties.'

'Do you think so?' Henrietta asked brightly. 'I think that's a good thing, for I would not wish them to become too attached to me. What experience have you of such things? Have you brothers?'

'No.'

His face was closed again, his expression shuttered. 'I take it, then, that life as Helen Ipswich's governess has fulfilled your expectations?'

'Yes, it has served its purpose admirably.'

'How fortunate for you. Now, if you don't mind, we will return to the more pressing subject of how you came to be in my ditch, then you may return to these duties you enjoy so much. No doubt your employer will be wondering what has become of you.'

'That is true. And the boys, too.' Though the notion of returning to Lady Ipswich's home was less appealing than it should be. Another of a rake's skills, no doubt, to beguile you and make you want to spend time in his company. Henrietta sat up straight and tugged at the dressing-gown belt. 'Well, then, to return to the subject, as you wish. Last night. Well, what happened last night was that I was knocked on the head by a housebreaker.'

'A housebreaker!'

Gratified by her host's reaction, which was for once just exactly what she had anticipated, Henrietta nodded vigorously. 'Yes, indeed. At least,' she added, incurably truthful, 'I am almost certain that is what he was, though I didn't actually see him steal anything. I was looking for Lady Ipswich's horrible dog, you see.'

'The dog who deprived you of your dinner?'

'The very same. I heard a noise coming from the shrubbery, so I went to investigate it, thinking, you know, it might be Princess—that's the pug's name—and then I heard glass breaking. I held up the lantern and saw him as clear as day for just a split second, then he leapt at me and hit me on the head. The next thing I remember is waking up here.'

Rafe shook his head slowly. 'But that's nonsensical. Even if it was a housebreaker, why on earth would he go to the trouble of taking you with him? It takes time and effort to heft a body on to a horse.'

Henrietta coloured. 'I am aware that I am not exactly a featherweight.'

'That is not at all what I meant. It is women who consider stick-thinness the essence of beauty. Men actually prefer quite the opposite. I find your figure most pleasing on the eye.' Rafe was not in the habit of encouraging young ladies with compliments, for they were likely to be misconstrued, but Henrietta Markham was so different from any young lady he had ever met that he spoke without considering the effect his words would have. 'It was no hardship to get you on to my horse. I meant merely it would be awkward if the man were slight, or elderly.'

Or one less muscled, Henrietta thought, her gaze lingering on her host's powerful physique. It hadn't occurred to her until now to wonder how, exactly, he had retrieved her from the ditch. Had he pulled her by the wrist or the ankle? Held her chest to chest, or maybe thrown her over his shoulders? And when she was on his horse, was she on her front with her bottom sticking up? With her petticoats on show? Her ankles? Worse? Feigning heat from the fire, she frantically fanned her face.

Rafe followed the train of her thoughts with relative ease, mirrored as they were in her expressive face, recognising the exact moment when she tried to imagine how she had been placed on Thor's saddle. Unfortunately, it turned his mind also to that moment. He had lain her crossways on her stomach with her bottom pointed provocatively up to the sky. Her dress had ridden up a little, exposing her ankles and calves. At the time, he had not been aware of noticing. Yet now, in his mind's eye, he found he could dwell appreciatively on the inviting curves of her voluptuous body as if he had drunk in every inch of her.

'Why,' he said tersely, reining in his imagination, once again disconcerted by having to do so, 'having gone to all that effort to abduct you, did your housebreaker then change his mind and abandon you in my grounds?'

'I don't know,' Henrietta replied. 'It doesn't make

any sense, I can see that. Perhaps he had evil designs upon my person and then changed his mind when he got a better look at me,' she said with a wry smile.

'If that was the case, then his taste was quite at fault,' Rafe said impulsively, bestowing upon her his real smile.

It quite transformed his face. Henrietta blushed rosily, but even as she struggled for a response, the smile was gone, as if a cloud had covered the sun. Utterly confused, she folded her arms defensively. 'You don't really believe a word I've said, do you?'

The dressing gown gaped. Rafe caught a glimpse of creamy flesh spilling from a plain white cotton undergarment. The rake in him would have allowed his glance to linger. He wanted to look, but it was his wanting that made him look resolutely away. *Nothing touches you any more.* The memory of his friend Lucas's words made Rafe smile bitterly to himself. True, thank God, if you didn't count the all-pervading guilt. He had worked very hard to ensure it was so and that was exactly how he intended it to continue. Wanting was no longer part of his emotional make-up. Wanting Henrietta Markham, he told himself sternly, was completely out of the question.

'You have to admit that it sounds a tall tale,' he said to her, his voice made more dismissive by the need to offset his thoughts, 'but my opinion is of little importance. I would have thought the more pressing issue for you is whether or not Lady Ipswich believes you.' He got to his feet purposefully. Henrietta Markham had been a very beguiling distraction, but the time had come to put an end to this extraordinary interlude and for them both to return to the real world. 'I will arrange for you to be taken back in my carriage. Your dress should be dry by now.' He pulled the bell rope to summon the housekeeper.

Henrietta scrabbled to her feet. He was quite plainly bored by the whole matter. And by her. She should not be surprised. She should certainly not feel hurt. She was, after all, just a lowly governess with a preposterous story; he was an earl with an important life and no doubt a string of beautiful women with whom to carry on his dalliances. Women who didn't wear brown dresses and who most certainly didn't lie around waiting to be pulled out of ditches. 'I must thank you again for rescuing me,' she said in what she hoped was a curt voice, though she suspected it sounded rather huffy. 'Please forgive me for taking up quite so much of your time.'

'It was a pleasure, Miss Markham, but a word of warning before you go.' Rafe tilted her chin up with the tip of his finger. Her eyes were liquid bronze. Really, quite her most beautiful feature. He met her gaze coolly, though he didn't feel quite as cool as he should. He wasn't used to having his equilibrium disturbed. 'Don't expect to be lauded as a heroine,' he said softly. 'Helen Ipswich is neither a very credulous nor a particularly kind person.' He took her hand, just brushing the back of it with his lips. 'Good luck, Henrietta Markham, and goodbye. If you return to your room, I'll send Mrs Peters up with your dress. She will also see you out.'

He could not resist pressing his lips to her hand. She tasted delightful. The scent of her and the feel of her skin on his mouth shot a dart of pleasure to his groin.

He dropped her hand abruptly, turned on his heels and left without a backward glance.

Just the faintest touch of his mouth on her skin, but she could feel it there still. Henrietta lifted her hand to her cheek and held it there until the tingling faded. It took a long time before it finally did.

Molly Peters, Rafe's long-suffering housekeeper, was an apple-shaped woman with rosy cheeks. Her husband, Albert, who alone was permitted to call her his little pippin, was head groom. Molly had started service in the previous earl's day as a scullery maid, ascending by way of back parlourmaid, chambermaid and front parlourmaid, before eventually serving, briefly and unhappily, as lady's maid to the last countess. Upon her ladyship's untimely death, Master Rafe had appointed Molly to the heady heights of housekeeper, with her own set of keys and her own parlour.

Running the household was a task Molly Peters undertook with pride and carried out extremely competently. Indeed, she would have executed it with gusto had she been given the opportunity, but even when the last countess had been alive, Woodfield Manor had seldom been used as a residence. As a result, Mrs Peters had little to do and was frankly a little bored. Henrietta's unorthodox arrival provided some welcome excitement and consequently induced an unaccustomed garrulousness in the usually reserved housekeeper.

'I've known Master Rafe all his life, since he was a babe,' she said in answer to Henrietta's question. 'A bonny babe he was, too, and so clever.'

'He has certainly retained his looks,' Henrietta ventured, struggling into her newly brushed, but none the less indisputably brown dress.

Mrs Peters pursed her lips. 'Certainly, he has no shortage of admirers,' she said primly. 'A man like Lord Pentland, with those looks and the Pentland title behind him, to say nothing of the fact that he's as rich as Croesus, will always attract the ladies, but the master is—well, miss, the truth is...' She looked over her shoulder, as if Rafe would suddenly appear in the bedchamber. 'Truth is, he's the love-'em-and-leave-'em type, as my Albert puts it, though I say there's little loving and a darn sight more leaving. I don't know why I'm telling you this except you seem such a nice young lady and it wouldn't do to— But then, he's not a libertine, if you know what I mean.'

Henrietta tried to look knowledgeable, though in truth she wasn't *exactly* sure she understood the distinction between rake and libertine. Certainly Mama had never made one. She was attempting to formulate a question that would persuade Mrs Peters to enlighten her without revealing her own ignorance when the housekeeper heaved a huge sigh and clucked her teeth. 'He wasn't always like that, mind. I blame that wife of his.'

'He's married!' Henrietta's jaw dropped with shock. 'I didn't know.' But why should she? Contrary to what his lordship thought, Henrietta was not a great one for gossip. Generally speaking, she closed her ears to it, which is why Rafe St Alban's accusations had hurt. In fact, she had only become aware of his reputation recently, a chance remark of her employer's having alerted her. But if he was married, it made his behaviour so much worse. Somewhat irrationally, Henrietta felt a little betrayed, as if he had lied to her, even though it was actually none of her business. 'I hadn't heard mention of a wife,' she said.

'That's because she's dead,' Mrs Peters replied quietly. 'Five years ago now.'

'So he's a widower!' He looked even less like one of those. 'What happened? How did she die? When did they marry? Was he—did they—was it a love match? Was he devastated?' The questions tripped one after another off her tongue. Only the astonished look on Mrs Peters's face made her stop. 'I am just curious,' Henrietta said lamely.

Mrs Peters eyed her warily. 'Her name was Lady Julia. I've said more than enough already, the master doesn't like her to be talked about. But if you're ready to go, I can show you a likeness of her on the way out, if you want.'

The portrait hung in the main vestibule. The subject was depicted gazing meditatively into the distance, her willowy figure seated gracefully on a rustic swing bedecked with roses. 'Painted the year she died, that was,' Mrs Peters said.

'She is—was—very beautiful,' Henrietta said wistfully.

'Oh, she was lovely, no doubt about that,' Mrs Peters said, 'though handsome is as handsome does.'

'What do you mean?'

Mrs Peters looked uncomfortable. 'Nothing. It was a long time ago.'

'How long were they married?'

'Six years. Master Rafe was only a boy, not even

twenty, when they were wed. She was a few years older than him. It makes a difference at that age,' Mrs Peters said.

'How so?'

Mrs Peters shook her head. 'Don't matter now. As Albert says, what's done is done. The carriage will be waiting for you, miss.'

Henrietta took a final look at the perfect features of the elegant woman depicted in the portrait. There could be no denying the Countess of Pentland's beauty, but there was a calculating hardness in the eyes she could not like, a glittering perfection to her appearance that made Henrietta think of polished granite. For some ridiculous reason, she did not like to imagine Rafe St Alban in love with this woman.

Taking leave of the housekeeper, she made her way down the front steps to the waiting coach, unable to stop herself looking back just in case the earl had changed his mind and deigned to say farewell to her himself. But there was no sign of him.

A large fountain dominated the courtyard, consisting of four dolphins supporting a statue of Neptune. Modelled on Bernini's Triton fountain in Rome, Henrietta's inner governess noted. Beyond the fountain, reached by a broad sweep of steps, pristine flower beds and immaculate lawns stretched into the distance. Like the house she had just left, the grounds spoke eloquently of elegance, taste and wealth.

The contrast with her own childhood home could not be more stark. The ramshackle house in which she had been raised was damp, draughty and neglected. A lack of funds, and other, more pressing priorities saw to that. Any spare money her parents had went to good causes. An unaccustomed gust of homesickness assailed Henrietta. Hopelessly inept her parents might be, but they always meant well. They always put others first, even if the others weren't at all grateful. Even if it meant their only child coming last. Still, she never doubted that they loved her. She missed them.

But she had never been one to repine her lot. Henrietta straightened her shoulders and climbed into the waiting coach with its crest emblazoned on the door, already preparing herself for the forthcoming, almost certainly difficult, interview with her employer.

Rafe watched her departure from his bedroom window. Poor Henrietta Markham, it was unlikely in the extreme that Helen Ipswich would thank her for attempting to intervene—if that is what she really had done. He felt oddly uncomfortable at having allowed her to return on her own like a lamb to the slaughter. But he was not a shepherd and rescuing innocent creatures from Helen Ipswich's clutches was not his responsibility.

As the carriage pulled off down the driveway, Rafe left the window, stripped off his boots and coat, and donned his dressing gown. Sitting by the fireside, a glass of brandy in hand, he caught Henrietta's elusive scent still clinging to the silk. A long chestnut hair lay on the sleeve.

She had been a pleasant distraction. Unexpectedly desirable, too. That mouth. Those delectable curves.

But she was gone now. And later today, so too would he be. Back to London. Rafe took a sip of brandy. Two weeks ago he had turned thirty. Just over twelve years now since he had inherited the title, and almost five years to the day since he had become a widower. More than enough time to take up the reins of his life again, his grandmother, the Dowager Countess, chided him on a tediously regular basis. In a sense she was right, but in another she had no idea how impossible was her demand. The emotional scars he bore ran too deep for that. He had no desire at all to risk inflicting any further damage to his already battered psyche.

He took another, necessary, sip of brandy. The time had come. His grandmother would have to be made to relinquish once and for all any notion of a direct heir, though how he was going to convince her without revealing the unpalatable truth behind his reluctance, the terrible guilty secret that would haunt him to the grave, was quite another matter.

By the time the coach drew up at her employer's front door, Henrietta's natural optimism had reasserted itself. Whatever Rafe St Alban thought, she *had* tried to prevent a theft; even if she hadn't actually succeeded, she could describe the housebreaker and that was surely something of an achievement. Entering the household, she was greeted by an air of suppressed excitement. The normally hangdog footman goggled at her. 'Where have you been?' he whispered. 'They've been saying—'

'My lady wishes to see you immediately,' the butler interrupted.

'Tell her I'll be with her as soon as I've changed my clothes, if you please.'

'Immediately,' the butler repeated firmly.

Henrietta ascended the stairs, her heart fluttering nervously. Rafe St Alban had a point—her story did seem extremely unlikely. Reminding herself of one of Papa's maxims, that she had nothing to fear in telling the truth, she straightened her back and held her head up proudly, but as she tapped on the door she was horribly aware of the difference between speaking the truth and actually being able to prove it.

Lady Helen Ipswich, who admitted to twenty-nine of her forty years, was in her boudoir. She had been extremely beautiful in her heyday and took immense pains to preserve the fragile illusion of youthful loveliness. In the flattering glow of candlelight, she almost succeeded. Born plain Nell Brown, she had progressed through various incarnations, from actress, to high flyer, to wife and mother—in point of fact, her first taste of motherhood had preceded her marriage by some fifteen years. This interesting piece of information was known only to herself, the child's adoptive parents and the very expensive *accoucheur* who attended the birth of her official 'first-born', Lord Ipswich's heir.

After seven years of marriage, Lady Ipswich had settled contentedly into early widowhood. Her past would always bar her from the more hallowed precincts of the *haut ton*. She had wisely never attempted to obtain vouchers for Almack's. Her neighbour, the Earl of Pentland, would never extend her more than the commonest of courtesies and the curtest of bows. But as the relic of a peer of the realm, and with two legitimate children to boot, she had assumed a cloak of respectability effective enough to fool most unacquainted with her past—her governess included.

As to the persistent rumours that she had, having drained his purse, drained the life-blood from her husband, well, they were just that—rumours. The ageing Lord Ipswich had succumbed to an apoplexy. That it had occurred in the midst of a particularly energetic session in the marital bedchamber simply proved that Lady Ipswich had taken her hymeneal duties seriously. Her devotion to the wifely cause had, quite literally, taken his lordship's breath away. Murder? Certainly not! Indeed, how could it be when at least five men of her intimate acquaintance had begged her—two on bended knee—to perform the same service for them. To date, she had refused.

The widow was at her *toilette* when Henrietta entered, seated in front of a mirror in the full glare of the unforgiving morning sun. The dressing table was a litter of glass jars and vials containing such patented aids to beauty as Olympian Dew and Denmark Lotion, a selection of perfumes from Messrs Price and Gosnell, various pots of rouge, eyelash tints and lip salves, a tangle of lace and ribbons, hair brushes, a half-empty vial of laudanum, several tortoiseshell combs, a pair of tweezers and numerous cards of invitation.

As Henrietta entered the room, Lady Ipswich was peering anxiously into her looking glass, having just discovered what looked alarmingly like a new wrinkle on her brow. At her age, and with her penchant for younger men, she could not be too careful. Only the other day, one of her lovers had commented that the unsightly mark left by the ribbon that tied her stockings had not faded by the time she rose to dress. Her skin no longer had the elastic quality of youth. He had paid for his bluntness, but still!

Finally satisfied with her reflection and her coiffure, she turned to face Henrietta. 'So, you have deigned to return,' she said coldly. 'Do you care to explain yourself and your absence?'

'If you remember, ma'am, I went looking for Princess. I see she found her way back unaided.'

The pug, hearing her name, looked up from her pink-velvet cushion by the fireside and growled. Lady Ipswich hastened to pick the animal up. 'No thanks to you, Miss Markham.' She tickled the dog under the chin. 'You're a clever little Princess, aren't you? Yes, you are,' she said, before fixing Henrietta with a baleful stare. 'You should know that while you were off failing to find my precious Princess, the house was broken into. My emeralds have been stolen.'

'The Ipswich emeralds!' Henrietta knew them well. They were family heirlooms and extremely distinctive. Lady Ipswich was inordinately fond of them and Henrietta had much admired them herself.

'Gone. The safe was broken into and they were taken.'

'Good heavens.' Henrietta clutched the back of a flimsy filigree chair. The man who had abducted her was clearly no common housebreaker, but a most daring and outrageous thief indeed. And she had encountered him. More, could identify him. 'I can't quite believe it,' she said faintly. 'He did not look at all like the sort of man who would attempt such a shocking crime. In actual fact, he looked as if he would be more at home picking pockets in the street.'

Now it was Lady Ipswich's turn to pale. 'You saw him?'

Henrietta nodded vigorously. 'Indeed, my lady. That explains why he hit me. If he were to be caught, he would surely hang for his crime.' As the implications began to dawn on her, Henrietta's knees gave way. He really had left her for dead. If Rafe St Alban had not found her... Muttering an apology, she sank down on to the chair.

'What did he look like? Describe him to me,' Lady Ipswich demanded.

Henrietta furrowed her brow. 'He was quite short, not much taller than me. He had an eyepatch. And an accent. From the north somewhere. Liverpool, perhaps? Quite distinctive.'

'You would know him again if you saw him?'

'Oh, I have no doubt about that. Most certainly.'

Lady Ipswich began to pace the room, clasping and unclasping her hands. 'I have already spoken to the magistrate,' she said. 'He has sent for a Bow Street Runner.'

'They will wish to interview me. I may even be instrumental in having him brought to justice. Goodness!' Henrietta put a trembling hand to her forehead in an effort to stop the feeling of light-headedness threatening to engulf her.

With a snort of disdain, Lady Ipswich thrust a silver vial of sal volatile at her, then continued with her pacing, muttering all the while to herself. Henrietta took a cautious sniff of the smelling salts before hastily replacing the stopper. Her head had begun to ache again and she felt sick. It was one thing to play a trivial part in a minor break-in, quite another to have a starring role in sending a man to the gallows. *Oh God, she didn't want to think about that.*

'You said he hit you?' Lady Ipswich said abruptly, fixing her with a piercing gaze.

Henrietta's hand instinctively went to the tender lump on her head. 'He knocked me out and carried me off. I have been lying unconscious in a ditch.'

'No one else saw him, or you, for that matter?'

'Not that I'm aware of.'

'In fact,' Lady Ipswich said, turning on Henrietta with an enigmatic smile, 'I have only your word for what happened.'

'Well, yes, but the emeralds *are* missing, and the safe was broken into, and so—'

'So the solution is obvious,' Lady Ipswich declared triumphantly.

Henrietta stared at her blankly. 'Solution?'

'You, Miss Markham, are quite patently in league with the thief!'

Henrietta's jaw dropped. Were she not already sitting down, she would have collapsed. 'I?'

'It was you who told him the whereabouts of the safe. You who let him into my house and later broke the glass on the window downstairs to fake a break-in. You who smuggled my poor Princess out into the night in order to prevent her from raising the alarm.'

'You think—you truly think—no, you can't possibly. It's preposterous.'

'You are his accomplice.' Lady Ipswich nodded to

herself several times. 'I see it now, it is the only logical explanation. No doubt he looks nothing like this lurid description you gave me. An eyepatch indeed! You made it up to put everyone off the scent. Well, Miss Markham, let me tell you that there are no flies on Nell—I mean, Helen Ipswich. I am on to you and your little game, and so, too, will be the gentleman from Bow Street who is making his way here from London as we speak.' Striding over to the fireplace, she rang the bell vigorously. 'You shall be confined to your room until he arrives. You are also summarily dismissed from my employ.'

Henrietta gaped. A huge part of her, the rational part, told her it was all a silly misunderstanding that could be easily remedied, but there was another part that reminded her of her lowly position, of the facts as they must seem to her employer, of the way that Rafe St Alban had reacted to her story. What she said wasn't really that credible. And she had no proof to back it up. Not a whit. Absolutely none.

'Did you hear me?'

Henrietta stumbled to her feet. 'But, madam, my lady, I beg of you, you cannot possibly think…'

'Get out,' Lady Ipswich demanded, as the door opened to reveal the startled butler. 'Get out and do not let me see you again until the Runner comes. I cannot believe I have been harbouring a thief and a brazen liar under my roof.'

'I am not a thief and I am most certainly not a liar.' Outrage at the accusations bolstered Henrietta's courage. She never told even the tiniest, whitest lie. Papa had raised her to believe in absolute truth at all costs. 'I would never, ever do such an underhand and dishonest thing,' she said, her voice shaking with emotion.

Lady Ipswich coldly turned her back on her. Henrietta shook her head in confusion. She felt woozy. There was a rushing sound like a spate of water in her ears. Her fingers were freezing as she clasped them together in an effort to stop herself shaking. She wished she hadn't left the sal volatile on the chair. 'When he hears the truth of the matter, the magistrate—Runner—whatever—they will believe me. *They will.*'

Lady Ipswich's laugh tinkled like shattering glass as she eyed her former governess contemptuously. 'Ask yourself, my dear, whose version are they more likely to believe, yours or mine?'

'But Lord Pentland…'

Lady Ipswich's eyes narrowed. 'What, prey, has Lord Pentland to do with this?'

'Merely that it was he who found me. It was his carriage which brought me back.'

'You told Rafe St Alban this ridiculous tale of being kidnapped?' Lady Ipswich's voice rose to what would be described in a less titled lady as a shriek. Her face was once again drained of colour.

Henrietta eyed her with dismay. Her employer had not the sweetest of tempers, but she was not normally prone to such dramatic mood swings. The loss of the heirloom had obviously overset her, she decided, as her ladyship retrieved the smelling salts, took a deep sniff and sneezed twice. 'It is not a ridiculous tale, my lady, it is the truth.'

'What did he make of it?' Lady Ipswich snapped.

'Lord Pentland? He—he…' He had warned her. She

realised that now, that's what he meant when he told her not to expect to be treated as a heroine. 'I don't think—I don't know exactly what he thought, but I suspect he didn't believe me, either,' Henrietta admitted reluctantly.

Lady Ipswich nodded several times. 'Lord Pentland clearly attaches as much credence to your tale as I do. You are disgraced, Miss Markham, and I have found you out. Now get out of my sight.'

Chapter Three

Wearily climbing the stairs to her attic room, Henrietta struggled with the resentment that welled up in her breast. She was furious and shocked, but also ashamed—for soon it would be common knowledge in the household. Most of all, though, she was petrified.

Sitting on the narrow bed in her room on the third floor, she stared blindly at the opposite wall while pulling a perfectly good cotton handkerchief to shreds. She had been dismissed from her post. Lady Ipswich had branded her a thief. Heaven knows what Rafe St Alban would make of that. Not that it mattered what Rafe St Alban thought. Not that he'd actually give her a second thought, anyway, except maybe to congratulate himself for not becoming embroiled.

'*Oh, merciful heavens!* If I am brought to trial, he would be called as a witness.' He'd see her clapped in irons in the dock, wearing rags and probably with gaol fever. She knew all about gaol fever. Maisy Masters, who had been teaching her how to make jam from rose-hips, had described it in lurid detail. Maisy's brother had spent six months in prison awaiting trial for poaching. Normally the most taciturn of women, Maisy had been almost too forthcoming on the subject of gaol fever. There was the rash. Then there was the cough and the headaches and the fever. Then there were the sores caused by sleeping on fetid straw and being bitten by fleas. Oh God, and the smells. She would *smell* in the dock. Maisy told her that the lawyers all carried vials of perfume, it was so bad. She would be shamed. Even if she was found innocent, she would be ruined. And if she was not found innocent, she might even be headed for the scaffold. Maisy had told her all about that, too, though she'd tried very hard not to listen. They would sell pamphlets with lurid descriptions of her heinous crime; they would come to watch her, to cheer her last few moments. Mama and Papa would…

Deep breaths.

'Mama and Papa are in Ireland,' she reminded herself, 'and therefore blissfully unaware of my plight.' Which was a blessing, for the moment, at least.

More deep breaths.

They wouldn't find out. They wouldn't ever know. They absolutely could not ever be allowed to know. She must, simply must, find a way to clear her name before they returned to England. Even more importantly, she must find a way to avoid actually being clapped in irons, because once she was in gaol she had no chance of tracking down the real culprit.

Though how she was going to do that she had no idea. 'No matter how you look at it,' she said to herself, 'the situation does not look good. Not good at all.' Just because she had truth on her side did not mean that justice would automatically follow. Malicious or not, Lady Ipswich's version of events had an authentic ring. And she had influence, too.

'Oh dear. Oh dear. *Oh dear.*' Henrietta sniffed woefully. She would not cry. *She would not.* Blinking frantically and sniffing loudly, she wandered about the confines of her bedchamber. She stared out of the casement window on to the kitchen gardens and wondered who was looking after her charges. They would be missing her. Or perhaps Rafe St Alban was right and they would quickly forget her. Though perhaps she would be too notorious for them to forget about her, once they heard that she was a thief. Or in league with one. Worse. Boys being boys, they might even admire her in a misguided way. What kind of example was that to set? She must speak to them somehow, explain. Oh God, what was she to do? What on *earth* was she to do?

Helplessly, Henrietta sank down once more upon the bed. Perhaps by tomorrow Lady Ipswich would have come to her senses. But tomorrow—maybe even by the end of today—would come the Bow Street Runner. And he would take her away to gaol until the next Quarterly Assizes, which were almost two full months away. She could not wait two full months to clear her name. And even if she did, how could she hope to do so with no money to pay anyone to speak on her behalf? She didn't even know if she was permitted to employ a lawyer and, even if she was, she had absolutely no idea how to go about finding one. The authorities would most likely summon Papa, too, and then…

'No!' She couldn't stay here. Whatever happened,

she couldn't just sit here and meekly await her fate. She had to get out. Away. Now!

Without giving herself any more time to think, Henrietta grabbed her bandbox from the cupboard and began to throw her clothes into it willy-nilly. She had few possessions, but as she sat on the lid in a futile effort to make it close, she decided she must make do with fewer still. Her second-best dress was abandoned and the bandbox finally fastened.

She spent a further half-hour composing a note to her charges. In the end, it was most unsatisfactory, simply begging their forgiveness for her sudden departure, bidding them stick to their lessons and not to think ill of her, no matter what they heard.

It was by now well past noon. The servants would be at their dinner. Lady Ipswich would be in her boudoir. Tying the ribbons of her plain-straw poke bonnet in a neat bow under her chin, Henrietta draped her cloak around her shoulders and cautiously opened the door.

Stealing down the steps in a manner quite befitting the housebreaker's accomplice she was purported to be, she slipped through a side door into the kitchen garden and thence on to the gravelled path that led from the stables, without once allowing herself to look back. At the gates she turned on to the road that led to the village. A short distance further on, Henrietta sat down on an inviting tree trunk with her back to the road and indulged in a hearty bout of tears.

She was not given to self-pity, but at this moment she felt she was entitled to be just a little sorry for herself. Already she was regretting her impulsive behaviour.

All very well to make her escape with some vague idea of clearing her name, but how, exactly, did she propose to do that?

The dispiriting truth was that she had no idea. 'And now that I have run away, they will think it simply confirms my guilt,' she said to her shoe. A large tear splashed on to the ground. 'Stupid, stupid, stupid,' she muttered, sniffing valiantly.

She had not a soul in the world to turn to. Her only relative, as far as she knew, was Mama's sister; Henrietta could hardly turn up on the doorstep of an aunt whom she had never met and introduce herself as her long-lost niece and a fugitive from the law, to boot. Besides, there was the small matter of the rift between Mama and her sibling. They had not spoken for many years. No, that was not an option.

But she could not go back, either. She had been badly shaken by the ease with which her employer had accepted her guilt, and that, on top of Rafe St Alban's scepticism, made her question whether anyone would take her side without proof. No, there was no going back. The only way was forwards. And the only path she could think of taking was to London. Such distinctive jewellery must be got rid of somehow and London was surely the place. She would head to the city. And once there she would—she would— Oh, she would think about that, once she was on her way.

What she needed to think about now was how to get there. Henrietta rummaged in her bandbox for her stocking purse and carefully counted out the total of her wealth, which came to the grand sum of eight shillings and sixpence. She gazed at the small mound of coins, wondering vaguely if it was enough to pay for a seat on the mail, realised she would be better keeping her money to pay for a room at an inn, returned them to the purse and got wearily to her feet. She could not remain on this tree trunk for ever. Picking up her bandbox, with the vague idea of obtaining a ride in the direction of the metropolis, she set off down the road towards the village.

The fields that bordered the wayside were freshly tilled and planted with hops and barley, sprouting green and lush. The hedgerows, where honeysuckle and clematis rioted among the briars of the blackberries, whose white flowers were not yet unfurled, provided her with occasional shade from the sun shining bright in the pale blue of the early summer sky. The landscape undulated gently. The air was rent with birdsong. It was a lovely day. A lovely day to be a fugitive from justice, she thought bitterly

For the first mile, she made good progress, her head full of fantastical schemes for the recovery of Lady Ipswich's necklace. The illicit hours she had devoted to reading the novels of the Minerva Press had not been entirely wasted. Before long, however, reality intervened. The straps from her bandbox were cutting into her hand; her cloak, the only outerwear she possessed, was designed for the depths of winter, not to be combined with a woollen dress in early summer. Her face was decidedly red under her bonnet and she could not conceive how such a few necessities as she carried could come to weigh so much. A pretty copse, where foxgloves and the last of the bluebells made vivid splashes of colour, failed to fill her with admiration for the abundant joys of nature. She was not in the mood to appreciate rural perfection. In fact, it would not be inaccurate to say that Henrietta's temper was sadly frayed.

By the time she finally approached her destination she was convinced she had a blister on her foot where a small pebble had lodged inside her shoe, her shoulders ached, her head thumped and she wanted nothing more than a cool drink and a rest in a darkened room.

The King George was a ramshackle inn situated at a crossroads on the outer reaches of Woodfield village. The weathered board, with its picture of the poor mad king, creaked on rusted hinges by the entrance to the yard, where a mangy dog lazily scratched its ear beside a bale of hay. Dubiously inspecting the huddle of badly maintained buildings that constituted the hostelry, Henrietta was regaled by a burst of hearty male laughter that echoed out from behind the shuttered windows. Not a place to trust the sheets, never mind the clientele, she concluded. Her heart sank.

The front door gave straight into the taproom, which she had not expected. The hushed silence that greeted her entrance proved that she had taken the patrons equally by surprise. For a moment, Henrietta, clutching her cloak around her, stared at the sea of faces in front of her like a small animal caught in a trap and the men stared back as if she were a creature fished from the deep. Her courage almost failed her.

When the landlord asked her gruffly what she wanted, her voice came out in a whisper. His answer was disappointing. The mail was not due until tomorrow. The accommodation coach was fully booked for the next two days. He looked at her curiously. Why hadn't she thought to enquire ahead? Was her business in London urgent? If so, he could probably get her a ride with one of his customers as far as the first posting inn, where she could pick up the Bristol coach that evening.

Suddenly horribly aware that the less people who knew of her whereabouts, the better, Henrietta declined this invitation and informed the landlord that she had changed her mind. She was not going to London, she informed him. She was definitely not going to London.

With a mumbled apology, she retreated back out of the front door and found herself in the stable yard, where a racing carriage was tethered, the horses fidgeting nervously. There was no sign of the driver. The phaeton was painted dark glossy green, the spokes of its four high wheels trimmed with gold, but there were otherwise no distinguishing marks. No coat of arms. The horses were a perfectly matched pair of chestnuts. Such a fine equipage must surely be London-bound.

Henrietta eyed it nervously, a reckless idea forming in her head. The seat seemed a very long way from the ground. The rumble seat behind, upon which was stowed a portmanteau and a large blanket, was not much lower. The hood of the phaeton was raised, presumably because the owner anticipated rain. If he did not look at the rumble seat—and why would he?—then he would not see her. If she did not take this chance, who knew what other would present itself? The spectres of the Bow Street Runner and Maisy Masters's tales of prison loomed before her. Without giving herself time to think further, Henrietta scrambled on to the rear seat of the carriage, clutching her bandbox. Crouching down as far as she could under the rumble seat itself, she pulled the blanket over her and waited.

She did not have to wait long. Just a few minutes later, she felt the carriage lurch as its driver climbed aboard and almost immediately urged the horses forwards. Only one person? Straining her ears, she could hear nothing above the jangle of the tack and the rumbling of the wheels. The carriage swung round past the front of the King George and headed at a trot out of the village. Sneaking a peak out of the blanket, she thought they were headed in the right direction, but could not be sure. As they hit a deep rut in the road, she only just stopped herself from crying out and clutched frantically at the edge of the rumble seat to stop herself from tumbling on to the road.

The driver loosened his hold on the reins and cracked the whip. The horses made short work of quitting the environs of Woodfield village. As they bowled along, Henrietta tried to subdue a rising panic. What had she done? She could not be at all sure they were headed towards London and had no idea at all who was driving her. He might be angry when he discovered her. He might simply abandon her in the middle of nowhere. Or worse! She did not want to think about what worse was. *Oh God, she had been a complete idiot.*

The carriage picked up speed. Hedgerows fragrant with rosehip and honeysuckle flew past in a blur as she peered out from under her blanket. Beyond, the landscape was vibrant with fields of swaying hops. She glimpsed an oast house, its conical roof so reminiscent of a witch's hat. They passed through a village, no more than a cluster of thatched cottages surrounding a water mill. Then another. Farms. The occasional farmer's cart rumbled past heading in the opposite direction. On a clear stretch of road, they overtook an accommodation coach with a burst of acceleration that had Henrietta grabbing on to the sides of the phaeton. The driver of the coach raised his whip in acknowledgement.

Jolted and bruised, cramped and sore, her head aching again, Henrietta clung to the seat and clung also to the one reassuring fact, that at least she had avoided Lady Ipswich's Bow Street Runner. She found little else to console her as they sped on through unfamiliar countryside and soon gave up trying. The events of the past twenty-four hours finally took their toll. Exhausted, shocked, bruised and confused, Henrietta fell into a fitful dose.

When she awoke, it was to find that the carriage had slowed. They seemed to be following a river, and it seemed wide enough to surely be the Thames. She tried to stretch, but her limbs had gone into a cramp. She was weighing up the risks of emerging from under the seat when they turned off the road through a gap in the hedgerow.

A swathe of grass rolled down to the wide, slow-moving river. Henrietta's heart began to pound very hard and very loud—so loud she was sure it could be heard. Should she huddle down further or make a break for it? Should she stay to brazen it out, perhaps even request to be allowed to complete the journey? Or should she take her chances with her very limited funds and even more limited knowledge of where she was?

The chassis tilted as the driver leapt down. He was

tall. She caught a glimpse of a beaver hat before he disappeared round to the front of the horses, leading them down to the water and tethering them there. It was now or never, while he was tending to them, but panic made her freeze. *Get out, get out*, she chided herself, but her limbs wouldn't move.

'What the devil!'

The blanket was yanked back. Henrietta blinked up at the figure looming over her.

He was just as tall and dark and handsome as she remembered; he was looking at her as if she were every bit as unwelcome an intrusion into his life as she had been this morning. 'Lord Pentland.'

'Miss Markham, we meet again. What the hell are you doing in my carriage?'

Her mouth seemed to have dried up, like her words. Henrietta sought desperately for an explanation he would find acceptable, but the shock was too much. 'I didn't know it was yours,' she said lamely.

'Whose did you think it was?'

'I didn't know,' she said, feeling extremely foolish and extremely nervous. His winged brows were drawn together in his devilish look. Of all the people, why did it have to be him!

'Get out.'

He held out an imperious hand. She tried to move, but her legs were stiff and her petticoats had become entangled in her bandbox. With an exclamation of impatience, he pulled her towards him. For a brief moment she was in his arms, held high against his chest, then she was dumped unceremoniously on to her feet, her bandbox tumbling out with her, tipping its contents—its very personal contents—on to the grass. Her legs gave way. Henrietta plopped to the grass beside her undergarments and promptly burst into tears.

Rafe's anger at having harboured a stowaway gave way to a wholly inappropriate desire to laugh, for she looked absurdly like one of those mawkish drawings of an orphaned child. Gathering up the collection of intimate garments, hairbrushes, combs and other rather shabby paraphernalia, he squashed them back into the bandbox and pulled its owner back to her feet. 'Come, stop that noise, else anyone passing will stop and accuse me of God knows what heinous crime.'

He meant it as a jest, but it served only to make his woebegone companion sob harder. Realising that she was genuinely overwrought, Rafe picked up the blanket and led her over to his favourite spot on the riverbank, where he sat her down and handed her a large square of clean linen. 'Dry your eyes and compose yourself, tears will get us nowhere.'

'I know that. There is no need to tell me so, I know it *perfectly* well,' Henrietta wailed. But it took her some moments of sniffing, dabbing and deep breaths to do as he urged, by which time she was certain she must look a very sorry sight indeed, with red cheeks and a redder nose.

Watching her valiant attempts to regain control of herself, Rafe felt his conscience, normally the most complacent of creatures, stir and his anger subside. Obviously Henrietta had been dismissed. Obviously her ridiculous tale of housebreakers was at the root of it. Obviously Helen Ipswich hadn't believed her. He hadn't expected her to, but despite that fact, he had sent her off to face her fate alone. Faced with the sorry and very vulnerable-looking evidence of this act before him, Rafe felt genuine remorse. Those big chocolate-brown eyes of Henrietta Markham's were still drowning in tears. Her full bottom lip was trembling. Not even the ordeal of lying in a ditch overnight had resulted in tears. Something drastic must have occurred. 'Tell me what happened,' he said.

The gentleness in his tone almost overset her again. The change in his manner, too, from that white-lipped fury to—to—almost, she could believe he cared. Almost. 'It's nothing. Nothing to do with you. I am just—it is nothing.' Henrietta swallowed hard and stared resolutely at her hands. His kerchief was of the finest lawn, his initials embroidered in one corner. She could not have achieved such beautiful stitchery. She wondered who had sewn it. She sniffed again. Sneaking a look, she saw that his eyes were blue, not stormy-grey, that his mouth was formed into something that looked very like a sympathetic smile.

'I take it that you have left Lady Ipswich's employ?'

Henrietta clenched her fists. 'She accused me of theft.'

He had not expected that. Unbelievable as her tale was, he had not thought for a moment that she was a thief. 'You're not serious?'

'Yes, I am. She said I was in cahoots with the house-breaker. She said I opened the safe and broke a window to make it look as if he had broken in.'

'A safe? Then whatever was stolen was of some value?'

Henrietta nodded. 'An heirloom. The Ipswich

emeralds. The magistrate has summoned a Bow Street Runner. Lady Ipswich ordered me to stay in my room until he arrives to arrest me.'

Rafe looked at her incredulously. 'The Ipswich emeralds? Rich pickings indeed for a common housebreaker.'

'Exactly. It's a hanging matter. And she—she—by implicating me—she—I had to leave, else I would have been cast into gaol.' Henrietta's voice trembled, but a few more gulps of air stemmed the tears. 'I don't want to go to gaol.'

Rafe tapped his riding crop on his booted foot. 'Tell me exactly what was said when you returned this morning.'

Henrietta did so, haltingly at first in her efforts to recall every detail, then with increasing vehemence as she recounted the astonishing accusations levelled at her. 'I still can't quite believe it. I would never, never do such a thing,' she finished fervently. 'I couldn't just sit there and wait to be dragged off to prison. I couldn't bear for Papa to be told that his only child was being held in gaol.'

'So you stowed away in my carriage.'

Rafe's eyes were hooded by his lids again. She could not read his thoughts. She had never come across such an inscrutable countenance, nor one which could change so completely yet so subtly. 'Yes, I did,' she declared defensively. 'I didn't have any option, I had to get away.'

'Do you realise that by doing so you have embroiled me, against my will, in your little melodrama? Did you think of that?'

'No. I didn't. It didn't occur to me.'

'Of course not, because you act as you speak, don't you, without thinking?'

'That's not fair,' Henrietta said indignantly. She knew it *was* fair, but that fact made her all the more anxious to defend herself. 'It's your fault, you make me nervous; besides, I didn't know it was your carriage.'

'As well for you that it was. Did you think what might have happened if it had belonged to some buck?' Rafe's mouth thinned again. 'But I forgot, it could not be worse, could it, for you are now at the mercy of a notorious rake. Consider that, Miss Markham.'

'I am considering it,' she threw back at him, angry enough now to speak the truth. 'This morning I was even more at your mercy, in your bed in my underclothes, and you pretended to but really, you made no real attempt at all to—to…'

'To what?' He knew he was being unfair, but he could not help it. Something about her exasperated him. She made him want to shake the innocence out of her, yet at the same time he was fighting the quite contrary urge to protect her. He didn't understand it. He didn't try. 'What, could it be that you are insulted by my gentlemanly behaviour? Did you want me to kiss you, Miss Markham?'

Colour flooded her face. 'Of course I did not. I was *pleased* you did not find me attractive.'

'But you are quite mistaken. I do.'

His tone was mocking, his expression almost predatory. His thigh was brushing hers. *How had he come to be so close?* She could feel the warmth of him, even through the heavy folds of her cape and gown. Though he had shaved this morning, she could already see a shadow of stubble on his jaw line. She felt as if she couldn't breathe. Or as if her breath had become sharp. It hurt her throat. Her pulses were pounding. She felt afraid. Not afraid, exactly. Apprehension mixed with excitement. And for some reason, it was a nice feeling.

She didn't know how the conversation had taken this turn. All she could think about was that Rafe St Alban had admitted that he found her, Henrietta Markham, attractive. Even though she knew for a fact that she wasn't beautiful. Mama was beautiful. Mama said that it was as well that Henrietta didn't take after her, because such beauty was dangerous. It attracted the wrong sort of man. It attracted men like Rafe St Alban. Except Henrietta wasn't a dangerous beauty and Rafe St Alban was apparently still attracted to her.

'Lost for words, most verbose Miss Markham?'

He was so close she could feel his breath on her face. She should move, but she couldn't. Didn't want to. 'I don't…'

'Such a notorious rake as you think I am,' Rafe said huskily, 'it seems only fair that I should live up to my reputation. It seems only fair, my delectable stowaway, that you should pay the price for taking advantage of me. Twice, now, you have given me no option but to rescue you. I am entitled to some form of reward.'

He hadn't meant to do it, but he couldn't seem to stop himself. He hadn't realised how much he had been tempted until he gave in and kissed her. He hadn't realised just how much he wanted to, until he kissed the little tilt at the corner or her mouth, which made her look as if she was always on the verge of a smile. He had meant it as only a small rebuke, a mild punishment, but she tasted so sweet, she smelled so fresh, of sunshine and tears, and her mouth was quite the most kissable he had ever seen, that it was he who was punished by the eruption of unwelcome desire. Uncontrollable desire. Her mouth was plump, pink and soft. A veritable cushion for kisses. He allowed his lips to drift over hers and kissed her again, an appetiser of a kiss. And then, when she made no move to pull away, he teased her lips open with his tongue and kissed her again, and for the first time in a very, very long time, Rafe forgot all about where he was and who he was and how things were, and lost himself in the simple pleasure of a pair of soft, welcoming lips and the delight of a soft, welcoming body.

For Henrietta, time stopped, though the birds still sang, the breeze still rustled in the tree above them. Her heart, too, seemed to stop. She was afraid to move, lest the spell be broken. Her first kiss. And such a kiss. His mouth so very different from hers. His touch on her shoulders, her back, moulding her into him. She allowed herself to be moulded. Then she began to relish it. She should be shocked, but she was not shocked. She was entranced.

When he released her she could only stare, clutching at his coat in a most undignified manner, raising a hand to her mouth in wonder. 'I've never been kissed before,' she blurted out, then blushed vividly.

'I could tell,' Rafe said.

'Oh. Was it—was I…?'

'It was very nice.' *Much too nice*—it had provoked a disconcerting reaction in him. He, who prided himself on his self-control, had felt something akin to abandon flare in him. Not lust, something more primal, more sensual. He shifted on the blanket in order to put some distance between them, to disguise the incontrovertible evidence of his own arousal.

'Oh.'

'I, on the other hand, am not nice. You would do well to remember that, Henrietta.'

The warning in his voice was unmistakable. When he laughed, he looked like a different person, but already the shutters were coming back down, his lids shielding his eyes, his mouth straightening. 'I think you would like me to think so,' Henrietta replied daringly.

'I thought you already did?'

An ominous silence followed as Henrietta tried desperately to assemble her thoughts. 'I did,' she admitted finally, 'but now I'm confused.'

He admired her honesty, though he would not dream of emulating it. He was confused himself. He shouldn't have kissed her. He had meant it as a punishment, but it had backfired. She had awoken something long dormant in him. A kiss with feeling. He didn't want to kiss with feeling, any more than he wanted to deal with the problem of what to do with her.

'I stopped here to eat,' he said, getting quickly to his feet. 'You must be hungry, too. Perhaps a full stomach will help us sort out this damned predicament you've placed me in.'

Henrietta watched in something of a daze as Rafe strode over to the phaeton and began to haul out a hamper, which she hadn't previously noticed, from behind his portmanteau. She touched her lips, which still tingled from his caress. He had kissed her! Rafe

St Alban had kissed her, and she had kissed him back. She was a shameless hussy!

Was she? She didn't feel shameless. She felt—she had no idea how she felt. As if she did not know if she was on her head or her heels. As if her brain was cotton wool. As if the world had turned upside down and deposited her in a strange land. She felt as if she had drunk too much of the cherry brandy one of the villagers gave Papa at Christmas, or as if she were dreaming, for nothing that had happened in the last few hours bore any resemblance at all to her usual life. Especially not that kiss.

She touched her lips again, trying to recapture it. Heady, like wine. Sweet, like honey. Melting. No wonder kisses led people astray. Another of Rafe St Alban's kisses and she would willingly have been led astray. Wherever astray was. A place inhabited by rakes. Rakes who preyed upon the innocent. Once again, Henrietta reminded herself to be on her guard. The problem was, there was a rebellious part of her, a part which Rafe's kiss had conjured into life, that wasn't at all interested in being on guard. Mama implied that what maidens suffered at the hands of rakes was unpleasant. What Henrietta had suffered had been quite the contrary. Surely Mama could not be wrong?

Rafe placed the hamper down on the blanket at Henrietta's feet. 'I often stop here on my journey between Woodfield and London, I much prefer it to a posting inn.'

He began to unpack the food. There was a game pie, the pastry golden brown and flaky, a whole chicken roasted and fragrant with sage-and-onion stuffing, quails eggs, cold salmon in aspic jelly, a Derby cheese and a basket of early strawberries.

'Goodness, there's enough here to feed a small army,' Henrietta said, looking at the delightful feast laid out before her with awe.

Rafe was busy with bottles and glasses. 'Is there? We are not obliged to eat it all, you know. Do you wish claret or burgundy? I'd recommend the claret myself, the burgundy is a little too heavy for alfresco eating.'

Henrietta giggled. 'Claret, please.'

'What's so amusing?'

'This. You and me, the earl and the governess, having a meal by the Thames. I've never seen such a delicious picnic in my life.'

'It's plain enough fare.'

'For you, maybe. I am used to much plainer at home.'

Rafe helped them both to a generous wedge of pie. 'Tell me more about your family.'

'There's nothing much to tell.'

'Are you an only child?'

'Yes.'

'And you have no other relatives?'

'I have an aunt, but I've never met her. Mama's family considered Papa beneath them. They did not approve of the match and liked it a lot less when they realised he intended to spend his life helping other people to better themselves, rather than doing the same for his own family.'

'You admire your father?'

Henrietta considered this. 'Yes, in a way. I don't necessarily agree with how he goes about things, nor indeed with his priorities, but he is true to himself. And to Mama.'

Her hand was hovering over a bowl of strawberries. Rafe picked one out and popped it into her mouth. The juice glistened on her lips. He leaned towards her, catching it with his thumb. Her tongue automatically flicked out to lick it clean. Awareness shot like an arrow through his blood, making him instantly hard. He leaned closer, replacing his thumb with his mouth. A brief touch, no more, enough for her eyes to widen, her lips to soften in anticipation, his erection to harden.

Enough and not nearly enough. 'You have the most kissable lips I have ever come across, Henrietta Markham, you should be aware of that, and consider yourself warned. Have you had enough?'

'Enough?' She stared at him in incomprehension. Could he see the way her heart was beating? The way her flesh was covered in goose bumps? Could he sense the way she turned hot, then cold?

'Have you had sufficient to eat? Because if you have, I feel it is time to address the thorny question of what the deuce I'm going to do with you.'

'Do with me? You need do nothing more than deposit me in London, if you please.'

'What do you intend to do there, go into hiding? This will not blow over, you know. The Ipswich emeralds are no fripperies.'

'I know. Do you think me an idiot as well as a thief?'

'I think you any number of things, but I don't think you're capable of stealing. You are far too honest.'

'Oh.'

'You are also far too quick to share your opinions,

even quicker to judge. You make wild assumptions based on nothing but hearsay, you see the world in black and white and refuse to acknowledge any sort of grey, but like your father, I suspect, you are true to yourself. I don't think you are a thief.'

She hadn't realised until this point how much it mattered. To be thought of so ill had cut her to the quick. Even though he was a rake, it mattered. 'So you believe me?'

'Poor Henrietta, you have had a torrid time of it these last few hours.'

'There are always people more unfortunate than oneself,' Henrietta said stoutly. 'That is what Papa says.'

Rafe looked sceptical, wondering what Henrietta's other-worldly father would make of his daughter's current predicament. 'Not so very many. You do realise that by running away you have made a difficult situation much worse?'

'I know, but—'

'Your doing so will be seen to simply confirm your guilt.'

'I *know*, but I could not think of any other—'

'By rights I should hand you over to the authorities, let you take your chances. You are, after all, innocent. The problem is you have, by your actions, behaved guiltily and worse, implicated me.'

'But no one saw me climb into your carriage, and...'

'They do know that I found you. They know that I was involved in sending you back to Helen Ipswich's. When it becomes also known that I left Woodfield at about the same time you disappeared, even a Bow Street Runner will put two and two together. You have placed me in an impossible position. I cannot turn you in without risking being found guilty by association, but neither can I in all conscience simply abandon you.'

Rafe was not a man given to chivalry. He was not a man much given to impulsive action, either, but Henrietta Markham's endearing courage, her genuine horror at the accusations levelled against her and the very real dangers that she faced, roused him now to both. Whether he wanted to be or not, he was involved in this farce. That his involvement would, of necessity, postpone the unpleasant task of putting his grandmother straight was a small bonus. 'I have no choice. I'll help you,' he said, nodding to himself. It was the only way.

'Help me to do what?'

'Find the thief. The emeralds. Whatever it takes to clear your name.'

'I am perfectly capable of doing that myself,' Henrietta said indignantly and quite contrarily, because for a moment there, when he had offered, her heart had leapt in relief.

'How?'

'What do you mean?'

'Have you contacts in the underworld?'

'No, but—'

'Do you have any idea how to go about tracing stolen property?'

'No, but—'

'Admit it, Henrietta, you have no idea at all how to go about anything, have you? No plan.'

'No, none whatsoever.'

Rafe's smile lurked. His pleasure at her admission was quite out of proportion. It was a small enough victory, but it felt significant. He liked that she did not prevaricate even when it cost her dear. 'Then it is very fortunate that I do,' he said. The pleasure he took in her smile was also quite out of proportion.

'You do?'

'Obviously you need someone to assist you,' Rafe said, allowing his own smile to widen. 'A man with contacts in the underworld, who can trace the stolen jewellery, the thief or ideally both.'

'Obviously,' Henrietta replied, feeling slightly dazed by the prospect. 'Next you will tell me how I should go about finding such a man?'

'There is no need. You have already found him. Me.'

Chapter Four

'You?' Henrietta said incredulously.

She was staring at him as if he had just escaped from Bedlam. Once more, he had to bite his lip to suppress his smile. 'I have an acquaintance in London who has any number of contacts in such circles,' Rafe explained. 'A prize haul such as the Ipswich emeralds should not be too difficult to trace for someone in the know.'

'You are making a May game of me, you must be. How do you come to know such a person? And even if you did—I mean do—I mean, I don't understand. Why would you?'

'Under the circumstances, you have left me no option but to help you sort out this appalling mess.' The prospect was surprisingly appealing, but Rafe chose not to share this information. Indeed, he barely acknowledged it himself.

But, annoyingly, Henrietta shook her head most decidedly. 'Truly, I am much obliged for your generous offer, but my plight is my responsibility.'

'You would be most unwise to refuse my offer of help.'

She chewed her lip. What other options did she have, really? What was worse, placing herself in the hands of a rake who might or might not have designs on her virtue, but seemed honestly to be intent upon clearing her name, or taking the risk of being imprisoned, perhaps condemned? What use was virtue if she was deported or dead? And for goodness' sake, it wasn't as if she was about to surrender her virtue, anyway. It wasn't as if her virtue was to be payment. *Was it?* Was kissing to be considered payment for his helping her? Was there a higher price to be paid? Would he expect more?

She was being ridiculous. No matter what his expectations, she would not oblige him and one thing of which she was certain was that he would not take what was not given. He could have done *that* this morning. She was perfectly safe from him. Provided she was sure of herself. Which she was. Of course she was.

Henrietta nodded to herself. Rafe St Alban was clearly the lesser of two evils. The only sensible option. She would be a fool not to accept his offer. 'You are right, I don't have any choice,' she said.

'Very sensible, Miss Markham.'

'I like to think I am.'

'So you will trust me?'

She hesitated, alerted by the hint of something in his voice. 'To help me. Yes, I will trust you to do that.'

'Very careful and very wise, Henrietta. An equivocal response.'

'Lord Pentland…'

'Rafe will do. I think we've gone well beyond observing the niceties.'

'Rafe. It suits you.'

'Thank you. Let me return the compliment. I have never before been acquainted with a Henrietta, but the name seems to be made for you.'

'Thank you. I think. I was named for Papa.'

The way he was looking at her was giving her a shivery feeling, as if she were standing on the brink of something. Was she really thinking of throwing her lot in with him, an incredibly, devastatingly handsome stranger who had a reputation? 'Won't people be expecting you in town?'

Rafe considered that. There was his grandmother, with her list of eligible brides waiting for his approval. There were no doubt a new stack of gilt-edged invitations on his desk, for the Season was in full swing. Despite his notorious reclusiveness—exclusiveness, as Lucas liked to refer to it—Lord Pentland's attendance at any party or rout or ball was a feather in the hostess's cap, so he continued to receive them by the hatful.

'Save for Lucas, to be honest, I don't think there's a single person who will really miss me, any more than I can think of a single engagement which I would actually enjoy attending.'

'Who is Lucas?'

'The Right Honourable Lucas Hamilton. One of my oldest friends. We met at the Falls of Tivoli while on our respective Grand Tours. Hadrian's Villa is near there, you know, so it's *de rigueur* to visit, though I have to say I was disappointed by it. We found we were both destined for Greece and met up again there. Lucas's ancient Greek put mine to shame. He's much more of a scholar than I, though he keeps that fact very quiet. Prefers to be known for his prowess in the ring.'

'He fights?'

Rafe laughed. 'Not professionally—though he'd be up for it, most likely, if it were offered. No, whatever you may say of him, Lucas is ever the gentleman. He boxes only with fellow gentlemen at Jackson's. He fences with fellow gentlemen at Angelo's. And he drinks every fellow gentleman who is up for the challenge under the table.'

'He sounds a very colourful character,' Henrietta said doubtfully.

'He does get into some scrapes when I'm not around to keep an eye on him.'

'It sounds as if he's very lucky to have you.'

Rafe's smile faded. 'I'm Lucas's friend, not his keeper. For reasons known only to himself, Lucas seems hellbent on self-destruction. He will do that whether I am there to take care of him or not. You know, I can't think why I'm telling you this. In any event it should only take a few days to clean this emeralds business up. Lucas can look after himself until then.'

'How can you know that it will only take us a few days?'

'Distinctive emeralds and a very distinctive house-breaker must leave a distinctive trail, if one knows where to look. I'm pretty sure we'll be able to track one or both down very quickly. At least, my friend will.'

'I'm very grateful for your help. Truly I am.'

'I am very glad to offer it,' Rafe said, surprising himself with the truth. She was dressed quite atrociously in badly cut and patchily darned brown. He had never seen quite such a lopsided bow on a bonnet, but she was looking at him as if her life depended upon him and he supposed that at present it did. 'Really and truly.'

Whatever the next few days held in store for him, it was unlikely to be boring. Anxious, now that he had committed himself, to be gone, Rafe set about untethering the horses.

Sitting beside him on the narrow seat of the phaeton, Henrietta was acutely aware of Rafe's presence. Her thigh brushed against his. She nudged his whip hand by mistake. *Was she insane to be setting out with him like this?* She knew almost nothing about him save that he was rich and titled and a rake and a very accomplished kisser. Probably on account of being a rake. And yet here she was, sitting nonchalantly—sort of nonchalantly—beside him. She *must* be mad! She ought to think so, and certainly her inner governess did think so, but Henrietta was finding it increasingly easy to ignore her inner governess.

What an odd picture they must make, she in her ancient cloak and out-of-date bonnet and he the epitome of fashion. She counted at least six capes on his drab driving coat. His gloves were of the softest York tan leather; his buckskins fitted so tightly that they looked as if he had been sewn into them; his black boots had light-brown tops, which she had once heard one of her charges describe as all the crack. It made her horribly conscious of her own shabby attire. She pulled the carriage blanket more tightly around her in an effort to disguise it.

'Are you cold?'

'No. Oh, no. I was just thinking that I wished my clothes were more appropriate for your elegant carriage,' Henrietta replied, 'I'm afraid governesses are not accustomed to dressing in silk and lace.'

'For what it's worth, I think silk and lace would suit you very well,' Rafe said, and then wondered at his saying so. The image was appealing. His thoughts seemed to be increasingly straying to the carnal. Maybe it was time he selected a new mistress from the many willing volunteers available to him. The idea filled him with ennui.

Henrietta, whose imagination ran rather to silk promenade dresses than lace peignoirs, was looking wistful. 'I have never owned a silk gown, or even gone to a ball. Not that I can dance. Anyway, Mama says that clothes do not make a woman.'

'Mama has obviously never visited Almack's on a Wednesday night,' Rafe said drily. 'What about Papa— what has he to say on the subject?'

Henrietta giggled. 'I don't think the topic has ever come up.' A few hours ago, the question would have set her on edge. She was no longer so nervous that she allowed her tongue to run away with her, though it could not by any stretch of the imagination be said that she was relaxed.

'Never?' Rafe said in mock astonishment. 'Has Papa no ambition to find you a husband?'

Annoyed by what she took to be implied criticism, Henrietta bristled. 'Papa would not consider a husband found at a dance to be particularly suitable.'

'How refreshing,' Rafe said ironically, 'and quite

contrary to the opinion of all the other papas of my acquaintance.'

'That does not make him wrong and there is no need to be so rude.'

'I apologise. I did not intend to insult your father.'

'Yes, you did,' Henrietta said forthrightly.

Rafe was not used to people saying what they meant and certainly not women, but Henrietta was not at all like any other woman he had ever met. 'I did,' he admitted, 'but I will endeavour not do so again.'

'Thank you.'

'You are most welcome. At least now I know why you have reached the ripe old age of what—twenty-one?'

'I am three and twenty.'

'Three and twenty, and you are still unattached. Most young ladies would consider themselves practically on the shelf. You must learn to dance, Henrietta, while there is still time.'

She knew he was teasing her because she could see his mouth twitch, as if he were suppressing a smile. 'Oh, you mistake the matter entirely,' she said airily. 'Papa and Mama have already introduced me to several eligible young men of their acquaintance.'

'What happened, did none of them come up to scratch?'

'If you mean did they propose, then, yes. And each one was more worthy and more sincere than the last.'

'And therefore unutterably dull and boring.'

'Yes! Oh, now look what you have made me say.'

'Henrietta Markham, you ought to be ashamed.'

'Oh, I am.' She bit her lip, but it was impossible not

to laugh when he looked at her just so. 'Oh dear. I know I *ought* to be, but…'

'But you are a romantic and you wish to be swept off your feet and cannot be ashamed of being disappointed by the worthy young men your father has presented to you?'

'What is wrong with that? Every woman wants to be swept off her feet. I mean, respect and worthiness are all very well, but…'

'You want to fall in love.'

'Yes, of course. Doesn't everyone?'

'Certainly everyone says so, though they rarely mean it. *I love you* is what people say when they think it will get them what they want.'

His mouth was still smiling, but it seemed to have frozen. 'That's very cynical,' Henrietta said, thinking of the beautiful woman in the portrait. She touched his sleeve sympathetically. 'I know you don't mean it, it is probably that you are still grieving.'

'What are you talking about?'

'Mrs Peters told me about your wife.'

'Told you what, exactly?'

'Only that she died tragically young. She showed me her portrait. She was very beautiful.'

'I don't wish to discuss her,' Rafe snapped. 'I see I shall have to take steps to ensure that my housekeeper is reminded of the value I put upon discretion.'

'Oh, *indeed*, it was not her fault, it was mine. I was surprised you had not mentioned—I said I did not know you were married, and then she said that you were a widower and then—oh dear, I'm so sorry, I didn't mean to get her into trouble. I didn't mean to intrude.'

'And yet you have done so. I will not tolerate people prying behind my back.'

'I was not prying, I was just curious. It's a natural enough thing to ask. After all, you have just asked me the same sort of questions about my family.'

'It is not the same,' Rafe said curtly.

'Very well, then, I shall keep quiet.' Henrietta folded her lips and her arms, and sat back, turning her attention firmly to the passing scenery. 'Very quiet,' she said, a few minutes later. She had said the wrong thing again, clearly, but how was she to know what was the right thing? What was wrong with him, that he couldn't even have a perfectly normal conversation about his dead wife? His dead, beautiful wife with the soulless eyes, who had presumably known him before he acquired the cynicism that he wore like a suit of armour.

Shifting in her seat, she took covert surveillance of the brooding bulk of man at her side. He didn't like to be questioned and didn't like to be contradicted. He most certainly didn't like to explain himself. Could such a man really fall in love? But then, maybe all those years ago he had been a different man. Maybe all those years ago he had been happy. He certainly wasn't happy now. What had happened to make him so? The question, which had hovered upon her lips almost from the moment she had first set eyes on him, refused to go away.

Henrietta continued to study him from the shadow of her poke bonnet. Five years he had been a widower. Five years was a long time. The Earl of Pentland could surely have his pick of marriageable ladies. *Why had he not remarried?*

'I beg your pardon?'

Only when he spoke did Henrietta realise to her utter horror that she had posed the question aloud. She stared at him, too stricken to reply.

'I have no wish to marry again.'

'You mean never?' Henrietta said incredulously.

'Never.' Rafe's tone was positively glacial, but he should have known by now that Henrietta would take no heed.

She did not, too astonished to even notice. 'I would have thought that you would need to remarry, if for no other reason than to produce an heir to pass the title on to. Unless—oh, it didn't occur to me, do you have a child already?'

It seemed a natural enough question given that he *had* been married, but she saw at once that Rafe did not think so. His countenance did an excellent impression of turning to granite.

'Nor did it occur to you that your impertinence knows no bounds,' he said. He cracked the whip to urge the horses into a gallop. An hour passed, with Henrietta increasingly conscious of the strained silence, of the anger simmering in the man sitting rigidly by her side, horribly aware that she had touched some very private and painful wound. He had visibly retreated from her; she could almost see the dark cloud which hovered over him. Miserably aware that she had been the one to summon it, albeit unwittingly, she was also quite unable to summon up the courage to do anything about it, for fear of being further rebuffed.

It was early evening as they neared London. The traffic on the road became noticeably heavier, forcing

Rafe to concentrate on his driving. Carts, drays and gigs jostled for position with lumbering stagecoaches, town coaches and other sporting vehicles. The mail thundered past in a cloud of dust.

Henrietta became more tense with every passing mile. Though the noise and bustle of the city-bound traffic were exciting and it was most certainly busy enough to give her ample opportunity to admire Rafe's consummate driving skills, she was concerned with more mundane matters. For a start she had almost no money. It was one thing to accept Rafe's help, quite another to be beholden to him. She had no idea how much a night at a London hostelry would cost, but suspected her meagre finances would not run to more than one or two.

She cleared her throat. 'I was wondering, shall we meet up with your—your friend tonight?'

He did not take his eyes from the road. 'Hopefully.'

'And when we have spoken with him, shall we—shall you—what do you intend to do then?'

Having negotiated a safe path between a dray heavily laden with beer barrels and a small gig, Rafe risked a glance over at her. 'I have no intention of abandoning you, if that's what you are worried about.'

'It's not that. Only partly. But you will want to go to your London home, will you not?'

'I sent no word ahead. Besides, I can't go there, not yet, just in case the Runner, finding me not at home in Woodfield Manor, decides to come to London to try to obtain an interview with me at my town address in Mount Street. They are dogged fellows once on the scent, apparently. So you see, I have no option but to stay with you and keep you company.'

'I suppose. When you put it like that,' Henrietta said, telling herself firmly that the relief she felt was everything to do with having a familiar face around and nothing at all to do with the excitement of it being that particular face.

As they crossed the river it was dusk, and quite dark by the time they pulled up outside the Mouse and Vole in Whitechapel. The inn was small, but surprisingly well kept, with its bedrooms facing on to a central courtyard and a large, busy taproom from which the hum of male conversation emanated into the cool night air. Rafe drove the carriage directly round to the stables, leapt agilely from the high seat and helped Henrietta down, removing her bandbox and his own portmanteau before handing the reins to a waiting groom, slipping him a coin and leading Henrietta not to the front, but to a small side door of the inn where she followed him through what appeared to be a boot room, and down a dimly lit corridor.

'If you don't mind my saying so, this seems a rather strange place for a man such as yourself to frequent.'

'But surely, Henrietta, a man such as I would be expected to hobnob with low life?'

For once, she failed to rise to the bait, being quite overcome with nerves now that they had actually arrived in London. A burst of song came from the taproom. A servant girl scurried by with a large bucket of coals. Rafe pushed open a small door under the stairs, and, telling her curtly to wait, not to leave the room until he returned, and on no account to speak to anyone, he dumped their luggage at her feet and left without another word.

Compared to the open carriage, it felt warm in the musty little parlour. Pushing back her cloak and stripping off her gloves, Henrietta pressed her forehead to the dusty window pane. Outside, she could hear the clump of horses' hooves in the stable yard. In the corridor, a muffled giggle, a male voice calling for someone called Bessie to fetch a mop. Where was Rafe? She idly drew a question mark on the glass. Why was he so unhappy? She drew another. Why was he so secretive about his wife? One more. And why—?

The door creaked open. Henrietta jumped. Rafe appeared before her, holding aloft a well-trimmed lamp. 'I thought you'd forgotten all about me.' Henrietta scrubbed at her question marks with her glove, flustered by just how quickly her heart began to beat at the mere sight of him.

Rafe closed the door and leant against it. 'There's good news and bad. I'm afraid Benjamin is away tonight, but Meg, his wife, assures me he'll be back tomorrow morning.'

'You mentioned good news?'

'Despite the fact that there is a much-anticipated mill—a fist fight—taking place less than a mile from here in the morning, Meg has managed to secure a room for us.'

'A room. You mean just one?'

Rafe nodded. 'We're lucky to get anything at all. That's the other bit of bad news, I'm afraid. We're going to have to share.'

'Oh. Cannot one of us spend the night here?' She indicated the empty parlour. Save for a rickety table and a narrow settle, there was no furniture. 'I'm sure I could…' she said dubiously.

'No. There is no lock on the door, it would not be safe given some of the clientele this place attracts. Besides,' Rafe said, levering himself away from the door and holding out his hand, 'you are exhausted. It's been a very long day. You need to rest and you shall do so in a bed. If it is your virtue you are worried about, let me assure you that I am far too tired to make any attempt to relieve you of it,' he said, ushering her out of the door. 'Tonight, at least.'

'I assume that is a poor attempt at a jest.'

'I haven't decided yet.'

Giving her no time to reply to this ambiguous comment, he led the way down the hallway and up the stairs. The room was small, but clean, with a wooden chair, a cupboard and a night stand upon which stood a spotted mirror.

And a bed. A solitary bed. And not a particularly wide one at that, Henrietta noted. 'I'll sleep on the chair,' she said, trying to keep the panic from her voice.

'Nonsense.'

'Or the floor. I could be perfectly comfortable on the floor, if you could ask Meg for some more bedclothes.'

'Henrietta, I can only speak for myself, but the events of the last twelve hours, while fascinating, have left me completely drained. Carnal thoughts are the last thing on my mind. Let me assure you that even Helen of Troy would not tempt me tonight. And you must be utterly exhausted yourself, after all you've been through.'

She nodded uncertainly.

'Then it is settled. There is no need for anyone to sleep on the floor. We will share the bed, I will refrain from undressing, and, to satisfy your maidenly modesty, we will place a pillow between us.'

Serious or teasing? On balance, she decided he was being serious. On balance, Henrietta decided, she was relieved because she was exhausted.

A tap on the door heralded a maidservant bearing a jug of hot water. Rafe, who was used to bathing daily and felt sweaty and dusty after the whirlwind carriage journey to London, nevertheless forced himself to do the gentlemanly thing, for he could see that Henrietta was eyeing the jug longingly. Not for the first time that day, he put her needs before his own. It was less difficult than he might have imagined. 'I'll leave you to freshen up,' he said, 'I'll go and organise some dinner for us.'

Alone, Henrietta stripped off her hat and cloak, her shoes and stockings, and made as good a *toilette* as circumstances would allow. Rummaging in her bandbox, she drew out her faded-red flannel nightgown, which, she thought, pulling it over her head, was voluminous enough, and practical enough to deter even the most determined of rakes. Not that she knew what determined rakes like Rafe did, exactly. Nor did she really know what Rafe meant specifically when he referred to carnal desires. It was, she had been led to believe by Mama, an exclusively male province. And yet, when she thought about the way he had kissed her, how it had felt when she had licked the strawberry juice from his finger, the shivery, tingly feeling came back and the goose bumps, too, and another feeling, a sort of indefinable longing—was that carnal desire?

Rafe, returning, bearing a tray upon which was their dinner, interrupted these thoughts. 'It's just the half-crown ordinary, meagre fare, I'm afraid,' he said, looking in vain for a table, eventually placing it carefully on the bed.

'Half a crown for an ordinary! Good heavens, I had no idea things were so expensive. I am afraid I cannot— The thing is, running away as I did, and I do not get paid until the end of the quarter—I'm afraid I don't have enough money,' Henrietta said. 'Actually, I don't suppose I'll get paid at all now.'

'There is no need to worry about money. I have more than sufficient.'

'There is every need. I am already enough in your debt.'

Rafe sighed. 'I might have known you would be contrary in this as in all other matters. Very well, if you insist, you can reimburse me when your parents return, but there is really no need.'

'There is every need,' Henrietta said determinedly. 'It is only right and proper.'

It amused Rafe that it didn't seem to have occurred to her that it was very wrong and even more improper that they should be sharing a room, never mind a bed. It should be refreshing, to encounter a female set on paying her way. It was certainly a novelty, yet Rafe was irked, for rather irrationally, the more she asserted her independence, the more he wanted to take care of her. 'I really have no interest in disputing the repayment of a paltry few shillings at present. Come, our dinner is getting cold.'

They perched on the edge of the bed to eat, Henrietta with her toes curled under her flannel nightgown, terribly aware of Rafe's proximity, trying desperately not to think of what was to happen next, and as a result unable to think of anything else.

Determined to put her at her ease, Rafe kept up a stream of inconsequential conversation. He was rewarded by seeing her making a reasonable meal, relaxing enough at the end of it to yawn. He, on the other hand, was anything but relaxed. In her faded, frumpy nightgown, with her curls corkscrewing wildly down her back, Henrietta aught to be quite unappealing, but he was finding her positively alluring. How came it about that such thick and opaque material somehow served to make him wonder all the more about what delights lay underneath?

When they had finished their repast, Rafe placed the tray outside the door and turned the key in the lock. Then he pulled back the covers of the bed, placing one of the pillows in the middle. 'Try to get some sleep,' he said, carefully averting his gaze as Henrietta clambered into the bed and pulled the covers up to her chin. Exhausted as he was by his sleepless night and the long day that had just passed, Rafe was beginning to wonder if he might be better off sleeping on the settle downstairs, after all.

Lying in bed, Henrietta tried to do as he had bid her, but the sleepiness that had enveloped her had melted away. She tried not to watch as Rafe stripped off his coat and waistcoat, removed his fob and snuff box and carefully wound his watch, before placing them under the pillow. She tried not to look as he splashed water on to his face, fastidiously scrubbed his hands, cleaned his teeth. He seemed indifferent to her presence.

She peeped out from under her lashes as he sat on the edge of the bed to remove his topboots, cursing under his breath as he did so. She supposed he must be accustomed to having a valet do such things for him.

His hose were next. He stood to take them off, then tossed them carelessly on to the floor beside his portmanteau. In which, no doubt, were at least two or three more clean pairs. The simplest of movements, pulling his shirt out of his buckskin breeches, only served to emphasise the muscles and sinews of the masculine body underneath. As he tilted his chin up to remove his neckcloth, which followed his hose on to the floor, the strong line of his jaw was revealed, the hard plane of his cheekbone, the straight nose in profile, without even a tiny bump to mar its perfection. Bending over to wipe the dust from his boots, she saw the long line of his leg, the perfectly muscled rear contoured under the leather of his buckskins.

Then he picked up the oil lamp and padded barefoot over to the bed, and Henrietta screwed her eyes tightly shut. The lamp was turned down. The bed creaked, the lumpy mattress sinking under his solid bulk. She lay rigid, hardly daring to breathe, never mind move. Beside her, Rafe sighed, shifted and sighed again.

He wasn't much closer to her than he'd been when sitting on the seat of the phaeton. He wasn't wearing that much less and she had on her all-encompassing flannel, but still it felt incredibly intimate. Illicit. She could hear him breathing, taking deep regular breaths. She could smell the soap he had used. The scent of his linen. A faint trace of leather from his buckskins. And something else. Something distinctively male, making her sensitive to her own distinctively female smell.

His hard, solid weight made her aware of her own soft curves. She was lying in bed with Rafe St Alban, whom she had met only this morning. Rafe St Alban who, in the space of just over half a day, had rescued her twice. Rafe St Alban, who was the most formidable, attractive, cynical, fascinating and very male man she had ever met. Not that she'd met many. But still, Henrietta thought, clinging to the sheet as Rafe turned away from her, on to his side, no matter how many more she met, she doubted she'd meet another quite like him. Her eyes gradually grew heavy. Rafe's deep rhythmic breathing was hypnotic. Though she could have sworn she would find sleep impossible in such circumstances, Henrietta nonetheless fell fast asleep.

Beside her, Rafe lay awake, wholly conscious of the soft bundle in faded-red flannel lying next to him. He never shared his bed. He visited his mistresses in their rooms, just as he had visited his wife in hers.

Julia. He allowed himself to think about her for the first time in years. It was like conjuring up a ghost. He could hardly even remember what she had been like in life, though he had no trouble at all recognising the customary combination of humiliation and guilt her name conjured up. The familiar litany of *what ifs* paraded through his mind with the order and precision of a well-drilled regiment. If his father had not died so

prematurely. If he himself had not been so steeped in
duty. If he had not been fresh from the excitement and
romance of his Grand Tour. If Julia had been younger.
If he had been older. If he had tried harder. If he had not
enforced the separation. If he had not taken her back. If
he had—or if he had not—it was always the same. The
outcome was always the same. The deep wells of guilt
were always the same. The heaviest of burdens, but one
he carried so habitually as to have become accustomed.
It would never go away.

Beside him, breathing softly, smelling sweetly, lay a
delectable, yielding bundle. Henrietta had neither Julia's
beauty nor her lineage, but she was neither cold nor
weak. Her flaws did not stem from vanity or selfish-
ness. She never prevaricated. What Henrietta thought,
she said. What she felt, she said, too. And what she
lacked in inches, she made up for in pluck. Any other
lady would have resigned herself to her fate, would have
accepted with alacrity his offer of help, but Henrietta
was made of much sterner stuff. She was like a pint-
sized crusader.

A *naïf*, Julia would have called her, looking down her
straight, little aristocratic nose. But she wasn't naïve,
just innocent. There was something about Henrietta's
lust for life, her *joie de vivre* and those kissable lips, that
hinted at a latent sensuality. Those delightful curves
would embrace him. Those sweetly curved lips he had
so tantalisingly tasted would succour him.

Rafe turned restlessly on the pillow, which he was
now convinced was filled with not-very-fresh straw. If
only it were Helen of Troy, and not Henrietta Markham
lying beside him, he would find sleep easily. He still

didn't understand it. No matter how many times he told himself she was out of bounds and therefore undesirable, his body would not be told. Rafe's erection strained against the soft leather of his breeches. Damned uncomfortable things to sleep in, breeches. It didn't seem to occur to Henrietta that no rake worth his salt would be doing so. Damned uncomfortable bed. Damned uncomfortable pillow. Damned uncomfortable and totally inexplicable desire. He would never sleep. Never…

Henrietta drifted awake. Through sleep-laden lids, she could sense the dawn light filtering in through the thin curtain. Already, the Mouse and Vole was sparking into life. The rumbling of a coach preceded the loud call of the driver for his passengers. A clanging bell and a shout of *dust-ho* announced the arrival of the rubbish cart. Outside in the corridor someone was whistling. She tried to move, but could not. Something lay heavy on her waist. Another noise, a soft thudding in her ear. She opened her eyes, then screwed them tight shut again. An arm it was, anchoring her. A chest it was, cushioning her head. Rafe's arm. Rafe's chest. And not a sign of the pillow that he had promised would separate them.

She was practically sprawled on top of him, like a limpet clinging to a rock. Her left knee was trapped between his legs. Buckskin-clad thighs. Rough hair on his calves. Bare skin. Male skin. *How on earth had this happened?*

Her breasts were crushed against his ribcage. Rafe's right arm pinned her securely to him. Her own left hand seemed to be curled into the opening of his shirt and her right arm was somewhere underneath them both. She tried to shift, but Rafe mumbled and tightened his grip. She wriggled and his arm left her waist, found her bottom and pulled her tighter against him. He felt—he felt—he felt…

Hard. Muscled. Solid. Powerful. Safe.

Not *that* safe. He was a man. She was acutely aware of him as a man. So very, very different from herself. She tried to move, just a little, just enough to detach her body from his, but her wriggling merely made his hold tighten, and when his hold tightened, though she knew she should put up more of a fight, what she really wanted to do was to submit. So she lay there quietly, telling herself that soon, very soon, she would move. Just not quite yet.

He smelled of sleep. She lay there, with her eyes closed, and let her body relax. Except her body didn't want to relax. Her body felt alive. Curiosity, her besetting sin, took hold. Why did he feel different? What did a man feel like? What did *this* man feel like? Questions, questions and more questions.

Idly, telling herself it wasn't really she, keeping her eyes closed tight so that she could maintain the self-deceit, Henrietta embarked on a tentative exploration. Her left hand was already there under his shirt, after all; she just had to let it drift a little. Up to his shoulder, down to the hard wall of his chest. Well-defined contours peaked by nipples that were hard but flat. Down next, along the concave line of his ribcage, into the dip of his stomach. She could feel him breathe under the palm of her hand. Feel the heat of his skin. Firm, taut stomach. The indent of his navel, the roughness of hair below.

She hastily withdrew her hand, shocked by her own boldness. She told herself she'd felt and seen enough. Then she started again. Back to his stomach, where she let her fingers linger, enjoying the contrast between smooth skin and rough hair that feathered a path for her hand to follow, down from his navel, disappearing under the barrier formed by the top of his breeches.

A droplet of sweat trickled down the valley between her breasts. She realised her nipples were as hard as hazelnuts, pressing against the cotton of her flannel nightgown. Not just hard, they were tingling, as if clamouring for some sort of attention. Still without allowing herself to think what she was doing, she pressed herself into his chest. A delightful *frisson* shot through her. Now she was even hotter.

She ran the palm of her hand back over the heat of Rafe's stomach. Shocked, but unable to stop herself, she tried to imagine her breasts, free of their protective flannel, pressed into the skin where her hand was. As she imagined, a ripple, like a tiny jolt of lightning, shivered from her belly down to the source of heat between her legs.

Henrietta, who was well read, both in materials considered suitable for a young lady and those ostensibly forbidden to her, was none the less rather vague about what Rafe had called carnal desires. What Mama had called her definitive experience was never elaborated upon. None of the women at the Poor House who had suffered at the hands of predatory men were inclined to enlighten her, either. The limited experience Henrietta had was thus universally negative. Nothing had prepared her for the fact that she might actually find it a pleasant experience, though now she came to think about it, she supposed it must be, else why would it be so many women's downfall? She had never been quite able to imagine *how*, exactly, physical contact might be pleasurable. Until now.

Now she could quite easily understand and could quite easily comprehend how it might make a person lose their inhibitions, cast caution to the winds and behave most improperly. She could understand that this hot, shivery feeling of anticipation, this tingling in her breasts, could be wholly addictive. She could understand why a person could be easily persuaded into going a bit further, and then a bit further still, until it was far too late for a person to stop.

She was going to stop. *She* was not so easily taken in. Indeed, she was truly about to stop when Rafe moved. The arm on her waist lifted, but only to tilt her chin. The arm on her bottom lifted, but only to allow his thigh to drape over hers. His mouth moved, but only to cover hers. Then he sighed. Then he kissed her.

His mouth was warm. His lips were unexpectedly gentle, the slight grating of his stubble a delightful contrast. His kiss was delicate, the kiss of a man who is all the time telling himself that he will not. The kiss of a man who knows he should not, but cannot resist.

Her touch, her innocent exploration, he had borne stoically. He had resisted encouraging her, though he had not stopped her. He could not have stopped her, any more than he could stop himself now from kissing, tasting, licking into the early morning heat of her. She was every bit as soft and yielding as he remembered. Her lips were even more infinitely kissable. Her body nestled into his perfectly.

Too perfectly.

He stopped. He did not want to, but he stopped. With a gargantuan effort he stopped—and immediately regretted it. But still he let her go and turned away to create a space. A cold space, a yawning chasm between them.

Henrietta opened her eyes. Was he asleep or just pretending? Had he kissed her because he wanted to, or was it some instinctive response to her touching him?

'I warned you about those lips of yours,' Rafe murmured.

So she had her answer and should have been mortified, for he had been awake all the time, and yet she was not. Virtue, Mama had always said, was its own reward. And Henrietta, despite the fact that she had always found it far more difficult than Mama to sacrifice her meagre pin money to good causes, to darn last winter's dress rather than have a new one, to wear woollen stockings instead of silk, had nevertheless believed her. Now she discovered that it was perhaps another subject upon which Mama's opinions were suspect. At this particular moment in time, virtue felt like a vastly overrated concept.

'Rafe, I—'

'Henrietta,' Rafe said over his shoulder, 'there are times when it is best not to attempt to explain—this is one of them. Let it suffice that I am doing the gentlemanly thing—for once in my life, and at great cost. Let me warn you that next time I will not. Now go back to sleep.'

Next time? She opened her mouth to tell him that there would absolutely and unequivocally never be a next time, if she had anything to say in the matter, but the words, for lack of truth, froze on her tongue. Not only did she doubt her ability to resist, she doubted that resisting was what she wanted. She leaned over, saw his eyes firmly closed, his lashes soft and sooty black on his cheek. Perhaps it was best not to deny it. Perhaps he would see a denial as a challenge. She shivered at the very idea, then pretended that she hadn't. Actions speak louder than words, she told herself firmly. There would not be a next time. Henrietta shuffled back to her own side of the lumpy bed and resolutely closed her eyes, trying to focus her mind on the not-inconsiderable issue of the missing Ipswich emeralds.

Chapter Five

Ex-Sergeant Benjamin Forbes, the landlord of the Mouse and Vole, was a swarthy man with a sabre scar that ran from the corner of his left eye to his earlobe, the tip of which had been severed, providing a very visible memento of the Peninsular campaign. Not tall, he was nevertheless powerfully built, with burly shoulders and a barrel chest. Possessing the muscular forearms of an army infantryman, these were maintained in civilian life by the regular hauling of ale barrels and the occasional spat with an unruly customer. He kept a clean house, but located as it was, near the rookeries of Gravel Lane and Wentworth Street, it was inevitable that things sometimes became somewhat confrontational. Ex-Sergeant Benjamin Forbes's vicious and efficient left hook ensured that any discord was quickly quelled.

He was in the taproom when Rafe and Henrietta came in search of him, sleeves rolled up, a large leather apron wrapped round his person, watching with an eagle eye the rounding up of the pewter pots by the porter-house boy. 'Lord Pentland,' he exclaimed, ushering the boy out and closing the taproom door firmly behind him, 'Meg said you was here. Sorry I wasn't around last night. Little bit of business to take care of.'

'Benjamin,' Rafe greeted the man with one of his rare, genuine smiles, shaking his hand warmly. 'You're looking well. This is Henrietta Markham. Sergeant Forbes, Henrietta.'

'Pleased to meet you, miss, and it's just plain Mr Forbes now, if you don't mind, been a good few years now since I left the king's forces,' he said, eyeing Henrietta curiously as he ushered them both into a seat by the newly lit fire.

A pot of fresh coffee and some bread rolls were called for. Rafe was served a tankard of frothing ale. Henrietta, intrigued as to the nature of the relationship between the two men, and self-conscious about what must seem her own rather dubious relationship with Rafe, sipped gratefully on the surprisingly good brew. As usual, curiosity got the better of her. 'Have you known Lord Pentland for long, Mr Forbes?'

'Nigh on six years now, miss. You could say I owe my livelihood to him.'

'Oh?'

'Rubbish, Benjamin,' Rafe said. 'You exaggerate.'

'Don't listen to him, miss. I was in a bad state when his lordship here first encountered me. Been in the army all my life, you see. Had no idea how to look after myself when they pensioned me off.' He laughed grimly. 'Not that there was much of a pension to speak of. His lordship stepped in and helped set me up here.'

'It was nothing, the least I could do. You'd earned it,

as far as I'm concerned, and you paid me back every penny.' Aware of Henrietta's too-interested gaze, Rafe took a long draught of ale.

'He's a good man, that's the truth of it,' Benjamin said, nodding in Rafe's direction. 'Despite the reputation he works so hard to maintain.'

'Enough of this,' Rafe said.

'Aye, and never one to take thanks, either,' Benjamin said with a wry smile. 'Why, even down at Saint—'

'I said enough, Benjamin,' Rafe said, curtly. 'You're not usually one to let your tongue run away with you. Henrietta is not interested in your eulogies.'

Henrietta, who was, in fact, very much interested in the innkeeper's revelations, was inclined to protest, but a warning shake of the head from Benjamin silenced her. 'Beg your pardon,' he said, 'don't know what came over me, only I thought—but there, it's none of my business. Tell me instead now—what it is I can do for you?'

'We're interested in some emeralds. A most distinctive set. Henrietta, here, has been accused of stealing them.'

This information, not surprisingly, made Benjamin's jaw drop, causing him to eye his benefactor's unusual companion with a fresh eye. Quality she was, anyone could see that, even if she was worse dressed than Bessie the parlourmaid on her Sunday off. What she was doing with his lordship, well, he had no idea. My lord's tastes ran to expensive bits of muslin and he'd never brought any of them here before.

But as he listened to Henrietta describing the circumstances of the theft, a tale so unlikely as to test his credulity to the limit, Benjamin began to see just what it was that had attracted his lordship to Miss Markham. It wasn't so much the way she looked, as the way her whole face came alive when she spoke. Those eyes of hers, the way they sparkled with anger as she described the accusations against her. The way she talked with her whole body, her hands, even her curls flouncing with indignation, the softer look on her face when she spoke of the shame it would cause her parents. And the way she looked at my lord, too, with something more than admiration as she described his coming to her rescue, and something much less respectful when she forced him to admit that he hadn't believed her story, either, at first. If my lord was not very careful…

But my lord was always careful, which made it all the more inexplicable. Maybe it really was a case of impulsive chivalry? 'So how can I help?' Ben asked when the interesting Miss Markham had finished her extraordinary tale.

'Come, come, Ben, it is surely obvious. A man such as Henrietta has described must surely be known to one of the cracksmen and receivers who frequent your taproom. And the Ipswich emeralds are themselves not exactly run of the mill.'

Benjamin scratched his head. 'Describe him to me again, miss.'

She did so and Benjamin stroked the line of his scar thoughtfully. 'Well, he certainly shouldn't be too hard to trace, a rum-lookin' cove like that, presumin' you know where to look, that is. And the emeralds?'

Henrietta wrinkled her nose. 'The setting is antique, linked ovals of wrought gold, each with a stone at the centre surrounded by diamond chips. The stone in the necklace is very large, and there are in addition two bracelets and a pair of earrings.'

Benjamin shook his head. 'Such distinctive jewellery is nigh on impossible to sell on without arousing suspicion.'

'So it should be quite an easy thing to track him down, then, shouldn't it?' Henrietta said eagerly. 'You will find him for me, Mr Forbes, won't you? Rafe— Lord Pentland was so sure you would and it would mean the world to me.'

'I'll do my best,' Benjamin said, patting Henrietta's hand reassuringly, 'but we'll need to be discreet. People who stick their noses into other peoples' business in the rookeries tend to get them bitten off, if you take my meaning.'

'I would not wish to put you in any danger.'

Benjamin laughed heartily at this. 'I can take care of myself, don't you worry.'

'Well, if you are sure, then I really am extremely grateful,' Henrietta said fervently.

'It's Lord Pentland you should be thanking, miss. I wouldn't do this for any other man in England. It could take a few days, though.'

'A few days!'

'That is not the end of the world,' Rafe said. 'Provided Ben can continue to put a roof over our heads, you are safe from the Runner here.'

'He's right, miss,' Benjamin said. 'Nobody would think to look for you here. You'd both best stay at the Mouse and Vole until I track down that housebreaker. And now if you'll excuse me, I've things to do.'

'Thank you, Ben,' Rafe said, holding out his hand.

'You save your thanks until you've got something to thank me for,' Ben said gruffly. Shaking his head, wondering what on earth Meg would make of the unlikely couple, he left the taproom in search of her.

Alone, Rafe turned back to Henrietta with a quizzical look. 'So, it appears we are condemned to a few more days of each other's company. Do you find the notion tolerable, Henrietta?' He captured her wrist, forcing her to meet his gaze. 'For my own part, I'm more than happy to act as your chaperon.'

She flushed. She wished she didn't flush quite so easily or so often in his presence.

'Now would be a good time for you to reassure me that you feel the same, Henrietta.'

She risked a quick glance, saw that unsettling look in his eyes, then dropped her gaze again, but already she could feel it, that sparkling feeling. Heat spread from her wrist, where his fingers were wrapped around it. Her skin seemed to tug, as if it wanted her to move closer. The image of him, created by her touch this morning, flashed into her mind. 'What would we do?' she asked, then blushed wildly. 'To pass the time, I mean? We can't stay here all day, can we?'

'Cooped up together, you mean? Don't you trust yourself, Henrietta?'

He knew it was unfair, but he could not resist teasing her. He liked to watch the flush steal up her neck and over her cheeks; it made him wonder where it came from. He liked the way she sucked the corner of her bottom lip, just showing the tip of her pink tongue. He liked the way the little gold flecks in her eyes glimmered, the way she looked shocked and excited and tempted—definitely tempted—at the same time.

He stroked her wrist with his thumb and felt the pulse jump beneath him. He slid his hand a little way under the sleeve of her gown, caressing the fragile skin of her forearm. She closed her eyes. Her lips parted. He stroked the crease of her elbow, wondering that he had never before realised what an erotic crease it was, thinking how delightful it would be to lick it, to find other such creases. 'The thing is, Henrietta, you need to be able to trust yourself, because for certain you cannot trust me,' he said, pulling her towards him over the table and claiming her lips.

Henrietta let out a soft sigh as he took her mouth; she shivered as his tongue slid along her lips and moaned as it touched the tip of hers. Velvet soft, darkly illicit, infinitely tempting, his mouth, his kisses, his taste. He deepened the kiss and she softened under the pressure, then returned it. That feeling again. Longing. Deeper this time, in her belly. She tried to move closer, but the table was in the way; she hit her hand on the half-drunk tankard of ale, which tipped over, making them both leap back.

She was breathing too fast. Looking over at Rafe, she noticed with some surprise that so, too, was he. His chest was rising and falling quite rapidly. There was a flush staining the sharp lines of his cheek bones. His eyes were dark, a night storm, the slant of his brows emphasised by his frown. His sleek cap of hair was ruffled—had she done that? She didn't remember. He looked every bit as darkly enticing as his kiss. Every bit as dangerous as his reputation. Not unleashed, not out of control, but as if he could be, and it was that, the idea of that, that was more exciting than anything.

Her lips were tingling. Her nipples were throbbing. There was a knot pulled tight in her belly. She had never felt like this. She hadn't realised she could feel like this. She'd never imagined this, whatever it was, existed. A clawing desire for something, a burning need for something. For someone.

She put a hand to her throat, feeling the pulse jump and jump. She watched wide-eyed as Rafe pushed the table away, then pulled her to her feet. The door flew open and the startled screech of the maidservant made her pull herself free; he shrugged and straightened his necktie as if nothing had happened, then nodded casually to the astonished maid before taking Henrietta's hand and leading her out of the room.

She followed him automatically back up to their bed-chamber. She assumed he was going to kiss her again, but instead he pulled her cloak from the back of a chair and draped it around her, putting her poke bonnet firmly on her head.

He'd been right about that passionate nature of hers. It would be the easiest, most delectable, most desirable thing in the world to take her now, but he could not. Dammit, he *would* not. 'I think we have just proved that it would be most unwise to stay cooped up together. What we both need is a distraction and some fresh air,' Rafe said firmly, tilting her chin to tie the knot, trying not to look at her lips, focusing on the ugliness of her bonnet in the hope that his persistent erection would subside.

'It was just a kiss, Henrietta,' Rafe said curtly, 'and

one of your first. When you have sampled a few more, you will, I'm sure, like all other young ladies, grow more blasé about such things.' Rafe picked up his hat. 'Now, do you want to see the sights of London or not?'

'Aren't you worried that you'll meet someone you know?' Henrietta asked, as they emerged from the forecourt of the Mouse and Vole on to the main thoroughfare.

Rafe grabbed her cloak to pull her clear, just in time, from the muddy splash made by the cumbersome wheels of a passing milk cart. 'London is a large city, I am sure we can manage to avoid my acquaintances easily; it is not as if we are planning on visiting anywhere particularly fashionable. Don't you wish to see the popular sights?' Even as he asked the question, Rafe wondered if he had gone a little mad, for the sights Henrietta would consider worth seeing would undoubtedly be those he made a point of avoiding, forcing them to mingle with Cits and bumpkins.

'Of course I do, but I doubt you have much interest in them,' Henrietta replied, with her usual frankness.

And as usual, it made him contrarily set upon a path he would never normally have followed. 'It will be enlightening to see the metropolis through your eyes,' Rafe said.

'You mean you will be able to laugh at my expense.'

'No.' He tilted her chin up, the better to see her face, which was in the shadow of that horrible bonnet. 'I may find your views amusing because they are refreshingly different, but I never laugh *at* you or mock you.'

'I know that. At least, most of the time I do.'

Rafe suppressed a smile. 'Good, now we understand one another, are you willing to put yourself in my hands?'

Henrietta nodded. 'Yes, thank you, I'd like that.' Out here, in the bustling street under a grey sky washed with a pall of sea-coal smoke, she realised that Rafe had been right to insist they quit the intimacy of their bedchamber. She *did* need some air, though fresh was not exactly how she'd have described this gritty, tangy London atmosphere.

They took a hackney into the city, down Threadneedle Street and past the colonnaded front of the Bank of England. At Cheapside, they abandoned the hack, for Henrietta complained she could see nothing through its small dusty window, and they walked, something of a novelty for Rafe. Henrietta tripped gaily along at his side, exclaiming at the buildings, the mass of printed bills that covered them, the street hawkers who sold their wares on every corner, oblivious to the dangers of carriage wheels, horses' hooves and pickpockets alike. Several times he was forced to steer her clear of noxious puddles while she gazed up admiringly at the architecture. Eventually, he tucked her arm securely into his and wedged her to his side in order to prevent her straying into the path of a carriage.

He liked having her there, so close. He liked the way she bombarded him with questions, never doubting that he would be able to answer. He also liked the way she trusted implicitly that he would keep her safe, even though she had no apprehension of danger. He liked the way she threw herself with gusto into drinking in the ambiance of the bustling city. She paused at every shop to peer in the windows. Drapers, stationers, confectioners, pastry cooks, silversmiths and seal cutters alike, she was quite indiscriminate, as enthralled by a display of pen nibs, ink pots and hot-pressed paper as she was by an array of ribbons, trimmings and button hooks.

Outside St Paul's, the beggars, hawkers, petty thieves and pamphleteers fought for space, pushing their wares under the noses of the better off, slipping their fingers into the pockets of the unwary, proclaiming their tales of woe from upturned crates. Henrietta, spotting a filthy urchin whose flea-bitten dog was making an extremely feeble attempt to dance on its hind legs, fumbled in her dress pocket for her purse.

'For God's sake, put that away,' Rafe said hastily, as they were immediately surrounded by a small crowd holding out their hands beseechingly.

'But the child—'

'Is very likely part of an organised gang. There are hundreds, if not thousands, of urchins like that, and very few are the genuine article. Here, let me, don't waste your resources, which you've already told me are pitiful enough.' Expertly flicking a shilling at the urchin with the dog, Rafe took advantage of the diversion and ushered Henrietta up the shallow flight of steps into the relative sanctuary of the cathedral.

'You didn't have to do that,' she said, tucking her purse out of sight again and shaking out her cloak.

'Well, before you add it to that mental list of debt you're totting up in your head, let me tell you that it was a gift. And don't bother trying to deny it, I know that's exactly what you were doing.'

Henrietta's smile was shaky. 'Oh, very well, and

thank you. I have to confess, I was very glad of your presence out there, it was quite overwhelming. I had not realised there could be so very many very poor people. It was a shock. You know, I could not at first fathom why everyone walks so quickly with their noses either to the ground or in the sky, I thought it was simply to give themselves an air of consequence, but now I suspect it is because they don't want to see what is around them.'

'And as I've also already pointed out,' Rafe said drily, 'most of the beggars, especially the aggressive ones, are on the fiddle, believe me.'

Henrietta looked dubious, for it seemed to her that that was precisely what people said when they wanted to justify their apathy, but though Rafe could certainly be both cold and cynical, he was not callous. 'You seem to be uncommonly well informed about life on the capital's streets.'

Rafe shrugged. 'It is common enough knowledge, God knows, there are enough of them. The younger boys start out stealing pocketbooks and silk kerchiefs, then they graduate to more lucrative work, assisting housebreakers, and pilfering from the docks. Foundlings, many of them, though some are sold into the trade by their families.'

'Sold! Good God, you cannot be serious.' She had thought herself well informed upon the subject of poverty through her parents' association with Poor Houses, but that had been in the rural countryside. Here, in the capital, the sheer scale of the problem was beyond her comprehension, the horrors it led to simply unbelievable.

Rafe's expression was bleak. 'I am deadly serious. I don't doubt that, for some of them, it's a case of too many mouths, but for others, it's just gin money. And though there's always the risk of the gallows, it's not as if life as a Borough Boy or Bermondsey Boy is as bad as life as a climbing boy. The gangs at least look after their own. It's in a sweep's interest to keep his boys thin.'

'You sound so—so resigned! Is there not something that can be done to help such families keep their children rather than *sell* them?'

'What do you suggest, Henrietta, that I adopt them all?' Bitter experience had shown him the futility of finding a solution to society's ills. Even the small private contribution he currently made was a mere drop in the ocean. Often, he felt it was futile.

Henrietta was startled by the acidity in his voice. 'Don't you care? You must care, for if you did not, you wouldn't know so much about it all.' She stared up at him, but his face was shaded by the brim of his hat. 'I don't understand. Why do you pretend not to care, when you so obviously do?'

His instinct was to shrug and turn the subject, but, perhaps because her large, chocolate-brown eyes were filled with compassion, perhaps because she refused to believe the worst of him, he chose that rarest of courses, to explain. 'Because if a child is unwanted, there is little to be done to change that.'

'That's a terrible thing to say.'

'The truth is often terrible to behold, but it must be faced all the same.' As he must face that fact every day, despite the funds and time he poured into his attempt at atonement.

'I had thought, in my own small way, through teaching, that I could make a difference, a contribution,' Henrietta said sadly. 'I see now it could only ever be the merest scratch on the surface of the problem.'

'Forgive me, Henrietta, it was not my intention to disillusion you. Your altruism does you credit. Do not let my cynicism infect you, I would not want that on my conscience.'

'I must admit, it's a little disheartening to hear such a bleak view of the world.'

'Then let us turn our thoughts to more uplifting matters. Come, you must see Wren's dome, it is an extraordinary and quite breathtaking spectacle.'

He was already assuming his usual inscrutable look. Henrietta was, however, becoming more attuned to the nuances of his expression. His mouth was always tighter when he was trying *not* to show emotion, his lids always heavier over his eyes. And his tone, too, was always more austere when he didn't want to talk about something.

She followed him as he led the way swiftly along the chequered floor of the nave, her mind seething with questions, but if her brief acquaintance with Rafe St Alban had taught her anything, it was that the direct approach rarely paid dividends. The subject was closed for now, but she added it to the growing list of things she was determined to discover about him before their time together ended: how he came to know so much about the tragic fate of foundlings, why he had helped Benjamin Forbes set up in business, what it was about

Lady Ipswich that prevented him from calling on her, or what happened during his marriage to the beautiful Lady Julia to make him so adamantly against ever marrying again. Then there were the contradictions. His knight errantry and his compassion did not sit with his reputation, any more than did his refusal this morning to take advantage of her.

With so very many questions requiring answers, it never occurred to Henrietta to ask a few of herself: what, exactly, she would do if Rafe kissed her again, or why, if she really did believe his reputation, she continued to place her trust in him? Instead, at Rafe's bidding, she looked up, and caught her breath at the magnificence of the dome of St Paul's, which seemed to fill the sky, and the questions that flooded her mind were concerned with architecture.

After St Paul's, they took another hackney cab and visited the Tower of London, where Henrietta shivered at the sight of Traitor's Gate and the Bloody Tower. Dutifully inspecting the Crown Jewels, she declared them to be, in her humble opinion, rather vulgar.

Rafe suggested that perhaps she refrain from inspecting them too closely, lest she get felonious ideas, making her laugh, declaring that such ostentatious jewellery should be left to men with a northern accent and an eyepatch, which earned them both a reproving look from the Beefeater.

For the small price of a shilling—which Henrietta added to her mental list of debts—they were shown the Menagerie, but here her more tender feelings were roused by the pitiful condition of the caged beasts. 'The grizzly bear looks as if he wants to cry,' she whispered to Rafe, 'and look at those poor lions, they look positively mournful. It seems a shame to keep such proud creatures so confined, something should be done.'

'Do you wish me to have them released? I don't think the people of London would be too pleased to have these creatures at large. They might look pathetic, but I am pretty sure they could still cause a fair bit of carnage.'

'Of course I didn't mean that!'

'Or perhaps you mean to solve two problems at the same time, release the lions and feed the Bermondsey Boys to them. I can't say that it's a particularly humane notion, but I'm sure there are some politicians who would claim merit for the idea.'

'Stop making fun of me,' Henrietta said, biting her lip to suppress a smile.

'Not of you, with you,' Rafe said, as they retraced their steps out of the Lion Tower, 'there is a difference.'

'I know, but I am so unused to either, I forget. It's different for you, I'm sure, you must have lots of people to laugh with, but I...'

'No, I cannot imagine that Mama and Papa, worthy as they are, are much *fun*,' Rafe said.

She tried to stifle her giggles, but could not. 'That is shocking, but it's also true, alas. I'm very much afraid that worthiness precludes any sense of humour. I fear I must be very, very unworthy.'

'And I am very, very glad that you are,' Rafe said, taking her by surprise and raising her gloved hand to his lips. 'Because despite what you might think, my life is not over-full of people I feel able to laugh with, either.'

'You must have friends.'

He hailed a hackney, instructing the driver to take them back to Whitechapel. 'Lots—at least, lots of acquaintances,' Rafe said, 'but since I have a reputation for being a bit of a cold fish…'

'I can't understand how, for it seems to me that one cannot be a cold fish as well as a rake.' She saw his smile fade and regretted her words immediately. 'I didn't mean…'

'I know exactly what you meant,' Rafe said, in his best cold-fish manner. 'I thought, however, that your experience of me would by now have taught you not to believe all you have heard. Obviously I was wrong.' For a moment, just a moment, he was tempted to put her right, but then he would have to explain why, and he could not bear to open that wound. Instead, he resorted to his old armour of anger. 'If you had my wealth and title, you'd be a cold fish, too. You have no idea what it's like to be the fawning target of every mama with an eligible daughter, and every Johnny Raw who claims to be a cousin of a cousin first removed and thinks the Earl of Pentland is their ticket into society, to say nothing of those who claim friendship only because they've been brought to *point non plus* and want me to tow them out of the River Tick.'

She was cowed by the vitriolic nature of his reply, but refused to be silenced. What he said explained so much…and appalled her so much. 'But, Rafe, not everyone is like that. Most people—'

'Most people are exactly like that. I've rarely met anyone who's not on the take in one way or another, and in my experience, the higher the *ton*, the more they'll try to take you for.'

'That's a horribly cynical way of looking at things.'

'Also horribly true,' Rafe said, with a saturnine look.

'No, it's not,' Henrietta declared roundly. 'I'm not saying there aren't people who are as you say—'

'Well, that's something, at least.'

Henrietta glared at him. 'But there are lots of others who aren't, only you won't give them a chance.'

'For the very excellent reason that the one time I did place my trust in someone they repaid it by deceiving me.'

Furious with himself for this unaccountable admission, Rafe clenched his fists, then he hurriedly unclenched them. *God dammit*, what was it about her that made him say such things? How was it that one minute they were laughing and the next minute she had him completely on edge? 'It was a long time ago and I don't wish to discuss it,' he said tightly.

'Yet another thing you don't wish to discuss,' Henrietta said, now equally furious. 'I would add it to my mental list, only it's becoming too long to remember. Why is it that you are permitted to block every subject of conversation, yet you feel free to interrogate me? Who took advantage of you so badly as to make you so bitter?'

'I don't wish to discuss it, Henrietta, not at any time and particularly not in the back of a hackney cab.'

'The driver can't hear us. Who?' Henrietta demanded, now so beside herself with fury that she did not realise she was treading on exceptionally thin ice.

'My wife,' Rafe snarled.

'Oh.' She felt as if she had been winded, so unexpected was the admission.

'Yes, you may well say *oh!* Julia married me for my money. And for the title, of course—such a very old one, and so vast the lands that came with it. She married me because I was one of the only men able to give her the position she felt her looks entitled her to. Are you happy now?'

'Rafe, I didn't mean...'

But he threw her hand off angrily. 'Yes, you did. I told you to stop prying, but you would not desist.'

Remorse squeezed her anger away. She gazed at him helplessly, aghast at having unwittingly inflicted such raw pain as he had so fleetingly displayed. His face was rigid with his efforts *not* to show it, his lips almost white. Nothing had prepared her for this. Her wretched tongue! 'Rafe, I'm truly sorry,' she said, as the hack pulled up at the Mouse and Vole. Rafe threw some coins at the driver and all but dragged Henrietta out of the cab and through the door of the inn. 'Go to the room. I'll have them send some dinner up for you.'

'But what about you? Won't you be joining me?' Henrietta asked in a small voice. 'Rafe, please...'

But he was already gone.

She spent a dreadful night. Though she should have been ravenous from the day's sightseeing, she could only pick at the pigeon pie steaming on the platter. At every footstep on the boards of the corridor, she held her breath, but none halted, or even hesitated as they passed. Miserably, she prepared for bed. Not even the luxury of an entire jug of hot water to herself, and complete privacy in which to make use of it, made any difference to her sombre mood.

Over and over, she replayed their last conversation in her head, trying to isolate a point where she could have turned the subject, avoided it, said something different or been more tactful, but to no avail. Rafe's shocking admission had come out of the blue. She had had no idea. Could have had no idea. Taking herself to task over the matter was pointless. Feeling guilty—and she did feel guilty, even though she knew it was misguided— was also pointless. How on earth could she have been expected to guess?

But logic was no real balm. Unwitting or no, she had ripped open an old wound and felt absolutely terrible. Pulling her red flannel nightgown over her head, tugging her comb through her tangled curls, cleaning her teeth and climbing into a bed which seemed somehow to have grown much larger and much colder, Henrietta bit back the tears, but as the clock in the church tower across the road struck midnight, she pulled the rough sheet over her head and allowed a single tear to escape from her burning eyes. And then another. And another still. Then she sniffed resolutely, and the next tear was refused permission to escape as she began to feel angry.

Not with Rafe, but with that woman. That woman, that beautiful woman with the cold eyes. How had he found out? When had she shattered his illusions? How much had he loved her? That was the question she found hardest to contemplate. Though it explained everything. No wonder he didn't want to marry again. A few years older than him, Mrs Peters had said Lady Julia was. Had she toyed with him, laughed at him? Henrietta clenched her teeth. It would have been a crushing blow to his pride. No wonder he kept his thoughts opaque.

No wonder he cultivated that forbidding air of his. He had been hurt. Obviously he had no intentions of being hurt again.

Henrietta brooded darkly. Such a marriage must have been very unhappy. Was he glad, when Lady Julia died? Relieved? Or did he feel guilty? People did, sometimes, when they wished for something awful and it came to pass. Maybe that was why Rafe kept the portrait of his dead wife on display, as a painful reminder, as a form of penance.

Maybe that was also why he had such a notorious reputation when it came to women. But she couldn't match that to his behaviour. In fact, the more she thought about it, Rafe's reputation didn't conform at all with her experience of him, the Rafe she knew. He just wasn't the type to exact revenge in such a manner. Much more the type to bury it all deep—which is exactly what he *had* done. Was he not, then, the womaniser gossip would have him? But was there not always fire where there was smoke? She couldn't understand it. She probably never would.

The church bell tolled one. Where was he? Was he going to stay away all night? Perhaps another room had become available. So much for his concern about her being alone here. Although Benjamin Forbes *had* been up to check on her several times, and to remind her to keep the door locked, so maybe he was still a little bit concerned. When she'd asked Benjamin where Rafe was, he'd just shaken his head. Did that mean he knew, or he didn't?

Where was he? His portmanteau was still here, she realised hopefully. Except that to someone as rich as

Rafe, a portmanteau or two was neither here nor there. Probably he had lots more of them in his London house. Which was probably where he was now.

Well, if he had abandoned her—though she couldn't quite bring herself to believe that he had—then she'd just have to set about sorting things out herself. 'It's what I was going to do, anyway, before he came along,' Henrietta said stoutly, plumping the pillow, which refused to be plumped, 'so there's absolutely no cause to be downhearted.' But despite the fact that she knew Benjamin Forbes would do his best, it wasn't quite the same as having Rafe by her side. Although she had known him for only a few days, and although she had thought herself quite inured to coping alone, the prospect of not seeing him again was most melancholy.

A spark of indignation flickered in her breast. How dared he do this to her? How dared he make her feel so—so—whatever it was he made her feel—and then just walk away. *How dared he!*

She plumped the pillow again. Then she buried her head under it, in an effort to stop herself thinking. Then she began to fret about how she would pay her shot. And then, finally, exhausted by all the thinking, Henrietta fell asleep.

Chapter Six

She was woken a few hours later, as dawn was rising, by a rattling at the door of the bedchamber. Startled, she sat up, her heart pounding, thinking she must have been dreaming. But the rattling came again, then a heavy fist pounded on the door.

Shaking, she edged from the bed and picked up the pewter candlestick, before creeping over to the door. The handle shook. 'Go away,' she hissed, so quietly that it was not surprising when the handle shook again. 'Go away,' she said, more loudly this time, 'or I'll scream.'

'Open the door, Henrietta.'

'Rafe?'

'Dammit, open the door before I break it down.'

Relief made her clumsy as she fumbled with the lock. Still holding her candlestick in one hand, she peered out into the corridor. It was him, leaning heavily on the doorframe. 'Where have you been?' He pushed the door open and stumbled over the threshold. Only then did she smell the brandy on his breath. 'You've been drinking!'

'Your powers of observation never fail to amaze me,' Rafe slurred, staggering towards the bed. 'I have indeed been drinking, Henrietta Markham. I have, in point of fact, been drinking copiously.'

'That much is obvious,' she said, pushing the door to and pulling back the curtains in order to let in the grey dawn light.

'An enormous amount,' Rafe agreed, dropping on to the bed and nodding vehemently. 'And you know what? It still wasn't enough.' He tried to rise, but his foot slipped.

Henrietta caught him just before he fell on to the floor. With an immense effort, she managed to push him back on to the bed, which he promptly tried to get back up from. 'More brandy, that's what I need.'

'That's the last thing you need,' Henrietta replied, pushing him with a bit more force.

He fell on to his back with a look of extreme surprise, which made her giggle. 'What are you laughing at?'

'Nothing,' she said, quickly covering her mouth.

'I like the way you laugh, Henrietta Markham,' Rafe said with a lopsided grin.

'I like the way you laugh, Rafe St Alban, though you don't do it nearly enough. You should try to sleep. You'll have a terrible head in the morning.'

'Got a terrible head now,' Rafe muttered, 'far too many unpleasant things whirling around inside it. All your fault.'

Endearing. It was not a word she'd ever have thought to associate with him, but that is how he looked, with his hair standing up on end and his neckcloth rumpled and his waistcoat half-undone. The stubble on his jaw was dark, almost bluish. His cheeks were flushed, his eyes slumberous. He looked younger and somehow vulnerable, the way his arms were spread out as if in surrender, one long leg sprawled across the bed, the other dangling over the edge. Henrietta edged closer. 'Rafe, I was worried about you.'

'Come here.'

She hadn't thought him capable of moving so quickly. Before she could get out of his reach, he had grabbed her by the wrist and pulled her down on to the bed beside him. Her breath left her in a whoosh. She was pretty certain she must look every bit as surprised as he had done only a moment before.

'Ha! That showed you, Henrietta Markham.'

'Let me go, Rafe. And stop calling me that.'

'Henrietta Markham. What else shall I call you? Miss Markham? Think we've gone beyond that one. Hettie? No, you're not a Hettie. Hettie sounds like a great-aunt or a chambermaid. Henry? Nope. Nope. Nope. You feel far too feminine for that.' Once more he took her by surprise, rolling her easily over so that she lay breast to breast, thigh to thigh, on top of him. 'Nice,' he murmured, running his hands over her, 'you have a very, very nice bottom, did you know that?'

'Rafe, stop it, you're drunk.'

'I am a little intoxicated, but that does not, I assure you most fervently, stop me from appreciating quite how delightful your bottom is. And, I may add, that touching it is quite delightfully delightful.'

His hands moulded her curves and settled her more firmly on top of him, and, though she knew he was in his cups, she couldn't help agreeing with him. What he was doing was quite delightfully delightful. His coat buttons were pressing into her side. She could feel his fob chain and his watch on her stomach. His chin was rasping against her cheek. He smelled of smoke and brandy and man. Of Rafe.

There was something else pressing into her thigh. She wriggled, in a half-hearted effort to escape, but his hands remained firmly on her bottom, and the something got harder. She realised what it was then and felt herself get very, very hot. Her breasts were flattened against his chest, but still she could feel her nipples harden. She only hoped that brandy and a shirt and a waistcoat would prevent Rafe from noticing. She wriggled again, telling herself she really was trying to free herself, but succeeded only in making Rafe moan and heard herself moan, too, as his arousal pressed more insistently on her thigh.

Her flannel nightgown was getting caught up around her legs. Perhaps if she waited, he would just fall asleep? Cautiously, she lifted her head, only to be met with the glint of slate-blue eyes revealed by very unsleepy lids. 'What are you going to do now, Henrietta? Wriggle some more? You have my permission to do so.'

'Where were you, Rafe?'

'My mind was clogged with poisonous memories. I thought to wash them away with brandy. It didn't really work.' He shrugged dejectedly. 'Did you think I'd abandoned you?'

'No. Yes, well, for a moment. But—no. You said you'd help me, so I knew you'd be back. Hoped you would be. Not that I couldn't have managed on my own if you didn't.'

'But I said I'd take care of you,' Rafe muttered, 'so I did come back. You have no idea how much—how *very* much—I'd like to take care of you at this moment, Henrietta Markham. I did tell you not to trust me, did I not?'

His meaning was quite unmistakable. His meaning made her stomach clench in anticipation—and a little in trepidation. One hand was trailing up and down her spine. It was warm through her nightgown, yet it was making her shiver. And that feeling was back again, tingling and zinging and filling her with a sense of recklessness. *How did he do that?*

'Do what?' Rafe murmured, and she realised she'd spoken out loud again. 'You mean this?' he said with a wicked smile, and how he did it she had no idea, but his hands were on her spine and her bottom, only this time without any material between them.

'Rafe!' One sweeping stroke, from the base of her spine along her back and back down again, played havoc with her breathing. Another, and she felt she could not breathe at all. 'Rafe,' she said again, only this time it was not a protest, but something more akin to a plea. A plea he seemed to heed, for he rolled her over on to her back and now his hands were on her sides, her flank, her stomach. 'Rafe,' she said, only it was more like a moan. And he moaned, too, cupping the weight of her breasts, his thumbs caressing the hard peaks of her nipples, setting her on fire with his touch, making her writhe and arch her back, and ache for more.

Rafe hitched her nightgown up further. In the pearly grey of the morning light, her skin seemed translucent. She was every bit as luscious, as perfectly curved, as agonisingly desirable, as he had imagined. He dipped his head, eager to take one of those rosy nipples into his mouth. He felt the rasp of his stubble on the tender flesh of the underside of her breast.

An image of himself, dishevelled and smelling of brandy, looking every bit the hardened rake Henrietta thought him, flashed into his mind and he paused. He would not. He could not. She did not deserve this. The demons she had aroused, the demons that sinking his aching shaft into her wet, welcoming flesh would exorcise, they were not her demons. He would not use her thus, no matter how much he yearned to.

Yearning. The word echoed round his mind as he pulled her nightgown back down, as he hoisted himself away from her too-tempting flesh, as he sat up shakily on the edge of the bed. Yearning. Not a word he normally associated with himself, but that's what he felt, looking at her. For the union that would be, he knew, the most sensual of all unions. Yearning for the intimacy it would bring. Yearning to feel something. Anything. To give and to receive in return. Yearning, too, for what he had lost for ever. Innocence. Optimism. Idealism. A belief in love. She had them still. He could not deprive her of them, not like this.

'I can't,' he said aloud.

'Do you feel ill?'

Soft arms round his neck. Warmth against his back. The tickle of curls on his cheek. Rafe closed his eyes and groaned. She had taken him literally. Despite his patently obvious arousal tenting his breeches, she had taken him literally.

Sweet irony. He should be relieved, for it were better

she thought him unable to perform than that he betray himself more completely. For she had been right, after all, Henrietta Markham—he was not the cold fish he thought himself.

'Rafe, do you feel ill?' Henrietta asked, slipping off the bed to kneel before him, testing his forehead with the back of her hand.

'Sick to the very pit of my soul, Henrietta Markham, that is how I feel.'

'Let me take care of you.'

He allowed her to help him with his boots. He allowed her to help him out of his coat and waistcoat, but not his breeches. He allowed her to tuck him into the bed, to bathe his brow and to pull the covers gently over him. He closed his eyes as she lay down beside him, not touching him, but not putting the pillow between them, either. The world swam. He closed his eyes tighter. Blackness, welcome, brandy-induced oblivion awaited him. He succumbed willingly to its siren call.

Rafe woke with a start. His head was pounding, his eyes felt as if they had been filed vigorously with a large rasp and his stomach was most decidedly queasy. He had drunk an immense amount of Benjamin's French cognac, far more than was his wont, for he hated to be foxed. Clutching his head, he rolled out of bed and only then realised he was quite alone in the room. Fumbling for his watch, which was still on its fob in his waistcoat pocket, he saw that it was just a little before noon and cursed quietly, fervently hoping that Henrietta had had the sense not to leave the inn without him.

Henrietta. As he tugged his shirt over his head, he

remembered, and groaned. What had he said? Splashing tepid water over his face, snippets of the conversation—if one could call it a conversation—popped into his head, making him wince. He'd left her alone all night. She'd have been perfectly justified in being angry with him, but she'd refrained from uttering even one harsh word. Casting a quick glance around the room, he was relieved beyond proportion to see her shabby bandbox still sitting in the corner, her cloak still draped over the chair.

He rang for fresh water; when it arrived, satisfactorily hot and plentiful, he stripped off his clothes and scrubbed himself thoroughly before shaving. A fresh shirt and neckcloth, clean hose, and he felt almost human again. Human enough for his body to stir at the recollection of Henrietta's soft and luscious body pressed into his. Human enough to imagine what it might have been like had he not stopped himself. Human enough to be both relieved and rather astonished that he *had* stopped himself.

And then he remembered why he had been so drunk in the first place and groaned again. As he struggled into his boots, the guilt resettled, seeming to weigh even heavier on him than before. No doubt because he had allowed himself to recall the reasons for it. God dammit! The rawness of it all made him acutely aware, now, of how far below the surface he had buried it all. Made him realise, too, that his defences were just that: safeguards, but no solution. That the perpetual ennui he suffered was not boredom, but unhappiness.

Shrugging into his coat and brushing his hair, Rafe considered resorting to the brandy bottle again. Sweet oblivion. Except it hadn't worked. He couldn't understand why so many of his peers chose to dip so deep so often. All it gave you was nausea and a head that felt as if it would crack open like an egg. What it didn't allow you to do was either escape or forget. In fact, he recalled with a shudder, the more he drank the more he remembered, all the tiny details he'd tried so very hard to obliterate.

Henrietta was the unwitting cause of it all, for he could see, even through his pain, that she had not meant to rake over his smouldering ashes. He could picture quite clearly the horror on her face. She had had no idea she was treading on forbidden ground. Why should she?

Ironically she was the balm, too, for she, and not the brandy, had finally given him the sweet oblivion he sought. Henrietta on top of him, under him, laughing with him, kissing him, in her hideous flannel nightgown and *not* in her hideous flannel nightgown. *Then* he had found something much more delightful to occupy his mind. Only then.

Sighing heavily, Rafe made his way downstairs to the coffee room. He needed breakfast. 'And bring me a tankard of porter immediately,' he said to the maid-servant.

It arrived within a few moments and so, too, did Henrietta in her brown dress with her brown eyes—more cinnamon than chocolate today, he thought—fixed upon him sympathetically. 'Have you a very sore head?'

Relieved, but not very surprised to discover that she was not the type of female to raise her grudges when a man was at his lowest, Rafe attempted a smile.

'Extremely,' he said wryly, 'but it serves me right. Have you had breakfast?'

'Ages ago. I've been helping Meg bake bread.'

'Is there no end to your talents?'

'Well, most people consider baking bread a basic skill, not a talent,' Henrietta said, as she seated herself opposite him and poured them both coffee from the steaming pot that Bessie had just served. 'I don't have any real talents. I can't play upon the pianoforte—in fact, Mama says I'm tone deaf—and although I can stitch a straight seam, I can't embroider.'

'And you can't dance, either,' Rafe reminded her.

'Well, I can only assume I cannot,' she pointed out, 'given that I've never had the opportunity to find out.'

'Would you like the opportunity?'

'Would you teach me?' she asked with a twinkle. 'Only I'm not so very sure that you'd be a particularly patient teacher, especially not at this precise moment. Probably, you'd end up furious with me.' Her face fell. 'Actually, that's pretty much guaranteed, because you always end up furious with me. I don't know how it is…'

'Any more than I do,' Rafe said feelingly. 'Perhaps it is your tendency to say the most outrageous things.'

'I don't. I don't mean to. I just—'

'Say what you think. I know.' Rafe took a sip of coffee. It was hot and bitter. 'Contrary to what you are thinking, I like it. Most of the time. I'm getting used to it. It's refreshing in its own way. Like this coffee.' He took another sip. The ache in his head was beginning to subside. He realised that Henrietta had not once, since that fateful morning when he had found her in the ditch, complained about her own headache, which must have been considerably more painful. And he hadn't thought to ask. He took another sip of coffee. 'I'm sorry,' he said.

Her startled look would have made him smile had it not first made him feel guilty. 'Sorry for what?'

'I shouldn't have gone off and left you alone like that last night.'

'You asked Mr Forbes to check up on me. He did. Often.'

'You're very generous. More generous than I deserve.'

'And you must be very hung-over to be so complimentary,' Henrietta said, with a chuckle.

He did not deserve such understanding. For a brief moment, he had the most bizarre wish that he did. 'I don't make a habit of getting so disguised,' he said. 'You have every right to be disappointed in me.'

Henrietta grinned. 'It helped to know that an appropriate punishment surely awaited you in the morning.'

Rafe's real smile made a brief appearance. 'Then you should be more than content, for I am paying a heavy price indeed.'

'Is it very painful? Shall I fetch you a compress?'

'Good God, no. What I need is some breakfast, that should do the trick.' He released her hand and sat back in his seat, his long legs sprawled in front of him.

'I heard Mr Forbes tell Meg to give you three eggs, he said you'd need them,' Henrietta informed him helpfully.

'Benjamin Forbes is a very wise man.'

Henrietta picked up a knife and put it down again. Rafe looked paler than usual. His eyelids were heavier.

He had cut himself shaving. A tiny nick, just below his ear. 'I was angry with you for a while last night,' she confessed. 'I am sorry, Rafe, but you cannot have expected me to know….'

'You're right.'

'I am?'

He could almost have laughed at her astonished expression, were he not aware of the rather miserable picture it painted of him. Unknown. Unknowable. He had prided himself on those qualities. His armour. Now Henrietta had pierced it and he was relieved. Glad, almost. He felt as if she were waking him from a torpor. It wasn't a full awakening—there were some scars that were so much part of his being that no one could heal them—but it was enough to tempt him with possibilities. Not least, the possibility of looking forward to the day, rather than simply enduring it.

'You are. On this occasion, Henrietta, you are quite right,' he said, smiling again. It was coming easier, his smile. Practice. That, too, was down to Henrietta. Henrietta, who was still playing with her knife, which meant she had something else on her mind. He waited.

She could feel his eyes upon her, but was not quite able to meet them, despite his surprising admission. After he'd fallen asleep, she'd lain awake until she heard the clattering of pans in the kitchen, just listening to him breathing, only just restraining herself from snuggling into his side. Though she hadn't really thought he'd abandon her, the relief of having him back again was immense. Despite what she knew of him, or what she'd *thought* she knew, despite all of Mama's warnings and despite her principled objections to his way of life, she was not immune to his charms. Far from it.

From the moment she first set eyes upon Rafe, tall, dark, dishevelled and brooding, she had known he was dangerous. It was not just his reputation, but the man himself. He had warned her several times not to trust him, and several times she had failed to heed him. She had paid no heed, either, to her own cautioning inner voice. She was a mass of contradictions, almost as many as he. Before she met Rafe St Alban, her life had been perfectly straightforward. Now though…

She picked up her knife again and began to trace a pattern in the grain of the wooden table with the blade. Now, nothing was at all clear. The more she knew of Rafe, the more she liked him, the more she was attracted to him, yet she still understood him so little. She knew now for certain he was no callous seducer. Last night had proved that.

Why had he stopped? *Why had not she?* Looking at him over the scrubbed wooden table, she wondered if he even remembered. *She* remembered only too well. Last night, she would have given herself to him willingly. Much, much too willingly. Without even thinking about it, until it was too late. Last night she had discovered a side of herself that she hadn't believed existed. A side that seized control of her principles and her morals and contemptuously discarded them—until morn, at least. Last night she hadn't recognised herself.

And that, Henrietta realised with a horrible sense of foreboding that was at the same time horribly exhilarating, showed how very far she had already come already to making him a present of the heart that was beating, as ever, far too fast in his presence. She must be more careful. She must be *much* more on her guard against her own weakness. She nodded to herself resolutely, then jumped as the knife was removed from her hand.

'It would be far safer for you to simply say what's on your mind, Henrietta,' Rafe said, putting the cutlery out of reach, 'you're in danger of cutting yourself.'

'It's nothing.'

'Which means it's about last night.'

She coloured. 'How did you know?'

'Would you rather pretend it didn't happen?'

'Yes. No.'

'No, you're not one of those young ladies who pretend, are you? It's one of the things I like about you.'

'Is it?'

Rafe laughed. 'Don't look so surprised, it's not the only one. I like the way you suck your bottom lip when you're trying to stop yourself saying something you suspect you shouldn't. You twist your hair around your middle finger when you're thinking and you wrinkle your nose when something unpleasant occurs to you. You never complain and you are always putting others before yourself even when, like me this morning, they don't deserve it. You are in turn infuriating and endearing, but at least you are never predictable. I never know what you're going to say next, any more than you do. Just when I think I want to shake you, you make me want to laugh, or you look at me just so, and I want to kiss that delightfully kissable mouth of yours. In fact, there are aspects of you, Henrietta Markham, that I find quite irresistible.'

'Oh.'

'You always say that when I've said the opposite of what you were expecting. Last night, Henrietta,' Rafe continued in a gentler tone, 'I was drunk, but not incapable. I was unshaven, reeking of brandy and reeling with unpleasant memories. You deserve better, far better, than that.'

'Oh.' His tone, even more than the words he spoke, moved her. A lump rose in her throat. She blinked several times, touched by his care for her, which was more than she had had for herself. 'Thank you,' she said softly.

Rafe squeezed her hand. 'It's the truth. You are a rather extraordinary person, Henrietta Markham, and your being quite oblivious of the fact is perhaps the thing I like about you most.'

The coffee room door swung open and Bessie arrived with Rafe's breakfast, a vast plate of ham and the promised three eggs along with the first of the loaves that Henrietta had helped make. 'Excellent timing,' Rafe said, picking up his knife and fork with relish. 'Kill or cure, I suspect.'

Benjamin sought them out after breakfast with an update. 'No firm word of either the housebreaker or the emeralds as yet,' he said, 'but don't despair, I'm waiting on a couple of fences getting back to me in the next day or so.'

Henrietta looked blank.

'A man who sells on stolen goods,' Rafe informed her, 'and before you ask, not a man with whom you will be pursuing an acquaintance. We'll leave it in Ben's capable hands.'

'What shall we do today, then, if I am not to be allowed to meet shady underworld characters?'

'Oh, I'm sure I can find some alternative form of excitement for your delectation,' Rafe replied with a rare grin. 'Leave it up to me.'

He took her to Astley's Amphitheatre in Lambeth, where the entertainment included bareback horse riding and a staged re-enactment of the Battle of Waterloo. While Rafe would normally scorn such spectacles, as he would disdain to mingle with the great unwashed, even he was forced to admit that the horses were exceptionally well trained, though most of the time his eyes were on Henrietta, rather than the sawdust-strewn floor of the stage. She leaned precariously out of their private box, her eyes huge with excitement, her cheeks flushed. Such a simple treat, yet he might as well have given her the Crown Jewels. Then again, now he came to think about it, perhaps not, because she'd said only yesterday that they were vulgar.

He set himself out to entertain her, by way of an apology. A novel experience, yet infinitely rewarding, for Henrietta found everything fascinating and her enthusiasm was infectious. Her absolute faith in his ability to answer her questions, from the latest fashions—fuller skirts, narrower waists—to the accuracy of Astley's battle charge—almost completely lacking—and the King's current state of health—confined to Windsor with gout—he found touching rather than irksome. What would, had it been suggested by one of his peers, have seemed a day out beyond tedium, turned out to be one of the most entertaining he could remember in recent years.

* * *

Afterwards, they ate in a chop house. With a little prompting, Henrietta was persuaded to confide some of her history. As ever, she was self-deprecating. He surmised she had been happy, but rather neglected, her parents more concerned with good works than the welfare of their only child, but recalling how prickly she had been about her sainted papa, he refrained from criticism. Recalling the yearning look upon her face as she gazed upon the *toilettes* of the Astley's audience, cheap imitations of the walking gowns and carriage gowns, full dress and half-dress worn by the *haut ton*, he wished he could make her a present of just one such, but he knew better now than to offer. Not only would her principles forbid such a thing, he would be drawing attention to her own shabby gown; though he detested the thing, it was such an integral part of her that he had come to feel something like affection for it.

They talked on, long after they had cleared their plates of lamb cutlets and thick gravy, oblivious of the comings and goings of other customers, oblivious of the curious looks cast them, he so well dressed and austerely handsome, she so vivacious and yet so dowdy. They talked and they laughed, and they leaned ever closer as the light fell and the rush lights were lit and the chophouse proprietor finally plucked up the courage to tell them it was well past closing.

'Goodness, where did the time go?' Henrietta said, blinking in the gloaming outside as Rafe hailed a hack. 'I've had such a lovely day, thank you.' Rafe's thigh brushed hers as he took his seat beside her in the hackney cab. She watched the driver's head bobbing in front of her through the small window, vaguely aware that they were crossing the river, for she could see the gas lamps were lit. She should be tired after her restless night, but she had never felt so alive. Rafe's leg lay warm against the folds of her cloak. His shoulder brushed hers. Though they were silent now, it was a comfortable silence for once.

Though it was not precisely comfortable. She was too conscious of the man beside her. Irresistible, Rafe had called her. Henrietta had never thought of herself in that way before. She liked it, though it made her nervous, for it contained all sorts of possibilities she suspected she couldn't ever live up to and knew she should not try to do so.

Today she had seen yet another side of Rafe, one she liked very much. One she could grow to like even more. Another side of him that failed to fit the image his reputation ought to have created. She'd thought it was that simple: Rafe was a rake, therefore he was unprincipled. Yet her experience of him was almost entirely the opposite. She just didn't understand it. She could no longer believe him capable of dishonourable behaviour, yet he had not denied it.

Henrietta chewed her lip. Thinking back, every time the subject came up, it had been she who accused and he who refused to comment. Could she have been a little too presumptuous? It was a fault of hers, she knew that.

As they pulled into the yard of the Mouse and Vole and Rafe took her hand to help her down from the carriage, doubt shook her once more. Why would Mrs

Peters, his own housekeeper, have warned her off if there had been no grounds to do so?

She followed him, through the side door, along the corridor, the draught from the taproom door making the wall sconces flicker. Gazing at his tall figure, his wide shoulders, the neat line of his hair, she felt the now-familiar prickle of awareness. Another contradiction, perhaps the most significant, her body's desire for him. A desire quite independent of her mind. She knew she should not, she knew that it was wrong, but her body insisted it was right.

Right or wrong, that was the key question. She wished she had an answer. She wished things didn't have to be so complicated. Or maybe it was Rafe who was complicated? Or she was simplistic? He said she saw things too much in black and white, and he'd been proved right about that several times now.

'Go on up, I'll go and see if Ben has further news,' Rafe said, interrupting the somewhat tangled strands of Henrietta's reasoning. A roar of anger came from the taproom, quickly followed by a louder roar. 'Sounds like he has his hands full,' he said with a wry smile. 'Perhaps now is not the best time to interrupt him.'

They made their way up the stairs to the sanctuary of their chamber. Placing the oil lamp by the bedside, Rafe drew the curtains together. Henrietta unclasped her cloak and placed it over the chair, cast off her gloves, tugged the ribbons of her bonnet and pulled it from her head. Rafe cast aside his coat and loosened his neckcloth. A cosy domestic scene. The thought struck them both at the same time. They caught one another's expression, smiled, looked away, embarrassed by the intimacy—or perhaps unwilling to acknowledge it.

'I had a lovely day. Thank you,' Henrietta said, picking up her hairbrush.

Rafe smiled. The smile that made her feel as if her heart were being squeezed, so she found she had to concentrate on breathing. 'I enjoyed it, too,' he said.

'Confess, you didn't expect to. I can't imagine that Astley's is the sort of place you visit regularly.'

His smile broadened. 'I confess, but I still enjoyed myself. You have the knack of making even the most tedious occasions refreshing.'

'Because I'm so green.'

'Because you are so Henrietta.'

She put her hairbrush down. 'Is that a compliment?'

'Yes.'

She picked her hairbrush up again, looked at it absently and then put it back down. 'Rafe, I wanted to—at least I don't want to but I feel I must. I don't understand and it's confusing me, and so...' She looked at him helplessly, trying desperately to find the words that would not put him instantly on the defensive.

'You are confusing me, too, for I have no idea what you're talking about.'

She bit her lip. If she hesitated now, then she would simply find herself wrestling with the same questions tomorrow, and before that there was tonight to get through, not that she had any intentions at all—far from it—and, anyway, he would not. Probably. So...

'Rafe, are you really a rake?' She could almost see his hackles rise; his brows were drawn together, winging upwards to give him a satanic look, his eyes stormy.

Oh God, why had she had to blurt it out like that? 'I didn't mean to—forget I said it.'

'But you did, so it is obviously troubling you.'

'Well, it is,' she said resolutely. 'I simply don't understand you.'

'What, precisely, don't you understand?'

If she touched him, he would freeze. Not that he would let her touch him. The barriers were invisible, but she could see them all the same. Touch-me-not. 'You,' she said, refusing to back down. 'I don't understand how someone with your reputation can be so—so—well, you just don't behave like a rake at all.'

'And how does a rake behave, Henrietta?'

'Well, they—well, they—Mama says that they seduce innocents.'

'And Mama would know, would she?'

'Yes, she would,' Henrietta said, her temper rising in response to his heavily sarcastic tone. 'She knows because she was seduced by one. Oh!' She put her hand over her mouth, but it was too late, so she blurted out the rest. 'She was young. He promised her marriage. They eloped together and he jilted her.'

'After he had seduced her, presumably.'

Henrietta's colour rose. 'There is no need to be so callous.'

'Surely, if you are to tar me with the same brush as your mother's seducer, you would expect me to be callous,' Rafe said.

Henrietta folded her arms across her chest. She would have the truth from him this time. 'You're not callous,' she said firmly. 'You're not callous and you're not irresponsible, and you're not shallow and you're not selfish.'

He ignored this. 'What happened to your mother?'

'She was devastated. She is very beautiful, not a bit like me, and she had had excellent prospects, but they were all ruined. She retired to the country; it was there she met Papa and he fell in love with her and she agreed to marry him and there was some sort of quarrel with her family over that because Papa is not rich or titled….'

'Your mother was?'

'I believe her family is a good one, but I have never met any of them. They disowned her—not because she was seduced by a rake—he had the benefit of being a well-born man, too—but because she married my father,' Henrietta said indignantly 'What happened to my mother, it was a terrible thing. Awful. It has shaped her whole life. Even though she is happy with Papa, there are times when she is just so sad. You cannot imagine.'

He could. A fading beauty self-obsessed with something that happened more than twenty years ago, too caught up in her own tragedy to admit to any sort of responsibility. He could imagine it only too well, for he had married one such. Now Henrietta had tarred him with the same brush as her mother's seducer and he wanted nothing more than to shake some sense into her. 'And so Mama has filled your head with tragic tales of seducers, has she?'

'She has taught me to believe that such men are to be avoided. That they have no morals. That—'

'So, I am not only a seducer of innocents, but I have

no morals? I wonder that you trust yourself with me, Miss Markham.'

'That's my point, Lord Pentland. I do trust you. You are patently an honourable man.'

'Oh please, Henrietta, don't colour me whiter than snow.'

'I'm not, but you are content to be coloured black as night, and I don't understand why,' she replied furiously.

'I have no intentions of explaining myself.'

'Why not? I explain myself to you all the time. Why should you not tell me—?'

'Because it is none of your business.'

'But it still matters to me.'

'Why?'

'Because it does.' She waited, glaring at him, but she was no match for Rafe's stony countenance. Henrietta gave an infuriated growl. 'I don't understand you and because of that I don't understand myself,' she said. 'Oh, for goodness' sake, if you must know, I just can't reconcile how I can feel—want—I just—last night! Last night, when you kissed me, I wanted you to—and then when you stopped I wished you hadn't. And yet I know you are a rake, so I ought not to want. But I do and that is what I don't understand,' she said, dashing away a tear with the back of her hand. 'And if you are a rake, why have you not seduced me? I don't understand that, either.'

Her brown eyes were sparkling with tears. Her bosom was heaving. She was flushed with mortification and temper. Rafe saw that revealing her mother's past had cost her dear, but not as dear as the frank and totally unexpected admission of her desire. The righteous fury he had been nursing dissipated like a cloud of steam. He took a step towards her and tried to take her hand, but she pushed him away.

'Your honesty puts me to shame, Henrietta.'

'That was not my intention.'

'Which is why it was so effective,' he said ruefully.

'I hate having to think ill of you,' she confessed in a whisper.

'You want to think me an honourable man, is that it, Henrietta?' Rafe countered harshly. 'You want me to deny my past in order for you to reconcile your conscience? I cannot do that. I am no saint, Henrietta. My reputation as a rake is not unfounded.'

She swallowed hard. She felt as if she were shrinking inside.

Rafe pushed his fingers through his hair, casting his eyes up to the ceiling where a cobweb hung from the corner of the plain cornicing. 'I can tell you the truth, if you like.'

Chapter Seven

Was he really contemplating this? 'I can't refute my actions, but I can explain them.'

It seemed he was. Rafe took a quick turn around the room. It mattered that she understood. Only now did he admit to himself how much her opinion of him counted, how hurtful had been her judgements. How had she come to be so important to him? He didn't know. He just knew she was. Telling her would be a relief, if not a release. He wanted to tell her.

He took another turn about the room. Henrietta was still standing in the middle of it, in her brown gown with her brown eyes, watching him. He owed her the truth. He took her hand and led her back over to the bed, sitting down in the chair opposite once more. She looked so compliant, yet there was a core of steel running through her. It gave her a strength of purpose, a solidly grounded moral certainty at her centre that he envied. He might not agree with all of her opinions, but at least she had them and she meant them. She had integrity. He particularly admired that.

Settling back in the uncomfortable wooden seat, Rafe subdued a craven desire to extinguish the lamp and make his confession in the dark. 'I was only nineteen when I married Julia,' he said, launching into his sorry tale before he could think again. 'Lady Julia Toward. She was twenty-three, the same age as you are now.'

Henrietta listened intently. Rafe's voice was not much above a whisper, but the bitterness was there, like a rusty blade hidden in the petals of a flower.

'She was very beautiful,' he continued, 'very beautiful and, though I did not know it, very unstable. She had been betrothed some two years before, but her fiancé died. I thought her over it when I met her. She said she was. I wanted to believe her. When you want something enough, you can persuade yourself of anything.'

Silence. Henrietta waited, biting back the urge to protest. She hated the implications of what he was saying. Despite the evidence—foolishly, she now realised—she had persuaded herself that he had not loved his wife.

'I was just returned from my Grand Tour and was as green as spring asparagus.' Rafe's voice was stronger now. 'My father had packed me off with dire warnings of the dangers of salacious Continental women, but in truth I was more interested in ancient history. I spent my time seeking out every set of crumbling ruins that Greece and Italy had to offer. Father died quite unexpectedly while I was still abroad. When I returned to England, it was to take up the title. I had always known it would be mine, but I hadn't expected it to happen so soon. I was not close to my father, but I was shocked and saddened by his premature death. There was no one else, you see. I have no siblings and my mother had died years before. There was just my grandmother, as there still is. She urged me to marry, saying I needed help in taking up the reins, and there was Julia, ideally positioned to do so. The perfect doyenne, was Julia, it was what she had been raised to be. And she was beautiful and claimed to love me. And I was ripe and ready to fall in love myself. I couldn't have been more primed. So we married.'

'Were you happy?' Henrietta asked. It was churlish of her, awful of her, but she wanted him to say no.

Rafe shrugged. 'At first. It's hard for me to remember, it's like looking back at a shadow play, but, yes, I suppose we must have been. Or I was. Julia was…' He broke off with a heavy sigh. 'You know, I have no real idea what Julia was. There were days when she seemed content, days when she simply withdrew into silence. She'd lock herself away in her bedchamber for up to a week, then she'd come out smiling and pretending nothing had happened. She would shower affection on me, then she would freeze when I touched her. She would drag me to every party we were invited to, wouldn't let me leave her side, then she would take to ignoring me. If I so much as danced with another women, she would wreak havoc, yet she would not allow me to make comment on her coterie of gallants—and, believe me, it was a large coterie. She was terrified that her looks would fade. Actually, she was obsessed with how she looked. It was the source of her power.'

He ran his fingers through his hair. 'I can see all that now. At the time it was a different matter entirely. At the time, I grew tired of her tantrums and tears. I grew tired, too, of her blowing first hot and then cold upon the physical side of our union. I stopped going to her room. I stopped wanting her. I stopped caring about her moods. I stopped loving her.'

Silence again, a deeply uncomfortable one filled with ghosts and spectres. Rafe gazed blankly into the past, forcing himself to relive those days, slowly easing the tattered bandages from the wounds he had garnered, testing to see how much they had healed. 'It was my fault, most of it,' he said bitterly. 'I didn't care enough and she saw that. She didn't love me, but she was terrified of losing me, and she could see that I was by this time—two years or so into our marriage—she could see that I was quite indifferent in the way that only callous youth can be. So she tried to get my attention in the only way she knew how, by making me jealous.'

He had been stroking the back of Henrietta's hand, a rhythmic caress back and forwards, but now he stopped. 'She took a lover. When I found out, she wept and pleaded, begging forgiveness, but when she saw I would not be moved, things turned vicious. She told me she'd never loved me. She told me she married me only for the title and the money. She told me she'd only ever loved one man and he was dead. She told me I could never satisfy her, that she'd taken countless lovers to our marital bed before this one, that I was not man enough for her. That I was not man enough for anyone.'

Rafe's voice was shaking. He was breathing hard, as if he had been running. A cold sweat prickled the small of his back, but now that he had started, he needed to finish, no matter how much it pained him. A flash of the humiliation that had engulfed him at the time struck him with an immediacy which took him aback. It was quickly followed by shame as he remembered how Julia had made him feel. He had forgotten the vicious sting of her barbs that had so effectively lashed his youthful ego, flaying his more innocent self, for a brief time quite destroying his confidence. It had been so long since he had vowed to prove her wrong, so long since he had stopped believing he had any point at all to prove, yet for a moment he felt again as if he did.

He plunged on, eager to conclude now, his words spilling out, staccato-like. 'I know now that it was mere bravado, designed to wound, but I didn't know then. I hated her for what she said. I ended our marriage then and there. A formal separation, but discreetly done. No notices in the press, nor any to her creditors. Julia was banished to an obscure estate, given an adequate allowance to live on, but it was punishment enough for her. Banishment from society and all the vanities and admirers who fed her ego. I punished her because I believed what she said. Then later, to my eternal shame, I continued to punish her because I felt guilty. I hadn't ever truly loved her. I shouldn't have married her, any more than she should have married me, yet we were stuck with one another, married but not married, in a state of limbo. I kept us there because I felt guilty. Because I had failed. I punished myself as well as Julia. I felt I deserved the misery as much as she.'

'Couldn't you have divorced?'

Rafe shook his head vehemently. 'No. God, no. An Act of Parliament, to say nothing of becoming the latest crim. con. for the gossips. No, that would have been a step too far for both our families.' He sat down heavily on the chair, dropping his head into his hands. 'You have to remember, I was young. I'm not excusing what I did, I'm just doing as you ask, telling you why. I was loaded with guilt at not having made Julia happy and humiliated by her jibes. I couldn't make any woman happy, she said. I was hurt. I vowed I'd never let anyone hurt me again. And I—I set out to prove her wrong.'

He faltered here. Having for so long refused to allow himself to remember, he had never questioned the actions he had taken to remedy his sense of humiliation. Having made the decision, he had acted and continued to act without reflection. But now, in the retelling, under Henrietta's clear-sighted, innocent gaze, he did reflect, and found himself on less solid ground than he ought to be. 'It was not so much revenge as—as—I don't know, I suppose it was shoring up my defences, rebuilding my ego. I swear to you, Henrietta, I have never once hurt anyone in the process. I have never seduced any woman who was not a willing partner and I have taken every precaution to ensure that I would not leave her with child, but I cannot deny that there have been very many such women over the years. I have learned to use sex as an emotional shield. I've learned to use it as a release mechanism, to stop me feeling.'

It hurt, his confession, and it pained her soul to see him so raw, to think of him as once so vulnerable, to see the glimpses of that vulnerability still. She loathed the beautiful woman who had spoken so cruelly, but she was not so blind as to think Julia solely to blame. The most painful part of what Rafe was saying was hearing his judgement—his flawed judgement—upon himself. No one could be more ruthless, more self-condemnatory.

'I have my own rules, my own form of morality, if you will,' Rafe continued harshly. 'I have never had any problem in playing by them. I don't engage with women who expect any more than a physical relationship. I don't sleep with the innocent or the vulnerable. I don't allow any real intimacy. Don't look like that, Henrietta—believe me, it's very possible to share your body with someone and feel nothing. It is possible to give and to receive physical pleasure without feeling real desire. I am a rake, Henrietta, but not the kind of rake you think me.'

'Oh, Rafe, I so much wish you were not *any* kind of rake.' How much she wished *that* she had not acknowledged to herself, until now. She had not appreciated how much she had longed for an explanation that would eradicate his past until Rafe made it crystal clear that he could not.

She was torn, moved to tears by the pain and suffering he had endured. There were angry tears for the wanton destruction of Rafe's innocence by Julia, but also for the route to retribution he had chosen. 'I know it is trite, but it is true, none the less: two wrongs don't make a right. I *wish* you had not behaved so.'

'But you understand, Henrietta, why I do? Did.'

Did she? He had trampled a ragged path through her preconceptions, that much was certain. He was not a rake. Yet he was. He had good reasons to feel as he did, but were they sufficient to justify his actions? 'I'm sorry. I do understand, but I can't condone your behaviour, Rafe. I know it's not for me to judge, I was not the one married to Julia, but still.' She shook her head. 'You've been so honest with me, I can't lie to you. I just— I don't know. Tell me what happened after you separated? To Julia, I mean, what happened to Julia?'

The sorrowful look in Henrietta's eyes made him experience something remarkably like remorse, though he suspected it was more for the pain of disillusioning her than wishing his past undone. Bitter experience had taught him just how pointless that was. 'We lived apart for three years. I gradually eased the terms of our separation. I didn't love her, but I cared enough to wish her happy, so when she suggested a reconciliation, vowing it was what she wanted, I was not entirely against it. My instincts were to refuse, but Julia was persistent and my guilty conscience was persistent and so, too, was my grandmother. There was still the issue of an heir, you see. So we were reconciled and then...'

Once again, Rafe got to his feet. He wrenched his neckcloth from his shirt and tossed it on to the floor. 'It was a mistake from the start. To end a sorry tale, she died tragically. Almost exactly five years ago. And despite my grandmother's renewed and extremely determined campaign for my re-entering the matrimonial stakes, I will never marry again. The whole thing was too painful. I don't want that kind of pain again. I am much happier and better off alone.'

And now she did understand the real punishment he was meting out on himself. Not just cutting himself off from pain, he would not think himself deserving of feeling. She understood that now and so much more of it made sense. 'Are you sure you are happier?' she asked softly, already fairly certain of the answer.

Rafe hesitated. 'I was. At least, I thought I was until you waltzed into my life,' he admitted with a rueful smile. 'I sometimes feel as if you have picked me up and thrown me into the air and I can never be sure if I have yet landed, or where. I hate it and it makes me furious, but it also makes me laugh and it makes me want more. You were honest with me, Henrietta, let me be completely honest with you. I don't know how you've managed it, but you make me want to break my rules. You've made it damned difficult not to, if you must have the God's honest truth. There, now you have it all. I wish I could be the man you want me to be, but I'm not and never can be.'

She put her fingers to his mouth. 'You are always telling me not to think in black and white—you should take a lesson from your own book. You are much more than you think you are, Rafe. I wish that you were not quite so determined to see yourself in the poorest possible light. Whether you will admit it or not, you are my knight errant, and whether you will admit to them or not, you have some extremely chivalrous qualities.'

Kneeling up on the bed, she wrapped her arms around his neck. He was not the man he ought to be, not the man he could be, but he was Rafe, and she would not change him even if she could, any more than she would change this moment. An intense need to provide succour swamped her. She was overwhelmingly relieved to be able to explain her own feelings, to have them almost legitimised. Mentally exhausted by the process, she became intensely physically aware. Rafe's pulse was beating at his throat. The scent of him, so achingly familiar, was in her nose. She wanted the taste of him on her tongue. Rafe was not the only one who was finding it difficult to keep to his own rules. She wanted his kisses. She longed for his touch.

Desire! His word, but it rang true. That is what she was feeling. Unconsciously, she nestled herself closer, feeling the rise and fall of his ribs against her breasts. Desire. Was it really so very wrong? She knew the answer, but chose to ignore it.

'Henrietta, if you keep doing that, I won't be responsible for the consequences.'

She didn't want him to be. She didn't want to think. She wanted to feel. She wanted him to feel. She pressed herself closer and looked up at him.

Eyes slate-blue, piercing, seeing too much, more than she was prepared to look at herself. Henrietta tried to look away, but he tilted up her chin. 'Henrietta, I don't want...'

'You do. You said you do. And I do, too. I know I should not, but I do. I can't help it.'

'Dear God, Henrietta...'

'Rafe, just kiss me.'

He kissed her roughly. His mouth was hard on hers, but her lips were so meltingly soft, it didn't matter. He kissed her and his doubts fled, too. This was right. This. And this. And this. His kiss deepened. He pulled her closer, wrapped his arms around her and found it. Sweet oblivion.

As Rafe kissed her, Henrietta's senses whirled. He had kissed her before, tenderly, teasingly, with a promise of more to come, but this time it was there, right from the start. Passion. She had no time to think, she could only respond, melting into his arms as he enfolded her, his lips hard on hers, his tongue plundering her mouth, thrusting into it in a way that made her body tremble, heat and shiver all at once.

His hands were on the laces of her gown. Knowing, expert hands—she wouldn't think about that. He kissed and he unlaced, and the gown fell open at the back; he pulled it down over her arms and she helped him—she didn't care that it was wanton, she wanted to be free of it as much as he wanted her to be. He discarded his own coat and waistcoat. She was in her cotton chemise and his hands were on the plain material, stroking, caressing, his lips tracing a path from her mouth down her neck to the valley between her breasts as his fingers plucked her nipples into an aching hardness that made her moan.

He said her name, breathed her name, his voice hoarse, his breath coming as fast as hers. He said her name as if she were beautiful; the way he touched her made her feel beautiful. The way he touched her made her feel hot. Made her feel restless. Made her feel as if there was something delightful waiting for her, if only he would kiss her more, touch her more. She ran her hands feverishly up his back, feeling the heat of his skin through his shirt, but it wasn't enough, so she tugged his shirt free from his breeches and felt his skin.

He kissed her again, his mouth drugging hers, hot and dark and full of promise. Forbidding and enticing and dangerous, just as she had known from the beginning he would be. She kissed him back just as deeply, just as passionately; she shivered more violently as he pulled her closer and she felt the thick weight of his arousal press solidly against her thigh.

She was sprawled on the bed now and he was looking down at her, his eyes glittering and stormy. His cheeks were flushed. His shirt was open at the neck. A sprinkling of dark hairs. She couldn't remember when he had lost his neckcloth. Or his boots. He knelt down on the floor and untied her garters, delicately peeling down her coarse woollen stockings as if they were made of the finest silk. He kissed her ankle, the faint pulse at the bone. It was as if he had kissed her innermost self.

She shuddered. Heat pooled in her belly. Her body tightened, as if readying itself. He pulled her towards him and untied her chemise, freeing her breasts. He kissed her mouth again, more urgently now. He tangled his fingers in her wildly curling hair, murmuring her name. Then his mouth fastened on her breast, his tongue flicking her nipple.

First one, then the other, he tended to her breasts, cupping their weight in his hands, his tongue flicking over each nipple in turn, his mouth searingly hot on them. Her body was stretched as taut as the rope the tightrope walker had balanced on at Astley's. She felt the same sense of giddy excitement, of precariousness.

She shivered, hot, then cold, hot, then cold. She arched her back. Her fingers clutched at his skin. His shirt was gone. She nuzzled her face into the rough hair of his chest, her hands roaming feverishly over his contours, the ridged muscles of his back, the line of his ribs, the dip in his abdomen. When he licked, she licked, too, and heard him gasp as she gasped. She pressed herself into him with abandon, relishing the hard length of his arousal, wanting more of him, more from him, more.

He pushed her back on the bed and removed her drawers, then kissed the soft inner flesh of her thighs. *What was he doing?* She didn't care, she just wanted him to keep on doing it. He was nudging her thighs apart. She was taut, expectant. 'Rafe.' She writhed on the bed. She arched up as he kissed her thigh again. 'Rafe,' she said more urgently, a plea. She tugged on his shoulders.

He was so hard it ached. She was so ready, there was no need to wait. He had never seen anyone so aroused. He had never felt so aroused himself. She was perfect, ripe and luscious and waiting for him. His erection throbbed. His stomach clenched. He had never wanted anyone so much. Never. *So why in God's name was he hesitating? Again!*

'Rafe?'

He kissed her mouth, her infinitely kissable mouth, and she wrapped her arms around him and he realised what it was. She trusted him. Completely. Implicitly.

He disentangled himself from her arms, ignoring her soft protest. He kissed her breasts and she stopped protesting. He kissed the soft roundness of her belly and felt her tremble. Then he dipped his fingers into the sweet heaven of her sex and felt her wet, hot, so ready for him that almost his resolution crumbled. He heard her say his name, then he kissed where his fingers had been and he heard her cry out with surprise and pleasure; he forgot all about his own needs and, for the first time in his life, took pleasure in attending only to someone else's.

Henrietta's eyes flew open as he kissed her there. And there. Oh God, and there. *What was he doing?* Should he not—should they not—was this right? Then her eyes fell heavily closed as he kissed her again and she surrendered to the sensations he was arousing.

She'd thought she couldn't experience any more sensation, but her body proved her wrong. Everything focused. There. Where his mouth kissed and his tongue licked and his fingers stroked. There. Where she was getting tighter and hotter and climbing higher. There. She couldn't breathe. She heard herself moaning, saying his name, over and over, saying *Rafe, Rafe, Rafe, please, please, please,* though she didn't know why; then he licked her again and she knew why, because that was exactly, exactly, exactly what she wanted, so that when he stopped she wanted to scream. Then he did it again and she did scream as finally the tension became too much and she broke, shattered, flew apart and apart and apart, and then flew again as he licked her again, holding her against his mouth as he kissed her so unbelievably intimately, kissing her again until she floated, curling her body into his as she descended from whatever plane of ecstasy she had inhabited, kissing her mouth, stroking her hair, saying her name, kissing her as if he really meant it, as if she truly was irresistible.

She opened her eyes to meet his, deep indigo, filled with undisguised passion. She was pressed so close to him she could feel his heart beating, slower than hers, but still fast. She waited, knowing there was more, wanting more. She could feel him hard and solid through his breeches.

He still had his breeches on!

He laughed, and she realised that once again she'd spoken out loud. 'I know,' he said.

'But…'

'It's better this way.'

'But you…'

'I am more than satisfied, if you are,' he said. And he meant it. 'Sleep, Henrietta.' He stroked her hair, her shoulders. He cupped her bottom, nestling her closer, and stroked her back. He kissed her eyelids. The tip of her nose. Though his shaft was still throbbing, he felt almost sated, strangely replete.

Her breathing was already slowing. Her hands were loosing their hold on him. He pulled the rough blanket up over both of them. Another night confined in those damned breeches, yet he didn't care. He wasn't in the least tired, but he had no intentions of moving.

Henrietta snuggled her cheek into the crook of his shoulder. She was floating again, on a cloud of blissful happiness.

She awoke next morning to the reassuring thump of his heart. She was still anchored to his side, one of her legs pressed between his thighs. She lay completely still, relishing the feel of him, the solidity of him, the scent of him, the warmth. One of his hands was wrapped around her waist. The other lay on her bottom. She became dimly aware of another sound. An urgent tapping at the door. It was Benjamin and he clearly had some news.

Shyly clutching the sheet around her, Henrietta sat up in bed. Rafe had already pulled on a clean shirt and she was acutely conscious of her own nakedness.

Sitting on the end of the bed, pulling on his boots,

Rafe tried very hard to ignore the alluring and delightfully naked bundle only a few inches away. Intimacy was something he was accustomed to eschewing, but this kind of intimacy, this waking up together, and getting dressed, and starting a new day together—he was finding that he liked it. At least, he liked it with Henrietta. Her hair was curlier than ever in the morning light. Her skin was creamy, rather than white. He liked the way her lips were smudged with his kisses. He dropped his boot.

'Rafe, we— Benjamin is waiting.'

But he kissed her, anyway, and, when her arms went around his neck and the sheet slipped so that her breasts were pressed against his shirt, he kissed her again.

Henrietta disentangled herself with extreme reluctance. Already her body was tingling with anticipation. It was intoxicating, this passion they shared.

She smiled at him, and he felt as if her smile tugged at something inside him. It was the strangest feeling. She had judged him, but she had not found him wanting. She trusted him. And she cared. Perhaps too much. He hadn't thought of that. He hadn't thought of that at all. *Why the hell had he not?*

Guilt made his own smile fade. Because he had not wanted to. He wished—he wished—but wishes were the stuff of fools and he was a fool no more. He turned back to the shaving mirror. 'I'll only be a moment more. I'll go down and order breakfast, you can make your *toilette* in private.'

The door closed and Henrietta got out of bed. The magic of the night had fled, leaving a grey dawning of reality. These last few days had been a flight of fantasy.

If Benjamin's news was positive, it would precede a return to the real world. So successful had she been in forgetting all about the accusations hanging over her head that she had no idea, in fact, what form, exactly, her return to reality would constitute.

She had no source of income. Even with her name cleared, it was unlikely in the extreme that Lady Ipswich would take her back and, knowing what she knew now about the lady's past, Henrietta was far from sure that she wanted to return in any case. She could go to Ireland if she borrowed the fare from Rafe, she supposed, but the very thought of facing Mama and Papa and the inevitable chaos that would surround them made her heart sink.

As she tied her garters and laced her shoes, a tear plopped down on to her hand. 'The thing is,' she said to her melancholy reflection, as she dried her face on a towel smelling of Rafe's shaving soap, 'the thing is that though, of course, I don't love him, I don't want to leave him just yet. Though I know I must.' She sniffed and picked up her brush, dragging it through her tangled curls roughly enough to explain the fresh batch of tears that collected in her eyes.

She cast down her brush and began to stick pins randomly into her hair. 'It is high time you faced facts, Henrietta Markham. Rafe St Alban will very soon— maybe as early as today—be leaving this inn and returning to his privileged life in London. You would do well to turn your mind to what you are going to do next, even if you don't have to worry about Newgate. Which is not yet a foregone conclusion.'

She pushed a final pin into her hair and surveyed the

dismal result. It would have to do. Taking several deep breaths, reminding herself yet again that there were thousands of people worse off than she was, Henrietta left the bedchamber.

Rafe was waiting for her in the coffee room with a substantial breakfast spread before him. 'Ben won't be a moment,' he said, helping her into a chair and pouring her some coffee.

Henrietta buttered a slice of bread, glancing at Rafe as she did so. His expression was impassive. 'You'll be able to go home, if the news is positive,' she said brightly.

'Home?'

'You must have a dozen things to attend to, lots of parties and such. You'll be pleased to finally have the comfort of your own bed, too.'

He had been about to take a bite of beef, but his fork remained suspended halfway to his mouth. 'You are eager to be rid of me?'

'No, of course not, only I am vastly conscious of the amount of time you have already wasted....'

Rafe put his fork back down on his plate, the beef uneaten. 'I don't consider it wasted time.' He took a sip of coffee. He hadn't thought about returning to his solitary life. He wasn't ready. 'Anyway, things are not that simple. Even if Ben has tracked down the housebreaker, he's hardly likely to readily admit to the theft, especially with the threat of the hangman's noose looming over him if he does.'

'Oh.' Henrietta bit into her bread and butter. 'I hadn't taken that into account.'

'Let us wait until we hear what Ben has to say,' Rafe said, as their host entered the room.

What Benjamin had to say was that he had, through a variety of mysterious contacts, tracked down a man who strongly resembled Henrietta's description of the housebreaker. 'Goes by the name of Scouse Larry. Looks like your man, all right, but he's a sneaking budge—a small-time thief, that is. Clothes, the odd piece of silver, is what Scouse Larry deals in, not gew-gaws and he's certainly not tried to fence anything like those emeralds you described, miss. If they'd been on the market, I'd have heard.' Benjamin tugged at his battle-scarred earlobe. 'I dunno, it's a rum 'un; something about all of this don't add up.'

'Well, there's only one way to find out, and that's to confront him. Will you bring him here, Ben?' Rafe asked.

But Benjamin shook his head adamantly. 'Wouldn't come. He'd think it was a trap and run, then we'd be back to square one. You'll have to go to him.'

Rafe pushed aside his empty plate and got to his feet. 'Where do I find him?'

Henrietta, too, pushed back her chair. 'Where do *we* find him, you mean. Let me just get my cloak.'

'Lord, miss, you can't go. Best leave it to his lordship,' Benjamin said, looking at her aghast. 'Scouse Larry's abode is in the stews of Petticoat Lane. It's a terrible place, full of cut-throats and cutpurses, to say nothing of the doxies and molls. Begging your pardon, miss, but you see, a rookery's no place for a lady.'

'Ben is quite right, Henrietta, you'll have to leave this to me.'

'No.'

'Henrietta…'

'Miss…'

'No. I'm coming with you,' Henrietta said determinedly. 'I'm the only one who's actually seen this Scouse Larry. Without me how will you know it's definitely the same man? And besides,' she continued before Rafe could comment, 'it's my neck that's in the noose, not yours. I want to hear for myself what this man has to say.'

'He is unlikely to say anything unless well recompensed. Something beyond your current means,' Rafe said.

Henrietta's face fell. 'I hadn't thought of that.'

Rafe sighed heavily. 'Have it your way, Henrietta, but if we manage to get out of Petticoat Lane the lighter for a few sovereigns alone, we should consider ourselves fortunate. I shall leave my fob and snuffbox here; you would be well advised to leave anything of value here, too. The cutpurses there will steal the clothes from your back if they are not fastened on tightly.'

Henrietta gave a little squeal. 'You mean you will take me, after all?'

Rafe sighed, but his mouth quivered on the brink of a smile. 'If I don't, you'll only follow me, anyway, and I'd rather have you by my side where I can at least keep an eye on you. Go and get your cloak. Just don't blame me if what you see gives you nightmares.'

The stews of Petticoat Lane were sordid beyond belief, a warren of narrow alleyways and blind cul-de-sacs, where the ramshackle tenements leaned precariously towards one another as if attempting a drunken kiss. What little light penetrated between the steeply shelving roofs was blocked by the lines of ragged washing strung out of windows on poles, and further filtered by the acrid smoke of sea coal belching from the chimney pots. Behind the buildings, a labyrinth of wooden stairs, precarious platforms and rotten ladders allowed the rookery's residents to flit unnoticed between the maze of lodging houses, gin houses and hovels where no Charley would dare give chase. In the lanes, the gutters were awash with the foul-smelling waste cast carelessly from the broken windows patched with brown paper. Flea-bitten dogs scratched themselves vigorously, skeletal cats scrounged waste heaps fruitlessly, for they had already been scavenged several times over by the hordes of barefoot urchins too young to be harnessed into a more formal life of crime.

Clutching her cloak tightly around her, Henrietta picked her way carefully through the detritus, trying hard not to breathe too deeply, for the stench was overpowering. Profoundly glad of Rafe's protective presence, she stayed as close to him as it was possible to be without tripping him up. She was utterly appalled at the destitution and vice on blatant display, horrified by the poverty and filth so close to the affluence of the London Rafe had shown her. Nothing, not even the beggars at St Paul's, had prepared her for this. She had had no idea that such a miserable life—if life it could be called—was being scraped out by so many people in their own capital. It made her feel very small, when she thought back to her own too-easily vaunted opinions. She knew nothing. She resolved to find out more, once this was over. It would give her a purpose, finding a way to really make a difference. And when she did, she told herself stoutly, she would feel a lot better.

Ahead of them, Benjamin strode confidently, looking neither to the right nor left, a stout cane held purposefully in his sabre hand. 'By the way, Meg told me this morning what you did for Mr Forbes,' Henrietta said.

'Meg should keep her mouth shut. It was nothing.'

'Meg doesn't think it nothing, and nor does Mr Forbes. If it hadn't been for you, she said, Mr Forbes would likely have starved.'

'She exaggerates. In any case, if Benjamin hadn't come to my rescue, I would likely have been killed.'

'Five of them, Meg said. Footpads. And in the middle of Piccadilly, too.'

'Yes, but it was nigh on two in the morning.'

'What were you doing out and about at that time?'

'Walking. I was just walking.' It was the night Julia had told him her news. Unable to believe it, completely taken aback by the conflicting emotions that swamped him, he'd gone walking to give his head time to clear. His first, most overpowering, feeling had been shock. He hadn't really believed it would happen. He hadn't actually thought about it becoming real. It was quickly followed by despair, for even so short a time after their grand reunion, he knew it had been a mistake to take Julia back. An even bigger mistake, an earth-shattering mistake, was the one he was going to have to deal with as a result.

A tug on his sleeve made Rafe realise he'd come to a stop in the middle of Petticoat Lane. 'You were miles away,' Henrietta said.

'And if we don't hurry up, so too will Benjamin be,' Rafe replied, drawing a curtain in front of his memories. 'Let us make haste and catch him up, this is not the kind of area to get lost in.'

Though Henrietta was desperate to ask what had brought that haunted look of his back, there were more pressing concerns. Like the straggle of urchins grabbing on to Rafe's coat-tails and her cloak, their saucer-eyed faces full of unspoken pleas. She knew that giving them money would be a huge mistake, they would be besieged, but still, her heart was smitten at the sight. 'There must be something to be done for those poor souls,' she said to Rafe. 'They are so dirty and so hungry.'

'And there are too many of them. I told you.'

'Yes,' she said sadly. 'But—'

'Here we are,' Benjamin said from up ahead, pointing to a dark alley. 'Up that set of stairs there—hold on tight, mind, they're coming away from the wall.'

The three of them made their precarious way to the first floor of the tenement. A sharp rap on the door with Benjamin's stick resulted in a shuffling noise on the other side, but the door remained resolutely closed.

'Larry, Scouse Larry!'

Chapter Eight

The door opened a fraction, sufficient for a face to peer out into the gloom of the stairwell. 'Who are you? What do you want? What's that mort doing here?'

Before anyone could stop her, Henrietta stepped forwards. 'I am the—the mort you hit over the head and left for dead in a ditch,' she said, 'and you are the oaf who did it.' She gave the door a violent push, which took the housebreaker sufficiently by surprise to send him staggering back into the room, allowing Henrietta, quickly followed by Rafe, to enter. Benjamin remained outside and on guard.

It was dark, was the overwhelming impression, and immensely stuffy, with smoke billowing from a fireplace over which was suspended a large iron pot. Smoke was billowing from that, too, and a smell of something rancid which, Henrietta suspected, had formed the basis for Scouse Larry's previous week's suppers.

The man himself was short, wiry of build, with a surprising shock of ginger hair and a pair of exceedingly bushy eyebrows. The patch was on his right eye, made of black leather and tied behind his head. Despite the heat of the room, he wore a greasy black greatcoat in addition to a green corduroy jacket, a navy waistcoat, a shirt that may once have been white, nankeen breeches and a pair of boots through one of which his bare toe protruded.

Having no option but to allow the small and horribly familiar female along with her intimidating companion into his lair, Scouse Larry retreated to his stool by the fire. 'I don't know what you're on about,' he said to Henrietta in a wheedling tone. 'Never seen you before in me life.'

Since she had awoken in Woodfield Manor, Henrietta had been too caught up in the chain of events that had followed to give the man who had assaulted her much thought. Even this morning, on their way through the stews to meet him face to face, she had been much more concerned with what he would tell her about the crime of which she had been accused, and had therefore been completely unprepared for the surge of anger that gripped her when she saw him—and recognised him instantly.

'Liar!' she exclaimed, making her way purposefully across to the stool on which the housebreaker cowered. 'Even without that eyepatch, I would know you instantly. That coat for a start,' she said, wrinkling her nose, 'it smells horribly familiar.'

Scouse Larry looked outraged. 'This here coat was given me by Honest Jack hisself. Look at them pockets, could have been made for a budge, pockets like these. Not much they can't hold.'

'They were certainly commodious enough to conceal whatever you used to beat me around the head,' Henrietta said indignantly. She pushed back her cloak and stood with her hands on her hips, her face flushed from a combination of the oppressive heat of the room and the fire of her temper. Watching her fearlessly confronting the man who, small as he was, had proved himself perfectly capable of overpowering her, Rafe felt a stab of pride, though he was not precisely certain that her tactics would prove helpful.

He hadn't expected her to rush into this as she had done. He hadn't expected to have to work so hard to keep his hands, which had instinctively formed into fists, by his side. It occurred to him for the first time that if he had *not* been out riding so early, if he *had* been able to sleep, then he would not have encountered Henrietta. She might well have died. That this pathetic excuse of a man, whose very existence he had sorely doubted, had been responsible for that made Rafe's blood boil. He could think of nothing more satisfying than beating the cur to a pulp.

His fists clenched tighter, but he restrained himself with some difficulty. Violence would not provide the answers they sought. Answers that would take them to the root of the conundrum, for now that he had set eyes upon Scouse Larry, Rafe knew for certain that he was no criminal mastermind. A dupe, at the tail end of things most likely. What they needed was to track down the dog that had wagged this particular tail. Ben was right. There was something rum about this whole affair. 'Who put you up to this? I refuse to believe you have either the brains, the skill or even the guts necessary to carry out such an audacious crime. Come on, man, out with it.'

The housebreaker reeled back in astonishment. 'Audacious crime? What audacious crime? What the hell you talking about?'

Henrietta cast him a contemptuous look. 'You know perfectly well what we're talking about. The emeralds.'

'You what?'

'The Ipswich emeralds. The heirlooms that you stole.'

'Ipswich emeralds!' Scouse Larry fell back on to his stool. 'I didn't. I did no such thing! I don't know— What do you mean?'

'Enough of this,' Rafe said sharply. 'The game is up. Miss Markham here remembers you perfectly. We want the truth. You can tell it to us or you can tell it to the authorities at Bow Street. There is a Runner there who will be more than happy to lend you an ear.'

'A Runner?' Scouse Larry's eyes darted from Henrietta to Rafe, his countenance ashen beneath the grime. 'Are you on the level?'

'I assure you. Lady Ipswich called in the Runners the morning after the crime.'

'The morning after you hit me over the head and left me for dead,' Henrietta said indignantly.

'I didn't mean— You got in the way. I panicked. I didn't mean— I didn't steal no emeralds, I swear. She promised. She promised it was a lark. I never thought— Bloody Norah! The double-crossing bitch!'

'Who?'

'What the devil are you talking about?'

'Her!' Scouse Larry growled. 'It was her.'

'Henrietta?' Rafe said incredulously.

'Who? No, bloody Lady La-di-da Ipswich. It was her that hired me.'

'Lady Ipswich! That is nonsense—why on earth would she want to steal her own jewellery?' Henrietta looked at Rafe in confusion. 'And why would she then accuse me when she must have known perfectly well— I don't understand.'

'Describe her to me and how you met,' Rafe said to Scouse Larry. 'I need proof that you are not spinning tales to save your neck.'

'I never spoke to her but twice,' Scouse Larry said sullenly. 'At the Assizes it was, she said she was looking for someone to do her a bit of an unconventional service, no questions asked. Offered to find me a witness to get me off—which she did—and a goodly purse to boot, so—like I said, I only spoke to her the two times, but I asked about later and I know it was her. Lady Helen Ipswich. My orders was to fake a break-in at her country estate and disappear. Which is what I would've done if Missy here hadn't 'ave stuck her oar in, opening her mouth as if she was about to scream fit to bust. I had to hit her.'

'You could have killed her.'

'I told you,' Scouse Larry said, turning to Henrietta, 'I panicked, no offence intended, miss.'

'And you did not steal anything?'

'I didn't even go into the bloody house. I told you, on me mother's life, I never stole no emeralds.'

'Though I doubt very much that your mother's life holds any value for you,' Rafe said, 'I believe you.'

'She sold them herself, I reckon.'

'I suspect you are right. Rundell & Bridge, on

Ludgate Hill most likely,' Rafe said. 'They have back rooms for such business, I've heard.'

'I still don't understand,' Henrietta said plaintively. 'Why, then, did Lady Ipswich accuse me of being an accomplice?'

Scouse Larry looked startled. 'Did she now?'

'Obviously your being able to identify the house-breaker queered her pitch, as they say,' Rafe said drily. 'And unfortunately this particular housebreaker is rather a distinctive one. Rather than take the risk of him being traced and blowing the whistle on her scheme, she decided to have you locked up where you could do no harm.'

'Let's face it, missy,' Scouse Larry said, nodding furiously, 'she done us both up like a pair of kippers.'

'Yes, she did,' Henrietta said, her voice faltering.

Rafe put a reassuring arm around her shoulders. She was piteously pale and shaking, obviously shocked to the core at the extent of Helen Ipswich's perfidy. 'What is this, my bold Henrietta?' he said breezily. 'Come, don't faint on me now, the floorboards here are quite unsavoury.'

'I won't. I don't faint,' Henrietta said with a wan smile.

'Of course you don't.' Anxious now to be gone, Rafe turned his attention back to Scouse Larry. 'We may need to call on you further if Helen Ipswich requires persuading to do the decent thing, but I sincerely hope not, for brief though this acquaintance has been, it is sufficient to make me quite certain I have no wish to extend it. Much as I'm sure you wish to disappear without trace, you will oblige me by remaining on hand until we have this matter cleared up. Present yourself at the Mouse and Vole tomorrow, by which time I will know whether or not Helen Ipswich requires convincing. You will, of course, be remunerated for your trouble, but in turn I require you to keep that mouth of yours firmly closed as to this day's events. Mr Forbes will inform me if you do not and I assure you,' Rafe said, his words all the more menacing for being so quietly spoken, 'that you will not be able to avoid the consequences.' As the housebreaker made to duck, Rafe grabbed him by the throat. His strong fingers tightened on the man's neck, making him gurgle. 'Are we clear?'

Scouse Larry gurgled again, his arms flailing help-lessly.

'Excellent,' Rafe said, letting go and allowing him to crumple to the floor. 'I'll take that as a yes. Come, Henrietta, I think our work here is done.'

Rafe took her arm. He left the room without a back-wards glance, giving her no option but to follow him. He strode so purposefully when they re-entered Petticoat Lane that both Henrietta and Benjamin struggled to keep pace with him, and though the questions buzzed around like a swarm of flies in Henrietta's mind, she had no breath to ask them. Once back out on Whitecha-pel Road, Rafe hailed a hack and helped Henrietta in. She was surprised, for it was but a short step to the inn, but also relieved, as her legs were really quite shaky.

'Benjamin will see you back,' Rafe said, nodding to the innkeeper to join her and closing the door behind him.

'But where— What are you going to do?' Henrietta asked, hurriedly lowering the window.

'Confront Helen Ipswich, assuming she has returned to town.'

'Then I'm coming with you.'

'No. Not this time. You are much shaken and most naturally upset by all of this. Besides, it is not beyond the realm of possibility that Helen Ipswich would have you arrested if you just turn up on her doorstep.'

'But what are you going to say to her? How will you make her— What will you do? Rafe, I don't want—'

'Henrietta, look at you, you are in no fit state for confrontations. Just for once, trust me to deal with the matter alone.'

'I do trust you,' she said, 'but—'

'Then act as if you do,' he replied tersely, signalling to the cabbie to go.

The horses pulled away. Leaning out of the window, she saw Rafe hail another hack, heading in the opposite direction.

'Do you think he'll be long?' she asked Benjamin forlornly.

The innkeeper patted her hand. 'No longer than he has to be, don't you worry.'

Which was much easier said than done, Henrietta thought.

As things turned out, Rafe took rather longer than he had anticipated. Lady Ipswich's town house was situated in Upper Brook Street, just on the other side of Grosvenor Square from his own mansion in Mount Street. Though it was too early to worry about the carriages making their way to Hyde Park for the afternoon promenade, the brief hackney trip through Mayfair was fraught, for it seemed to Rafe that almost every house they passed belonged to an acquaintance he wished to avoid.

At the junction of Mount Street and Park Street, the hack was caught up in the chaos caused by a high-perch phaeton whose horses were rearing in the traces. The impatient driver, more flash than substance, was ignoring his groom's attempts to rein them in and lashing them into a frenzy with his inept handling of the whip. A town coach and barouche were attempting to pass, one either side of the phaeton, and the carriers of a sedan chair were shouting contrary directions in a misguided attempt to assist. It took almost fifteen minutes for the road to clear, for most of which Rafe had an almost unobstructed view of the porticos of his own house. Strange to say, he dwelt not on the ample supplies of clean clothes, the starched sheets and feather mattress of his own bed, nor even the prospect of a copper bath filled with copious amounts of steaming hot water. The bare, unheated chamber he shared with Henrietta at the Mouse and Vole seemed more like home. His own mansion, richly furnished and sumptuously carpeted, held no appeal at all, for it did not contain Henrietta.

Depending upon the success of his visit to Helen Ipswich, Henrietta could be freed from danger as early as this evening. Free to leave his protection. Free to carry on with her life. Without him.

He would miss her terribly. The realisation took him aback. He couldn't decide whether to be more astonished at the simple fact itself, or at the fact that it was Henrietta, of all people, who had invoked such alien feelings in him.

He would miss her. *How the hell had that happened?*
He had no idea, but somehow, in the space of a few short
days, being with Henrietta Markham had become an
addiction. She made him laugh. She looked out at the
world from behind those big brown eyes of hers in a
refreshingly different way. He liked the way she looked
at him, too. He more than liked the way she made him
feel. Those infinitely kissable lips of hers—no, he had
certainly not drunk enough of those. Just remembering
her delectable body spread beneath him made him hard.

He wasn't ready to let her go. He *would not* let her
go. Surely, dammit all, he could find a way of keeping
her with him for a little longer? As the hack pulled
up outside the late Lord Ipswich's town house, Rafe
racked his brain for a solution. Obviously he could not
set her up as his mistress. Appealing as the idea was
of swathing her in the silks and laces she admired, of
granting her some of the luxuries she had always been
deprived of, he knew her better than to suggest such
an arrangement. Unwilling to even let him pay for her
shot at the inn without keeping a tally, she was hardly
likely to allow him to pay the rent on a house for her.
In any case, it felt wrong. He couldn't say why it felt
wrong, but it did. No, he could not offer to make her
his mistress. There must be another way. 'God dammit
to hell, there must be!'

It was the fop, stopping in mid-mince to stare, that
made him realise he'd caught Henrietta's habit of speaking aloud. It was the same fop, eyeing him through a
jewelled quizzing glass, which made Rafe aware of his
somewhat dishevelled appearance. In Whitechapel, he
had been, compared to the local denizens, the picture of

elegance. Here on his home turf in the smart environs of Mayfair, his creased coat and dull boots made him look decidedly shabby. He cast an anxious look around, then ascended the front steps to the town house two at a time. At least the knocker was on the door, which meant his quarry had, as he had hoped, returned to town.

Rafe was solemnly informed by her butler that, most unfortunately, Lady Ipswich was not at home at present. That same butler, knowing Lord Pentland by reputation, couldn't help wondering what on earth had happened to make the famously modish and austere Earl appear so rumpled. 'Madam is at Somerset House for the annual exhibition, my lord,' he said. 'Perhaps if you would care to call round later, or leave your card?'

'I'll wait,' Rafe said firmly, handing over his hat and gloves, giving the astonished retainer no option but to show him into the first-floor drawing room and offer him refreshments.

Rafe had refused tea, Madeira, claret and brandy, and had spent the next hour pacing up and down the room, careful to keep away from the long windows that looked out on to the street lest anyone passing glance up and recognise him. As his wait grew longer and his patience wore thin, the state of cold fury that had enveloped him at Scouse Larry's abode returned with a vengeance.

Denied the cathartic effects of planting a facer on the housebreaker, he was determined to exact revenge on Henrietta's behalf and his thoughts had taken a vicious turn. Though he could not forgive Scouse Larry for his callous treatment of Henrietta, Rafe could at least appreciate that the man had only taken on the job in order to save his neck. Helen Ipswich was a different matter. Her flamboyant lifestyle was obviously outrunning her widow's portion, and he suspected her favours were not so much in demand as they once had been. No doubt she was deep in dun territory, too deep to rely on the pluckings of a few pigeons to pull her out, else she would not be resorting to selling off the family heirlooms.

It wasn't surprising. Selling off heirlooms would mean little to a woman forced to sell her body. He didn't blame her, in a way. He'd seen it himself too often, urchins born into penury biting the hand that fed them, robbing food from their adoptive families. Force of habit, born of necessity. He could see why Helen Ipswich wouldn't place too high a value on a set of emeralds, even if they had been in her husband's family for hundreds of years. Even if they weren't hers to dispose of, but rightly belonged to her eldest son.

Though he would refuse to recognise her socially, Rafe had no personal gripe against women of her ilk. Helen Ipswich had done well for herself, some would say. That she'd done it on her back made her bad *ton* in the eyes of most. True, she'd lied, cheated and cuckolded her husband, which made her contemptible and self-seeking and selfish, but Rafe was in no position to judge anyone harshly. What she had done to Henrietta, on the other hand, was far beyond contempt. For that, she would be made to pay.

Rafe paced the length of the salon for the hundredth time. Picking up a brass toasting fork from the hearth, he swished it to and fro in time to his steps. 'Heartless bitch!' he exclaimed, remembering Henrietta's white-faced shock as she realised the infamous way she had been used, her sheer disbelief that another human being could treat her so cruelly. Henrietta, who was more concerned about what agonies her parents would suffer if they ever found out, than she was by the possibility of rotting in Newgate. Henrietta, the most honest, brave, truly good person he had ever met. What might have happened to her had she not stowed away on his phaeton he couldn't bear to imagine.

The salon door opened. Dropping the toasting fork, Rafe saw that it was bent over upon itself, mangled beyond repair.

'Well! This is indeed a fine way to treat my hospitality,' Helen Ipswich said, eyeing the ruined article with astonishment. 'I assume this is not a social call, my lord?'

When informed by her butler that the Earl of Pentland had called unannounced and was awaiting her inside, Helen Ipswich had been at first extremely pleased. After all these years, her standoffish country neighbour was calling on her. Perhaps she was finally going to be accepted by the *haut ton*. Those prized vouchers for Almack's would be hers this Season. At last!

Her triumph was short-lived, however. As she discarded her bonnet and anxiously checked her reflection in her boudoir mirror, several things colluded to disabuse her of her initial optimism. It was four in the afternoon, well past the time for morning calls. In any case, single gentlemen did not pay morning calls unaccompanied—not unless they had a certain purpose in mind, and she knew for a fact that Rafe St Alban was not one of those. The man was a rake, but he did not rake with the likes of her. And come to think of it, the card of invitation she had sent for her last rout party had been politely declined and by his secretary at that—she doubted it had even reached his high-and-mighty lordship's eyes. No, whatever had brought Rafe St Alban here, it was neither to exchange polite pleasantries nor offer improper contracts.

In her drawing room, as she looked up into his hard countenance, at those slate-grey eyes of his that met hers with cold contempt, Helen Ipswich repressed a shudder. There were few people capable of intimidating her, but there was something about this man that warned her he was not to be trifled with. Wisely, she refrained from extending her hand and instead took a seat, disposing the full skirts of her salmon-pink walking dress elegantly around her. 'Well, my lord, I am sorry to have kept you waiting. If you had perhaps informed me that you intended calling....'

'I did not know until a short while ago that it would be necessary.' Rafe remained standing, ignoring her suggestion that he be seated. 'I have come upon a matter of some import.'

Now that she had had a chance to recover her nerves, Helen Ipswich coolly appraised her unexpected guest. He looked tired and his boots were far from the glossy perfection for which he was famed. His coat, too, was somewhat creased, and as for his neckcloth—it looked as if it had been tied without a mirror. 'We have not seen you in town this last while,' she said sweetly.

'Since we have very few acquaintance in common, that is hardly surprising,' Rafe replied curtly.

'I believe you were in the country until recently, like myself. A shame you did not see fit to call on me then,' Helen Ipswich continued, through gritted teeth.

'With luck, this will be my first and last visit.'

'Sir, you are impertinent.'

'And you, my lady, are a fraud.'

Lady Ipswich gasped. 'How dare you!' Beneath her delicately applied rouge, her cheeks flushed. 'I will not stand to be insulted in my own home.' Frantically trawling through her memory for a clue as to what on earth Rafe St Alban could possibly hold against her, Helen Ipswich found herself at a temporary loss. Then a truly horrible thought occurred to her, but it was instantly dismissed. She had covered her tracks too well. She flicked open a fan and applied it vigorously. 'La, my lord, I am sure I have no idea what you are talking about,' she said more confidently.

Rafe forced himself to take a seat opposite her, crossing his legs, taking his time to calm himself, to order his thoughts. Helen Ipswich was definitely rattled. He recrossed his legs. 'Then I shall enlighten you,' he said laconically. 'I require several things, none of them negotiable.'

Helen Ipswich raised a delicately plucked brow. 'Indeed? You will forgive me if I tell you, my lord, that you are impertinent. The days are long gone when I entered into any non-negotiable deal.' She permitted herself a small smile.

Rafe's brows snapped together. 'You will discover to your cost, my lady, that if you do not heed me, then the next deal you will be negotiating will be with the Newgate gatekeeper.' Ignoring her protest, he got to his feet and began to list his demands. 'The first, and most important, thing I want is for the outrageous allegations made by you concerning Henrietta Markham to be withdrawn.'

Lady Ipswich put a hand to her mouth to suppress her gasp of horror. She had no intention of going down without a fight. 'Ah, yes, Miss Markham,' she said with admirable control. 'You have surely not fallen for that cock-and-bull story she told you?'

'You mean the one where she was hit over the head by a housebreaker, then accused by you as an accessory and threatened with incarceration? Not only do I believe her, I have irrefutable proof that she is telling the truth.'

'What proof?'

'Why, the best proof of all, from the horse's mouth,' Rafe said carefully. He watched as the full import of what he had said sank in. Even Helen Ipswich's perfect maquillage could not disguise the grey tinge to her complexion. Her hands were visibly shaking.

'I've met the gentleman you employed to fake the break-in, who goes by the somewhat colourful sobriquet of Scouse Larry, and had a most enlightening conversation with him.'

Helen Ipswich's mouth dropped open most unbecomingly, her fan clattered to the floor, but she made a valiant attempt to pull herself together, sitting up straight in her seat and clasping her fingers tightly together. 'You have quite lost me, I'm afraid.' She sounded as if a sharp stone had caught in her throat. 'I have no idea what you're talking about.'

In contrast, Rafe's tone was smooth. 'He was not over-eager to confess, your stooge, but he was even less eager to go to the gallows for a crime he did not commit. When he found out that you'd duped him, he was most keen to cooperate. The facts are irrefutable. You paid him to fake a break-in in order to cover your own tracks. You'd already sold your emeralds by then. What was it, gambling debts?' He could tell by the way she flinched that he'd hit the mark. 'Don't you know that you shouldn't play if you can't pay, my lady? Very bad *ton*. But then, how would you know?'

'I did not—'

Rafe raised a hand imperiously. 'Do not even attempt to deny it. You will call off that Runner of yours, tell him there was no robbery. Tell him your emeralds were away being cleaned at the jewellers and it slipped your mind. Tell him the housebreaker was a figment of your fevered imagination. Tell him the whole thing was a mean trick being played on you by one of your friends. Tell him anything you like, provided you make it clear there was no crime.'

'But I can't do that. I'll look a complete fool.'

'If you don't, that will be the least of your worries. I'll make you a social outcast, a pariah. To say nothing of ensuring that it is known you are reduced to selling off your children's inheritance.'

Lady Ipswich clutched at her bosom.

Rafe settled back into his chair. Helen Ipswich looked like a whipped cur. 'Let's face facts—were it not for the protection of your dead husband's name, you wouldn't even be tolerated on the fringes of society, as you are now. Your reputation is as flimsy as gossamer; one puff from me and you will be quite gone. Do you really want that?'

'You wouldn't.'

'You know perfectly well that I would and I could.'

She did, perfectly well. It was one thing for the Earl of Pentland to look down his aristocratic nose at her from a distance, but quite another for him to publicly spurn her, and that was all it would take for uncomfortable questions to be raised and all those years of discretion undone. 'How can I tell them it was a mistake? What the devil do you care, anyway, about that damned governess? A mere nobody! Why, she—'

Rafe was towering over her before she could move to avoid him. She shrank back in her chair, her hands instinctively at her throat as if to prevent him throttling her—for that is what he looked as if he would do.

'Unlike you, Henrietta Markham has scruples. Not only is she innocent, the accusations you have levelled upon her weigh extremely heavy. She has been crushed by your maligning her. God dammit, she was in your employ. You were responsible for her. Could not you of all people understand what it is to be alone and helpless? Deception is your stock-in-trade, my lady. I'm sure you will come up with some plausible tale to tell the authorities. I don't give a damn what it is, provided you succeed. Do I make myself perfectly plain?'

Helen Ipswich nodded slowly.

'And I want it done now. Today. At once. Or I fear the rumours will begin to fly, and the paste copies you have no doubt had made of your damned emeralds will be subject to rather closer inspection than they can bear. Are we clear upon that, too?'

Another reluctant nod. Helen Ipswich licked her lips.

They felt dry and thin, despite the carmine she had applied earlier.

'Then I will take my leave, madam. I trust our paths will not have to cross again.'

'I will ensure that they do not,' Helen Ipswich said, through very gritted teeth. 'I will do as you ask.'

'I never doubted it,' Rafe replied contemptuously. 'Self-preservation often walks hand in hand with self-interest. You are endowed with an acute sense of both. I will bid you goodbye.'

The door closed behind him. Helen Ipswich sat for some moments, pleating the elegant fringe that bordered her walking dress, her mind seeking frantically for another way out, darting first one way and another, like a rat in a trap. But there was no other way and she was never a woman to waste energy repining over lost causes.

With a resigned sigh she rose, rang the bell by the fireplace to summon her butler and demanded that her footman be sent immediately to Bow Street and not to return without either the magistrate or a certain Runner, as she had important news for them. Then she set her mind to the tricky task of fabricating a plausible story to tell them.

Henrietta paced up and down the bedchamber at the Mouse and Vole, anxiously checking the time on the clock tower outside. She felt as if she had been whirled too fast in a country jig. Her mind was positively reeling. To have been falsely accused was bad enough, but to discover it had been a quite deliberate act! That someone could be so utterly self-serving, and that someone then turn out to be her employer, was beyond belief. And yet it must be true. Why would Scouse Larry lie?

In the course of these last three days at the Mouse and Vole, while Benjamin had attempted to track down the thief, she had almost forgotten the shame and horror of the accusations levelled against her. Now they returned with full force. When she thought of how close she had come to being arrested, of the real possibility that she would have been found guilty—dear heavens, she felt as if she might faint for the first time in her life. And all because Lady Ipswich needed money. Not that she could really need money, not in the way those people in Petticoat Lane needed it. That was real need! And not even need such as that would justify putting two other innocent lives in danger. A criminal Scouse Larry might be, but he didn't deserve to be hanged. Henrietta's blood positively boiled.

'Let Rafe make her confess,' she said fervently. 'Please, let Rafe make her confess and let her beg for forgiveness on bended knees,' she added, warming to the subject. 'Let her promise to change. Let her see the error of her ways. Oh, and let her call off the Runners. Please let her call off the Runners.'

Where was Rafe? Perhaps Lady Ipswich was not in town, after all. Would he have travelled back to the country in search of her? What if he could not persuade her to drop the charges? What if she simply denied it all? But Rafe would find a way to persuade Lady Ipswich. Most likely he was late because—because…

Where was Rafe?

The clock outside chimed another hour. The time was passing interminably slowly. Pulling a pair of woollen stockings, which were long overdue for darning, from her bandbox, Henrietta threaded a needle and sat down on the bed. He would be back as soon as he could. She had utter faith in him, even if she had no idea where he was and what he was doing.

She set a neat stitch, then paused, her needle in mid-air. She missed him. She would miss him a lot more in the very near future, when all of this was over. It was a most melancholy fact, and she wished fervently that it had not occurred to her just now, but the thing she had most wanted, to clear her name, was now the thing which would deprive her of her heart's desire.

Her heart's desire.

She loved him.

Oh, dear heavens! She loved him. She was in love with Rafe St Alban. Her needle dropped into her lap. She loved him. It was ridiculous. Impossible. And absolutely, irrefutably true. The Honourable Rafe St Alban, Earl of Pentland, Baron of Gyle and who knows what other titles he possessed—*this* man, *this* one, was the love of her life. Of course he was!

Of course. The smile that was tugging at the corners of her mouth faded. She could not be in love with him. But why else did she feel as she did whenever he was near her? That tingling, bubbling, breathless feeling—what else could that be but love? Why else did she desire him and only him, save that she loved him? Why else had she never felt any of this before? Because she hadn't met him. Because she was still waiting to meet him. Because she would only ever feel any of this for him. Only him.

She loved him. Surely love conquered all? Surely

love could redeem and reform? Surely if he knew—if he could see—if he could…

'Could what, Henrietta?' she asked herself. 'Love you?'

She shivered. Rafe said he could never love again. Rafe said he would never marry again. But Rafe had also said that Henrietta made him break his own rules.

'He said I turn his world upside down,' she said, picking up her needle. 'He said I make him feel. Surely one feeling can lead to another, more profound feeling?' In the first flush of optimism that love inspires, she thought it might. The desperate yearning to have it so ensured that any doubts were banished to the cold recesses of her mind, forbidden even the faint tapping on the window of reality. She loved him. She longed for him to love her. It could happen. It would!

The clock chimed another hour. Her needle was making very desultory progress on the threadbare patch of her stocking, so entranced was she by the dreams she was weaving, that she was barely aware of time passing, until the door opened. Needle, stocking and her spare skein of wool went flying as Henrietta launched herself at the tall figure in the doorway.

Chapter Nine

'You're back. You've been an age. I've been so worried.' Her arms were around his neck before she could stop herself, her body pressed safe against his.

Rafe kicked shut the door, but made no attempt to disentangle himself. He closed his eyes and wrapped his arms around her and leant his chin on her curls and breathed in her scent. It felt so good. She felt so good. 'Lady Ipswich was out when I got there. I had to wait,' he said.

'But you saw her?' With her cheek pressed against his chest, her voice was muffled.

'Yes, I saw her. And it took a bit of persuasion, but she admitted to it all in the end. She will call off her Runner.'

'Oh, my God! I can't believe it. Really? Truly?'

Henrietta raised a shining face to his. Her eyes were dark chocolate-coloured tonight, the gold flecks in them more pronounced. She looked as if he had just given her something priceless. Perhaps he had. 'Really,' Rafe said, planting a kiss on her upturned nose. 'Truly.'

'And I will be cleared of all her accusations?'

'All of them.'

'Oh, Rafe! You're wonderful. I never doubted— But I didn't know how and— But you are simply marvellous.' She pressed a fervent kiss on his gloved hand. 'Sit down and tell me *everything*.'

Rafe laughed. Tossing his hat and gloves on to the table, he pulled her down on the bed beside him and gave her an account of his interview. He could not have asked for a more enthusiastic or grateful audience. Henrietta clapped her hands, praised his ingenuity and positively hissed at Helen Ipswich's perfidy, as if she were the audience at a melodrama. He had thought he understood how much of a burden the crime had weighed upon her, but he realised, seeing her unalloyed delight at it being removed, how much he had underestimated it. He felt good. He felt he had done something good for the first time in ages. 'So, you can now stop fretting about Newgate,' he said, stroking a wayward curl from her cheek.

'And gaol fever,' Henrietta said with a chuckle. The relief was so intense, she felt almost drunk with it. 'I can't tell you how much this means to me,' she said before placing a hand on his shoulder and brushing his cheek with her mouth. A thank-you kiss, no more. But the taste of his skin made her lips linger and he moved his face just a fraction, so that they lingered on his mouth. 'Sorry, I didn't mean— I just wanted to...' She tried to shuffle away from him, but he restrained her. She tried to ignore the sharp stab of awareness that accelerated her breathing. 'Are you hungry?'

'Ravenous,' Rafe murmured, nuzzling his cheek against hers.

'Shall I— Would you like me to ask Meg to send up some food?'

'I'm not that kind of hungry,' Rafe said, kissing her. Then he kissed her again, pulling her closer, absorbing the feel of her, the softness, the curves, the sweetness, the delicious taste of her, with every part of him. He kissed her and she wrapped her arms around him and pulled his head down and kissed him back just exactly as if she felt the same.

Passion flared and quickly, greedily, consumed them. Their kisses fired it, the memory of their previous pleasures fuelled it, the traumatic events of the day lent it an edge of desperation, stood them high on a precipice from which they yearned to tumble.

Henrietta kissed and clutched and moaned and pressed her lips, her breasts, her thighs, closer and closer to the man she loved so desperately, the man she so desperately wanted to love her back. Clothes ripped and were frantically discarded. Rafe's hands on her face, on her arms, her shoulders, her waist, stoked heat and fire and flame, making her burn, searing her, so that the slow build, the gentle climb, to her first climax seemed tame by comparison. This heat, this wild desire, this not-to-be-denied, aching, pulsing need, was beyond anything she had ever dreamed of. If she did not—if he did not—she would die. She would die, anyway, of this, and she didn't care.

His teeth nipped at her lower lip. His tongue thrust against hers. His hands moulded and melded, making of her whatever he wanted and making her want it, too. Vaguely, she heard her laces rip, felt a flutter of a breeze as her gown fell to the floor, then heat again as he picked her up and threw her on to the bed. His chest was bare. Sweat highlighted the broad sweep of his shoulders, the ripple of his muscles, the flex of his sinews. As he lay down on the bed beside her, she rained kisses over him, panting wildly, careless of the picture she made, caught up in this feral, elemental need to take and be taken, to absorb him, to be absorbed, to climb until she could no longer breathe, to heat until she ignited.

She struggled out of her chemise. Wearing only her stockings and garters she lay back on the bed, watching entranced as he removed the remainder of his clothing. His chest heaved with his efforts to breathe. His manhood stood magnificently erect, curved and proud, making her own muscles clench in anticipation.

He kissed her again, on the mouth. He kissed her nipples, sucking each into an aching sweetness that made her writhe. His hands dipped into the damp folds of her sex, making her writhe all the more. He muttered her name. She clung to him, pressed herself against him, kissed him and writhed again as his fingers stroked her sex, quickly, quickly, not quickly enough. She wanted this, and him, and now. She loved him. She wanted him to love her. She wanted to show him how much she loved him. If he knew—if he could see—if he could feel how much, then surely...

'Now, now, now,' she muttered, clutching at his back, her fingernails scoring down his spine, sinking into the taut curves of his buttocks. He stroked her harder, kissed her harder and she felt herself high on a cusp, and clung to it, waiting, clinging, panting. 'Now, oh please, now,' she panted, clutching at his shoulders as she tipped over and began to fall.

Rafe kissed her deeply. The contractions of her climax were unbelievably exciting. He was throbbing, pulsing in response, his shaft so hard he thought it would explode, yet still he had to ask her.

'Are you sure? Henrietta,' he said, breathing hard, 'are you sure?'

'Rafe, please. I want— I'm sure. I promise. Please.'

He couldn't resist any more. He couldn't wait any more. Right now, it felt as if his whole life had been hurtling towards this moment. Tipping her bottom up, he angled himself carefully and entered her, and had to stop, wait, stop, because the sensation of her pulsing around him was almost too much and he didn't want it to be over, not yet, not ever, not yet.

She was tight and hot and wet. He pushed, past the slight resistance of her maidenhead into the glorious heat of her, and caught his breath on a harsh cry. He had never, never, never... 'Henrietta. Oh God, Henrietta.' He thrust and moaned, and felt her cleave to him and hold him and enfold him, the sweetest, most intoxicating feeling. He thrust again and this time she was there with him, and again, and she was there, too, and again, as if they were made for this, as if this were some secret only they could share.

She had thought herself lost in the heights of ecstasy, but now she knew it was but a false summit. All of him, all of his hard velvet thickness, was inside her and she had never dreamed, never, that it could be so marvellous, this filling and emptying, filling and emptying, and each time he filled her more, finding depths in her that she couldn't believe existed, taking her higher with him with each thrust, spiralling her up and up and up until she really was at the top, giddy with being at the top, burning and freezing with being at the top, and he thrust high inside her and she toppled over the edge of the abyss, feeling as though she would pass out from the intensity of it. Then she felt him swell and withdraw just before his own climax exploded, making him cry out, a low groan dragged from him, which he seemed reluctant to release.

He held her so tightly that she could not breathe. Tears tracked down her cheeks and she made no attempt to stop them. He licked them away, saying he was sorry, and she stroked his silken crop of hair and told him that no, no, no, he hadn't hurt her, not even a little.

He planted a soft kiss on the cushion of her lips. Nestling her close, he couldn't have said how he felt, even if he tried. He felt strange. Utterly sated, utterly empty and yet somehow quite complete.

Henrietta's heart came slowly back down to a level that allowed her to breathe normally. She lay mindless, aware only of Rafe's arms around her, his legs over her, luxuriating in the euphoric aftermath of what had been, for her, a life-changing experience.

She had made love to the man she loved. For those ecstatic, blissful minutes he had been inside her, they had been joined. One. Surely he had felt it, too? He cared. He really cared. He did not love her, but despite all the warnings he had given her, as she lay replete, she allowed herself to hope that he might, one day. He was an honourable man. He would not have made love to her unless he had meant—*meant what?*

How could she be so sure he meant anything at all? This had always been an interlude for Rafe, an escape from whatever it was in his own life that he was trying to avoid. She had always had much more at stake. Her good name. Her freedom. She just hadn't expected to lose her heart as well. But she had, irrevocably.

Propping herself up on her elbow, Henrietta forced a bright smile. 'So, this will be the last night we will be required to stay here,' she said, determined at least to say it before he did. 'You will think me foolish, but I have come to think of this little room as home.'

Rafe twined one of her curls around his finger. 'No, I don't think you are foolish, I myself have become inordinately fond of this pokey little room, if not the unutterably uncomfortable mattress. Henrietta, have you given any thought to what you will do next?'

Her heart began to beat frantically. She tried to quell the panic, tried to cling on to her certainties, but of a sudden they seemed not to be so certain. He would not love. He would not marry. He had said so, but she hadn't listened. Was he about to brush her off politely? The utter contentment of their lovemaking fled like a thief from the scene of a crime. 'I don't know,' Henrietta said. 'However Lady Ipswich clears my name, I doubt she'll give me a reference and, without one, I am not like to find a new position very easily.'

'I have to admit, I have become used to being your protector these last few days.'

'Oh.' Her heart stopped, then started again even more quickly. Now she felt quite sick. She daren't hope, but she hoped all the same. She pushed herself upright, the better to see his face. Eyes indigo blue. A slight smile. Oh God, please. Please. Oh please.

'It is a position I am loath to surrender just yet,' Rafe said.

Just yet! If she had been standing, her knees would have given way, crumpling like her hopes. Whatever he was offering was not of a permanent nature. 'Just yet?' She sounded as if she was being strangled. She felt as if she was. 'What do you mean?'

'You told me you had no wish to go to Ireland to join your parents, I'm assuming that you haven't changed your mind?'

'No, I haven't, but…'

'And from what you've told me, you've no other relatives who would take you in?'

'There is my aunt, Mama's sister, but…'

'No doubt some crotchety old widow who lives in seclusion in the country, surrounded by her cats.'

'Well, actually, she—'

'No, we need to find you somewhere to stay in London, till your parents return. Clearly you cannot stay with me. Tempting though it is to offer, I know that would be wholly inappropriate.'

Rafe frowned, tapping his finger on the sheet. 'I have it!' Why had he not thought of it before? 'I've got the perfect solution.'

'What?' *What?* Hope again, irrational hope, flaring up like a candle caught in a draught. 'What is it, Rafe? What have you not thought of before?'

'My grandmother.'

'Your grandmother?' Henrietta's face fell. 'What has your grandmother got to do with me?'

'She is in her ninth decade and, in my opinion, much in need of a companion.'

'She does not sound to me like someone who needs a companion,' Henrietta said dubiously, having conjured up a fairly accurate picture of the indomitable Dowager Countess. 'And even if she did, I still don't understand what it has to do with me.'

'Don't be obtuse, Henrietta, I mean you would be a perfect companion for her. You are neither of you reticent when it comes to expressing your opinions, nor indeed are either of you short of opinions, come to that. I think you will suit very well. My grandmother lives most of the year in London. I could do with visiting her more often—she is my only close relative, after all,' Rafe said, with growing enthusiasm. 'And though she is elderly, she is fiercely independent and takes great pride in having a full engagement book,' he continued, so taken with his idea that he failed to notice Henrietta's horrified expression as realisation of what he was actually proposing dawned. 'You wouldn't be tied to her apron strings, there would be plenty of time for you and me to continue with our—our—to continue to spend time together. You will want to see more of London,' he concluded ingeniously. 'What could be more natural than that I act as your guide? What do you say?'

She said nothing, unable quite to believe what she was hearing, equally unable to believe that he could so misread her character. What he was proposing sounded remarkably like a proposition. An improper one. What he was proposing sounded—it sounded—it sounded like something a rake would say!

'Henrietta? What do you think?'

'I'm not sure what to think,' she said, praying that he would say something, anything, to contradict her assessment of his motives.

'I don't want to let you go. Not yet. I've come to—you must know that I have come to care for you, Henrietta. I thought you had come to care for me.'

She stared at him, nonplussed. He had no idea how much she cared. No idea at all. Just as she had underestimated how determined he was to limit his own feelings. He had warned her. It was her own fault.

'Henrietta?'

'You're asking me to be your mistress.'

'No! I would not…'

'Then what are you suggesting?'

'I just wanted— I want— I thought you wanted…' Rafe ran his fingers through his hair, frowning heavily. This wasn't going as it should. 'I am simply trying to find a way of not ending this.'

'Ending what?' Henrietta demanded. She hadn't realised how high she had been flying the flag of her hopes. It fluttered down to earth now, in total freefall. 'Did you think that by dressing it up as something else I wouldn't realise what it was you were asking? Do you really think I rate myself so low as to consider such a proposal, let alone what it says of your opinion of your unwitting grandmother, from whose house our *affaire* is to be conducted.'

'Henrietta, you're twisting it all. I just want—'

'To have me available whenever you fancy slaking

your thirst,' she said bitterly, resorting to the language of the Minerva Press, her only reference point for such a conversation. 'I know perfectly well what you want.'

'That is a disgusting way to put it.'

She threw herself out of the bed, snatching her chemise from the floor and pulling it over her head. 'It was a disgusting offer.'

Was it? He hadn't meant it that way. He could see now that he had worded it badly, but dammit, he hadn't had time to think it through. Why could she not be less judgemental? Anger rose, spiced with bitterness and a shard of fear. He could not lose her. Pushing back the sheet, he strode over to her and tried to pull her back into his arms, but she pushed him away.

'God dammit, Henrietta, what is wrong with my simply wanting to find a way for us to spend a little more time together?'

'No! I won't let you—'

'What? Persuade you? Force you?' His anger, fuelled with frustration, boiled over. 'I thought you knew me better by now. I have never—'

'No, you have not. Never. You are quite right,' Henrietta admitted, with a defiant tilt of her head, curls flying wildly round her shoulders. 'All this is my fault. I thought that you—that I— I thought— I thought…' She stopped, her breathing ragged.

'Henrietta, can't you just—?'

'No! Leave me alone. Please, Rafe. I can't. I just can't.' She poured herself a glass of water from the carafe by the bed and took several slow sips, willing herself to calm down. It was not his fault. It was her fault. She hadn't listened. But she hadn't listened because she didn't want to. 'What an idiot I've been,' she muttered.

He had pulled on his breeches. Bare-chested, still glistening with sweat from their lovemaking, his hair standing up in spikes, he looked devastatingly handsome. Her heart ached with love for him. There was confusion and hurt and anger in his stormy eyes. And desire, too. She recognised it, for he had taught her very well.

For a moment, a terrible moment, she considered saying yes. She considered surrendering her principles and her will to his, just so that she would not have to say goodbye. There would be time—days, weeks, maybe even months, before he tired of her—to share more lovemaking, to build more memories. She swayed, but then pulled herself upright. It would be wrong. She could not be happy, knowing that what they were doing was wrong. It was one thing to make love in hope. She could not imagine doing so without it. She loved him. She would not have that love tainted by selling it. She would not allow herself to enter into such a demeaning relationship. Not even with Rafe. Especially not with Rafe.

She had no option but to leave. He had left her nowhere to go. Henrietta's hopes finally crashed to earth and shattered painfully. Like the heroines of the Minerva Press, she felt as if her heart was breaking. She did not want to deny him, but deny him she must, for her own sake. 'Rafe, I can't.'

It was the resolution in her voice that made him realise she meant it. That core of steel at her centre, which he had so admired. 'May I ask why not?'

'It's not enough for me.'

'Henrietta, it's more than I've ever offered anyone else since…'

'I know,' she said. 'I understand that it's more than you've offered since—since Julia, but it's still not enough.'

'Is it my reputation?'

She shook her head. 'No. I would wish—but I cannot undo. If I thought that you—that you cared enough, would come to care enough, it wouldn't matter. But I don't, you see, and I—I do. Care. Too much to put up with anything less. You see, we are from different worlds. We've always known that, Rafe, but we forgot, here. I forgot, anyway.' The tears were burning her eyes, but she wouldn't let them fall. She had only her dignity left. She clutched it around her like a swaddling blanket. 'I'm sorry.'

'I see.' He wanted to protest. To persuade. To show her by kissing her just how much she was throwing away, just how much they would both lose. But the armour he had worn for so long, and his own rakish morality, prevented him. 'I see,' Rafe said again, deliberately turning away from those big brown eyes, lest he see the hurt, lest he allow it to persuade him into something he would regret. As he picked his shirt up off the floor, he felt the dark cloud that had been his faithful companion until Henrietta had banished it, returning like a whipped cur in from the cold. He almost welcomed it. At least it was familiar. At least he knew how to manage it.

He finished dressing, throwing the rest of his possessions carelessly into his portmanteau. 'I think it's best if I sleep elsewhere tonight. In the morning, we can make arrangements for whatever you want to do.' He looked at her now, willing her to change her mind, willing her to tell him not to go.

'I'm sorry. I wish— I'm sorry.'

He shrugged.

'Rafe. Thank you. For everything. Don't go like this.'

'I am only going down the hall. I'll see you in the morning. Goodnight, Henrietta.'

'Goodbye, Rafe.'

He closed the door, subduing a horrible feeling that he was missing something important, suppressing the almost irrepressible desire to go back. Setting off in search of Benjamin, it felt as if he was walking away.

On the other side of the door, Henrietta stood frozen. Her heart seemed to crack in two. But she would not compromise herself, she told herself firmly. She would not, for if she did she was doomed. As she set about packing up her possessions into her shabby bandbox, she told herself so several more times and the tears streamed unnoticed down her face.

Chapter Ten

Two weeks later

'Well, my dear, let me take a good look at you.'
Lady Gwendolyn Lattisbury-Hythe surveyed her niece
through the silver lorgnette she habitually wore on a
ribbon hung around her neck.

The thick glass gave her eyes a fishy look, Henrietta thought, shifting nervously from one foot to the
other. Even after two weeks in her company, during
which time Mama's estranged sister had treated her with
unwavering generosity, refusing to discuss the estrangement which, she said, was ancient history, Henrietta still
found her aunt rather formidable.

Lady Gwendolyn was the relict of an eminent
Whig who had, like his friend Mr Fox, divided his
time between vociferous occupation of the opposition
benches and an equally dedicated occupation of the
faro table at Brooks's. Fortunately for his spouse, Sir
Lattisbury-Hythe's fortune was considerable and his

luck rather more consistent than that of the late Mr Fox's. It had run out somewhat spectacularly one evening three years previously when, with his foot heavily bandaged from the gout, he fell down the main staircase of his country home and cracked his head open on the marble plinth upon which a bust of the Roman Emperor Tiberius was mounted.

Sir Lattisbury-Hythe's son Julius inherited the title, but not his father's temperament, being inclined towards the Tory and disinclined to sharing any more of the family fortune with Brooks's. With his mousey wife and fast-multiplying brood of mousey children, parsimonious and staid Sir Julius was content to occupy the stately pile in Sussex in which his father had met his maker, thus leaving Lady Gwendolyn free rein of the town house from which to enjoy her extremely busy London life and equally free to lament the shortcomings of her anodyne first-born.

She did both with gusto. Her parties and breakfasts were always granted the ultimate epithet of being labelled a sad crush. Despite her Whig alliances, Lady Gwendolyn was a close friend of Lady Cowper, that ardent Canningite and most powerful of Almack's patronesses, whose wit was as dry and as sharp as her ladyship's own. This Season, however, had proved a little flat for Lady Gwendolyn who, having successfully fired off each of her three daughters in consecutive years, had no chicks left to launch and only a granddaughter of some eight summers to plan for. Thus, Henrietta's wholly unexpected arrival upon her doorstep, when she had just returned from a tedious night watching the unfortunate Mr Kean being pelted with rotten fruit at Drury Lane Theatre, provided a most welcome diversion.

Too numb from the shock of her sudden flight from the Mouse and Vole to worry about the reception which might await her at the house in Berkeley Square, Henrietta's only thought had been to seek the sanctuary of a roof over her head and some time to come to terms with things. She scarcely remembered that first night, and indeed had proved incapable of providing any coherent answers to her concerned aunt's many questions. Fortunately, Lady Gwendolyn, an eminently practical woman, had taken one look at her strained, lily-white face and, deciding tomorrow was time enough for explanations, packed Henrietta off to bed with strict orders to sip upon a cup of warm milk and sleep without waking until morn.

Exhaustion had set in, and Henrietta had been only too happy to oblige. When morning had come, though the heavy weight of self-blame still threatened to suffocate her, she was determined not to show it. She had been a fool. She had allowed her desires to cloud her judgement, persuading herself that Rafe would change just because she longed for him to. The scars inflicted by his marriage to Lady Julia would not heal because he would not let them. His care for her was sincere, but shallow, and he would not allow it to deepen. Rafe was not incapable of love, but he had chosen to be.

'And the point is,' Henrietta had told herself stoically that first morning in Berkeley Square, as she woke to find a pot of hot chocolate by her bed, a huge copper bath placed behind a screen by the fireside of her chamber, 'the point is that anything less than love would only ever make me unhappy. I could perhaps sacrifice myself and my principles for someone who loved me, but not for someone who doesn't.'

She had had a very lucky escape, she had told herself firmly as she sank into the luxuriously scented water and soaped her hair. 'At least, in time, I'm sure it will feel so,' she had said mournfully, for the painful ache in her heart could not be ignored. 'In time I am sure I will accept that it could never have been and I will hardly miss him at all—or even think of him. In time.'

She had tipped a kettle of warm water over her hair to rinse out the suds and wash away the flurry of tears that dripped down her cheeks. She would not cry! She would not pity herself! This pain she was feeling was completely self-inflicted. She had fallen in love with a man who had encased his heart in ice, whose solution to pain was to numb himself, lest he feel anything of any sort again. It should be a comfort to know that she had not succumbed to the temptation of his improper offer. She would not allow her love, her precious love, to be contaminated or sullied or defiled. She had done as she ought, in walking away with her self-respect, if not her heart, intact.

'And soon, I am sure that will make me feel a lot better,' she had told her reflection forlornly, for there was no escaping the fact that part of her wished she had never left Rafe in the first place. There was a shameful, most shameful bit of her, that would have accepted his proposition, and no amount of talking to and taking in hand and resolution would make it go away entirely.

'What I need to do now is concentrate on the future,' she had muttered, pulling on her brown robe. And so it was the future that she raised with her aunt on that first morning, but Henrietta's notions did not at all meet with Lady Gwendolyn's approval. 'My niece a lowly governess!' she had exclaimed in horror, upon hearing Henrietta's somewhat truncated explanation of how she had come to arrive in Berkeley Square, following what she described as an unwarranted dismissal from her position, careful to make no mention of either emeralds or earls.

'I can't say I'm surprised that your tenure with Lady Ipswich ended in acrimony,' Lady Gwendolyn said. 'In fact, I'm rather glad of it. I had no idea that your mother had detached herself quite so fully from the world as to think that Helen Ipswich was a suitable person to entrust you to—however, I will say no more on that subject. But as to any notion of you taking up another similar position—absolutely not! And as to the notion you have of becoming a teacher in that school in Ireland!' She patted Henrietta's hand and tutted. 'Well, my dear, let us hope that it is all pie in the sky, like the rest of your mother's notions. No, don't protest, you are a sensible chit and I am sure you know as well as I do that it's true. I am simply glad that you had the good sense to come to me when you did, Henrietta. You must place yourself in my hands. I think I can promise to find you some brighter future than toiling away as a mere governess.'

She smiled benignly and Henrietta had tried very hard to smile back, even though at that moment a brighter future seemed a very long way off. 'It has been a great sadness to me that we have never met,' Lady Gwendolyn continued. 'Though I can quite understand the loyalty you must have to your mother, it does seem a shame that you have never felt yourself able take up any of my invitations to visit.'

Henrietta looked at her aunt in dismay. 'But I never received any invitations.'

'Well! That certainly explains a lot,' Lady Gwendolyn said tartly. 'Your father's doing, no doubt. I have never met him, but—'

'Oh, no, Aunt, Papa would not have…' Henrietta faltered to a halt. 'I think it must have been Mama,' she said, blushing. 'She is very—very— She has very strong views on the evils of society. On account of her—her misfortune.'

Lady Gwendolyn tapped her lorgnette in the palm of her hand. 'Well,' she said eventually, deciding that discretion was the better part of valour, much as she longed to set her niece straight, 'well, we will say no more on that subject, either, but be assured, Henrietta, that I am most pleased to have you here.'

'Oh, Aunt, and I am most pleased to be here,' Henrietta said, giving her a hug.

Lady Gwendolyn felt herself adequately rewarded. Henrietta was really unexpectedly charming, with surprisingly excellent manners, given her rusticated upbringing. The Season was well underway, but that was rather an advantage than not, for people were at that stage where a new face was most welcome. It could not be a formal launching, for apart from the fact that Henrietta seemed strangely and most adamantly opposed to the notion of finding a husband, even Lady Gwendolyn recognised she had not the authority to find her niece a match. No, not a launching, but she would show Henrietta off to the world, get her a bit of town polish and dress her to advantage, all of which would stand her in good stead for the future. It would also be fun. That her sister Guinevere would be appalled by the whole thing went without saying, which made Lady Gwendolyn all the more determined to carry it off.

Henrietta had at first been extremely reluctant, for the very last thing she wished was to bump into Rafe again, to say nothing of the fact that she was struggling not to give in to the urge to hide herself in her bedchamber most days and not come out. She reminded herself resolutely every morning that she had no wish to see him at all. Ever. As the days progressed, she missed him with an increasing intensity that was horribly difficult to hide. Several times she had found herself under her aunt's penetrating gaze and been forced to make up a white lie about missing Mama or Papa or Lady Ipswich's sons.

Soon she had run out of excuses. A few tentative enquiries informed her that Lord Pentland's town house was closed, apparently, the knocker off the door, the shutters fastened. That, coupled with Rafe's self-confessed dislike of the *ton* and its soirées, meant any encounter was highly unlikely. Henrietta began to wonder if perhaps the diversion of a month or so under her aunt's wing would be just what she needed to help her forget all about the reclusive earl, so that when Lady Gwendolyn shrewdly suggested that her niece would, in fact, be doing her a great service by accompanying her to her various engagements, her own daughters all being out of town, Henrietta was finally swayed, and Lady Gwendolyn was able to write a triumphant letter to her sister informing her of her daughter's elevation in the world.

The next two weeks had been a whirl of dress fittings, shopping trips and dancing lessons—an activity at which Henrietta was most adept, which proved to be a decidedly double-edged sword, for she could not help recalling Rafe's offer to teach her, could not help wishing herself in Rafe's arms, could not help resenting the dancing teacher for not being Rafe, then could not help but chide herself for being so very ungrateful.

She was overwhelmed by Aunt Gwendolyn's generosity and the sheer number of day dresses, promenade dresses, evening gowns and ball gowns she seemed to think a bare minimum requirement, to say nothing of the silk stockings, satin slippers, kid boots, shawls, pelisses, hats, bonnets, gloves and reticules with which to accessorise them. For the first time in her life, Henrietta felt silk next to her skin. Her chemises were of the finest lawn, lace trimmed, and there was not a trace of serviceable white cotton in her wardrobe anywhere— nor anything brown; she was determined she would never wear anything brown ever again.

She wished that Rafe could see her in her new clothes. She was terrified that he would. Tying the garters of her silk stockings, or shaking out a lace ruffle on the sleeve of her gown, she would catch herself wondering what he would think, how he would look, what he would do if only—and then the lump would form in her throat, the tears would collect in her eyes and she hated herself for being so weak.

She accompanied her aunt on a round of morning calls. She sat in her box at the opera, took ices at Gunter's and took her place in the barouche as it made its sedate way round Hyde Park at five in the afternoon. She attended several select parties, at one of which she met the rather intimidating Lady Cowper who promised her vouchers for the exclusive Almack's. Occasionally, the novel delights of Aunt Gwendolyn's glittering world stopped her thinking about that little bedchamber in the Mouse and Vole, but more often than not the contrast was too obvious to be ignored.

She felt as if she were living a double life. She felt as if she were wearing a mask. She felt lonely and angry at Rafe for making her so. She felt guilty at the lack of pleasure she took when Aunt Gwendolyn was making such an effort to entertain her. While she ate and talked and went to the play and listened to the latest gossip, she wondered what Rafe was doing and who he was with. She did not think he would miss her, though she missed him desperately. When she slept, which she did not do very well, she dreamed of him. She awoke heated and drenched in perspiration, filled with an aching longing. Time and time and time again, when she was out in the town coach with Aunt Gwendolyn, she thought she saw his elegant figure striding a little distance ahead and her heart leapt into her mouth, but it never was him.

She missed him. More than anything, she missed him. So many things she wanted to tell him, to see his lip curling in disdain at some foible she had witnessed, or the smile that turned his eyes from stormy to indigo. She felt haunted.

'There, I think that will do.'

Aunt Gwendolyn's voice brought Henrietta abruptly

back to the present, making her jump, forcing her to
plaster her smile back on to her face. The figure in
the mirror, who looked like a very splendid version of
Henrietta, jumped and smiled rather wanly, too. 'I beg
your pardon, Aunt, what did you say?'

'You were miles away, my dear. Are you nervous
about tonight? You need not be, it is a private ball,
there will be twenty, thirty couples only, quite a small
affair. Now, tell me what you think of the gown. I think
Madame LeClerc was quite wise to insist on the colour,
though it is most unconventional for a débutante. And
before you say it again, I know you're not a débutante in
the strict sense, but this is nonetheless your first Season.
And you have still not told me what you think.'

'I think I hardly recognise myself,' Henrietta said,
surveying her reflection in amazement. Her curls had
been pinned high on top of her head and fixed in a knot,
with ringlets falling in artfully crafted natural tendrils
on either side. Two hours it had taken the coiffeur to
achieve the effect; so many pins had he used that Henrietta felt her head must topple over with the weight
of them, though the result was undoubtedly extremely
pleasing, making her look a little more mature and, if
not sophisticated, at least a little less naïve. The dress,
her first ever ball gown, was a full robe of burnt-orange
silk cut in the French fashion, with a natural waist and
a skirt that belled out from a sash, a shape which suited
her curves. Indeed, Henrietta was concerned that far
too much of her creamy bosom was on display, for the
ruched décolleté was so low as to skim her shoulders,
forming one line to the intricately puffed sleeves. It was
hard to refrain from twitching the sleeves up higher.

She still could not quite believe the modiste's assertion that a combination of *mademoiselle*'s bosom and the excellent cut of the robe would keep it in place. A ruffle, the same rich golden colour as the sash, formed the hem of her gown, weighted with an intricate pattern of beading, the same pattern repeated again in the fringed shawl that Aunt Gwendolyn now draped over her shoulders.

'Mama always says that clothes do not make a woman,' Henrietta said wistfully, remembering Rafe's comment about Almack's when she'd told him the same thing, 'but I am not so sure now that she is quite right.'

'My sister was ever a featherbrain,' Lady Gwendolyn replied tartly. 'Clothes matter, as she knows perfectly well. Your mama was used to have the most exquisite taste, my dear, and you seem to have inherited it. Look at yourself. Really, I suspected you had potential when I first laid eyes on you clad in that dreadful brown gown, but I have to say, Henrietta, you have exceeded my expectations. You really are quite charming.'

Henrietta blushed. 'Am I? Really?'

Lady Gwendolyn clucked. 'You will have to learn to take a compliment in a more elegant manner than that, my dear. A lowering of the lids, a polite thank you, or, you are too kind, not an over-eager request for more.'

'Oh, I did not mean—in any case I am sure that it will not—that I will not— I'm sorry.'

'Silly puss. Come now, or we will be late. There is a fine line to be drawn between being too early and arriving with the bumpkins, and too late and arriving with the jug-bitten.'

* * *

'No! It's my first night back in town, I'll be damned if I'll spend it traipsing round a ballroom with a series of doe-eyed debs whose conversation is as insipid as their dancing is uninspired, just because you've promised your sister you'll drag me along.' Rafe poured himself a small glass of port and pushed the decanter down the table towards his friend. 'I am not a trophy to be paraded. Damn it all to hell, Lucas, I'm not going and there's an end to it.'

'Please, Rafe, do it for me. You know what Minerva's like. She fixes you with that stare of hers and it's like being confronted by a basilisk. I found myself saying yes before I even realised. Just an hour, I promise, then we'll pop down to White's.'

'I'm not in the mood for cards, any more than I'm in the mood for dancing.'

The Right Honourable Lucas Hamilton took a pinch of snuff from an elegant silver box, sneezed, took another pinch and poured himself a generous measure of port. He was a tall man, and an exceptionally thin one, whose gaunt cheeks and slightly sunken eyes had inevitably earned him the unwanted appellation of the Cadaver. His constitution was actually extremely hearty; indeed, some would say almost obscenely robust, given the maltreatment it endured and despite his willowy frame—which, were he a young lady, as Rafe delighted in pointing out, would be most fashionable.

Downing his port in one swallow, Lucas poured himself another. 'You're not much in the mood for anything, my dear chap. Even less so than normal, if I may make so bold an observation. What's got into you and where have you been these last weeks, anyway?' he asked, sliding the decanter back up the table. 'We expected you back in town an age ago.'

Rafe shrugged. 'Rusticating. I find the solitude suits me.'

'If you don't mind my saying so, you look much the worse for it. In fact,' Lucas said, 'you look like the devil.'

'Thank you, Lucas, I can always rely on you for a frank opinion.'

His friend laughed. 'Well, someone has to tell you.' He took another pinch of snuff. Rafe didn't just look like the devil, he looked as if he hadn't slept in days. He was thinner, too, and just a little more touchy than usual. Despite the fact they were dining tête-à-tête, he had remained monosyllabic throughout. 'All joshing aside, Rafe, I'm worried about you. Not woman trouble, is it?'

Rafe started. 'What makes you say that?' he snapped.

Lucas raised his eyebrows. 'Good God! It *is* a woman! Don't tell me…'

'I have no intention of telling you anything. *Not* that there is anything to tell.' Rafe pushed back his chair and got to his feet. 'If you are done drinking my cellar dry, then let us go to this blasted party of your sister's. The sooner we get there, the sooner we can leave.'

'You mean it? You'll need to change, you know, Minerva's a stickler for evening dress, so, if you don't mind, I'll continue helping myself to some more of this excellent vintage while you do so.' Lucas drained his glass, got leisurely to his feet and picked up a full decanter from the side table. If Rafe would rather dance with insipid debs than exchange confidences with his oldest friend, he must be in a really bad way.

Standing in front of the mirror in his dressing room, Rafe was thinking much the same thing. In the two weeks that had passed since he had knocked upon her chamber door to summon her for breakfast and discovered Henrietta gone, he felt as if he had been to hell and back.

Stark disbelief had been his first emotion as he looked round the empty bedchamber, at the chair that no longer had her cloak draped over it, the nightstand bereft of her brushes, a scraping of dust on the floorboards where her bandbox had been, the neatly made bed, even the pillows plumped clean of any sign of their passionate lovemaking. He'd found himself, rather preposterously, looking under that bed, as if she might have been hiding there, but all he'd found was the stocking she had been mending. He had it still, in his own portmanteau.

Neither Benjamin nor Meg had any idea what had happened. No one had seen her leave. Disbelief had given way to fear. She had no money. She had nowhere to go. The thought of her without a roof over her head, perhaps wandering the streets of Whitechapel, was terrifying. He'd combed those streets that night, stopping hackney drivers and night watchmen and anyone who would listen, asking them if they'd seen a young lady in a brown cloak, but no one had.

She'd mentioned an aunt, but he had no idea where that aunt might be. He waited in vain for word from her, a note, a letter, an offer to reimburse him for the expenses he had incurred on her behalf, anything. In Mount Street, with the knocker still removed from the door, fear gave way to anger. Didn't she realise how worried he'd be? Time dragged inexorably. He missed her smile and her laughter and her enthusiasm and her blurting out anything and everything the minute she'd thought it; and he missed her big brown eyes, and the way she looked at him, and kissed him and... He realised, though it cost him dear to admit it, even to himself in the dark of night, that he missed her like a part of him was missing.

Devil take it, how dared she do this to him!

Dammit to hell, where was she? Closeted in his town house, the dark cloud of depression that was his customary companion returned with a vengeance, but now there was no prospect of it lifting. Finally granting his butler permission to have the house opened up, Rafe paid his long-overdue visit to his grandmother, who took the news of his absolutely confirmed bachelorhood better than expected, being rather more concerned by the state of his health than his marital status. The victory that would have granted him a small crumb of comfort before he met Henrietta now meant nothing to him.

Allowing his valet to help him into his black evening coat, standing listless while that man gave a final finicky polish to his shoes and handed him his hat, gloves and cane, Rafe felt as if his life were one long, endless trek through an interminable tunnel without a glimmer of light at the end.

Walking the short distance to Grosvenor Square, he listened with half an ear as Lucas recounted some tedious *on dit* about his sister Minerva's husband's brother's attempt to race one of the new hobby-horses against the real thing in Hyde Park at promenade time, a feat that resulted in the bolting of the latter and the destruction of the former.

At Grosvenor Square, there was the usual crush of coaches and sedan chairs. Flambeaux lit the wide set of steps. A plethora of footmen in scarlet livery relieved the gentlemen of their outerwear, and Rafe and Lucas joined the queue of people waiting to be greeted by their hosts. Automatically returning greetings, nodding curtly, shaking the occasional hand, bowing when necessary, Rafe was already counting down the minutes until he could escape. Two dances at most, he thought. He would leave it up to Minerva to find him appropriate partners. At least he would be spared a waltz, which Lucas's sister thought improper.

The greeting line was long, comprising Minerva, her husband, various relatives and hangers-on. The girl, Lucas's niece, for whom all this rigmarole was in aid, had inherited the Hamilton stature and was, like her mother and uncle, thin and bony and too tall. She appeared to have none of Lucas's wit and unfortunately all of Minerva's basilisk stare, but she'd go off all the same, Rafe thought cynically, as he waited impatiently while she wrote down his name on the card dangling at her wrist, for the first country dance.

The crush was unbearable. It was too hot. Too bright. Too noisy. And the tray of claret was too far away. Pushing his way through an ante-room into the ballroom in search of one of the elusive waiters, Rafe was accosted by a formidable woman, resplendent in lavender, a mauve turban with purple feathers on her head, and a silver lorgnette held to her eyes, giving her a haddock-like appearance.

'Lord Pentland.'

Rafe bowed. One of his grandmother's younger cronies. A Whig. Husband was a friend of Fox. Tedious son. Clutch of daughters. He remembered now that the youngest had been rather amusing. 'Lady Gwendolyn.'

'I thought you were in the country.'

'As you see, I am returned.'

'I didn't expect to see you here. You so rarely bless us with your presence.'

'I came to oblige a friend.'

'Oh, Minerva's brother, of course. Lanky fellow, what's his name?'

'Lucas.'

'That's it. No doubt Minerva will have engaged you to dance with that daughter of hers. Unfortunate gal, favours her mother rather too much and has even less conversation—you'll be bored to tears.' Rafe smiled tightly and made to bow his leave, but Lady Gwendolyn tapped his arm with her closed fan. 'Just a moment, I've got someone I'd like to introduce you to. I think you'll find her a much more amusing dance partner. Has a refreshing habit of speaking her mind, just like you. You'll like her. She's my niece.'

'You are very kind, but I fear…'

'My sister's child, she is come to visit me for a few weeks. Where is— Oh, there you are, my dear, what were you doing lurking behind the pillar like that? Come here and make your curtsy. Lord Pentland, may I introduce my niece, Miss Markham.'

'Henrietta!'

'Rafe!'

Lady Gwendolyn looked from one to the other. Both were white as sheets. 'Surely you two cannot be acquainted?' But she was speaking to thin air.

Rafe pushed his way through the crowd, ignoring the curious eyes that followed them, keeping a firm grip on Henrietta's wrist, which left her no option but to follow him, no time to draw breath nor to protest nor to shake off the rush of blood to her head, which made her so dizzy that she couldn't be sure it was actually him.

But it was unmistakably him, pulling back a heavy curtain to reveal a large window embrasure, dragging her behind him into the space, where she blinked and shivered in the relative dark after the blaze of the brightly lit ballroom, in the relative cool after its oppressive, near-tropical heat. Rafe released his grip and Henrietta sank gratefully on to the padded window seat, staring blankly up at the imposing figure resplendent in full evening dress.

She was shaking. Her brain was refusing to function. Her mouth was opening and closing, but no sound was coming from it. He was here. Standing right in front of her, looking every bit as tall and dark and unfairly handsome as he always did. He was here; her heart was pounding and her breathing wasn't functioning properly and she had been wrong, so wrong to think she could cure herself of him, because here he was and all she wanted to do was hurl herself into his arms.

'Rafe. I didn't expect—I thought…'

'Where the hell have you been?'

For a few brief moments he had been simply, over-whelmingly, relieved. For something less than the minute it took him to drag her into this relative sanc-tuary, Rafe felt a surge of joy that picked him up like a huge wave. Then he tumbled from zenith to nadir as reality broke over him. She was not dead. She was not hurt. She had not been arrested and she had clearly not attempted the journey to Ireland alone. What a complete fool he had been to worry so much about her!

Cold fury rent him, the fury of a man who realises he has behaved completely out of character to no purpose at all. After these two weeks of not knowing, after two weeks of cursing her for making him miss her, and two weeks of nights tortured by dreams so vivid he woke up sweating and hard and aching, what he wanted was to vent his spleen on the person responsible. 'Well? Have you nothing to say to me? I came to your room to find you gone. Not a trace, save a stocking. No one knew what had happened. Not Benjamin, not Meg, no one.'

Henrietta could only stare at him in amazement. His anger was so unexpected. It hadn't occurred to her that she would need to explain. 'It was over between us,' she said faintly. 'I thought my going in such a way was for the best. To say goodbye would be too painful. For me, at least. I thought that was obvious.'

'For God's sake, Henrietta, I'd no idea what fate had befallen you. Did it not occur to you that I would be beside myself with worry? Well?'

His hands were on her arms now, dragging her to her feet, his firm grip bruising the exposed flesh between the tops of her long kid gloves and the delicate puffed sleeves of her gown, but she hardly noticed. Her teeth were chattering so much she could hardly speak. 'I didn't think I'd see you again. I didn't *want* to see you again.' She wriggled free from his grasp and slumped back down on to the window seat. 'Of course it didn't occur to me that you'd look for me, Rafe. Why would you? We had nothing more to say to each other.'

'*You didn't think I'd look for you?* God almighty, Henrietta! I knew you had no money. I thought you had nowhere to go. I know your opinion of me is not high, but surely you do not think me so heartless as not to care what happens to you?'

'I'm sorry. I'm sorry, I was not thinking straight. I should have let you know I was safe and well. I did not mean to cause you any more upset, quite the contrary. For that I beg your pardon.'

Rafe sank down on the window seat beside her. His thigh brushed hers, warm through the silk of her gown. Henrietta tried to move away, but he tilted her chin and scrutinised her blatantly. 'You scrub up very well, Miss Markham. I'm surprised. You led me to believe your aunt was some impoverished spinster who lived in the country.'

'I never said that. I hadn't ever met Lady Gwendolyn; it was you who assumed she lived in the country.'

'And you who made no effort to contradict me. I know what I offered you was not to your taste, but I did not deserve to be treated with such contempt.'

'Rafe, I did not—I would not! If you only knew,' Henrietta said wretchedly. 'It is not the improper nature of the proposal you made, it is what it implies of your feelings for me. Or lack of feelings.'

'You know nothing of my feelings.'

'I know you don't have any.'

'You think I don't care? What possible grounds have you for making an assumption like that?'

'I think you won't allow yourself to care. I think you are afraid to care!'

'You're damned right I am. If you knew—if you had any idea…'

'That's my point entirely, Rafe, I don't. Despite what you told me of your marriage, I still don't. Why are you so determined to deny yourself any chance of happiness?'

'Because I don't deserve it!'

'What on earth do you mean by that?'

'I can't offer you more than I already have Henrietta. You've made it perfectly clear it's not enough and I respect your decision. But I have reasons.'

'What reasons?'

'Good reasons, or rather horrible reasons.'

'Then tell me. Make me understand. At least that would be something. Please, Rafe.'

He stared at her for long moments. Make her understand. It would indeed be something. At least then she might not think so ill of him. He didn't like her thinking ill of him. 'Dammit, why not?' he said abruptly. 'In fact, I'll do better than that, I'll show you.'

'Show me what?'

'Not tonight, tomorrow. I'll call for you at ten.'

'But, Rafe…'

'Tomorrow.' He made a sketchy bow and left, pushing his way through the crowd, oblivious of the resentful looks aimed at him by his hostess and her daughter, who was now bereft of a partner for the next dance, of Lady Gwendolyn's gimlet gaze, or Lucas's infuriated one.

By the time Henrietta had sufficiently recovered from the shock of the encounter, he was gone. The room seemed to be full of tall men in black evening coats. It didn't help that the second dance was already forming. She edged her way forwards, only to have her toes trampled by a young lady in dusky pink, practising an over-energetic change. Desperately, she began to work her way round the perimeter of the floor, certain that if she could just reach the main staircase she would catch him before he left, quite uncertain of what she would say if she did, but there were just too many people in her way. It was impossible.

'My dear.'

'Aunt Gwendolyn!'

A firm hand on her back propelled her into a salon set aside for the rest and recuperation of the ladies. 'Sit here, my dear, while I summon the carriage.' Her aunt pushed her gently into a *chaise-longue*. 'My niece is overcome with the heat,' she said to the other two occupants of the room, one of whom was pinning up the lace ruffle of the other's ball gown.

Henrietta did as she was bid. When the carriage was called, she protested weakly that she was perfectly capable of going back to Berkeley Square alone, but Aunt Gwendolyn, whose nose for scandal was by now positively twitching, and whose genuine concern for her niece's welfare was matched only by her desire to hear her niece's account of her acquaintance with the aloof Lord Pentland, would not hear of it.

* * *

She held her tongue for the duration of the coach journey. Once home, she allowed Henrietta time to go upstairs to dispense with her finery while she herself removed her jewellery and replaced her ball gown with a wrapper. Only then did Lady Gwendolyn tap lightly on the door of her niece's chamber.

Henrietta was sitting at the dressing table, staring sightlessly at the mirror, but upon her ladyship's arrival she jumped to her feet and fixed a smile upon her face. 'Dear Aunt, I have been thinking that perhaps London does not suit me, after all. I have been thinking that—'

'Never mind that, child. How came you to be acquainted with Rafe St Alban?'

'Oh, it is nothing,' Henrietta said airily. 'Merely he was Lady Ipswich's neighbour and we came across one another in—in passing. The acquaintance is not of long-standing. It is—it is nothing.'

'It didn't look like nothing to me. The pair of you were staring at each other as if you'd both just seen a ghost.'

'Rafe was— Lord Pentland was not expecting to see me, being unaware of my relationship to you. I expect that was it.'

'Henrietta, has anyone ever told you that you are the most appalling liar, my dear? Just exactly like your mother. Her face is an open book, too.'

'Oh.'

'Precisely. Now, stop prevaricating and tell me what Rafe St Alban is to you.'

Henrietta opened her mouth to speak, but found she could not utter the polite lies which she knew she ought.

Her mouth trembled. Tears filled her eyes. 'Everything,' she sobbed. 'Rafe St Alban is everything to me and I am absolutely nothing to him and— Oh, Aunt Gwendolyn, I love him so much.'

It was not to be expected that such an admission would fill her ladyship's heart with joy. In fact, Lady Gwendolyn's jaw dropped. She groped in vain for her lorgnette. 'But how came you to be—when—what?'

'Please don't ask me to explain.'

But Lady Gwendolyn, a veteran wife of a veteran politician, was relentless. It was like extracting teeth, requiring skill and determination on her part, and resulting in a great deal of suffering on the part of her niece, but she was soon in command of the entire sorry tale.

'You do realise, my dear, that Rafe St Alban is a hardened womaniser? If any of this got out, you would be ruined, for no one would believe it possible for you to have spent so much time in his company without losing your innocence.'

'He is not a womaniser,' Henrietta protested. 'He does not—he only—he's not that type of man. I know he is a rake, but he's not a rake of the worst kind.'

'Well, I was not aware that there was any such thing as a good rake,' Lady Gwendolyn said with a raised brow, her worst fears confirmed.

'Well, that is what Rafe is. He only—he doesn't—he is not a seducer,' Henrietta declared, oblivious of the fact that her words only served to confirm to her aunt that that was exactly what Rafe St Alban was. 'And, anyway, I don't care about what other people say about him except—oh, I could not bear it to reflect upon you, dear Aunt, when you have been so kind.'

Henrietta threw her arms around her aunt. Lady Gwendolyn, a woman not much given to demonstrative gestures, patted her head awkwardly. 'There now, if you assure me that you are—are—that you have nothing to worry about in that direction,' she said, her customary frankness deserting her.

'There is nothing for *you* to worry about, Aunt,' Henrietta replied, not quite meeting her eyes.

Lady Gwendolyn pursed her lips, vastly relieved that Henrietta was her niece and not her daughter. 'Well, so we must hope,' she said drily, casting up a silent prayer that both their hopes would not be misplaced.

Chapter Eleven

Rafe spent an anxious night, pacing back and forwards in his bedchamber. Casting off his evening clothes, he pulled on a silk dressing gown. It reminded him of the brocade one Henrietta had worn that day at Woodfield Manor. She'd looked lost in it. And endearing. And he'd been unable to take his eyes off those lips of hers. Infinitely kissable, he'd called them.

A familiar clenching in his gut made him pace the room restlessly. Throwing open the casement, he gazed out on to the street. Not a sign of life. Not a light in any other window. Just a few streets away, in Berkeley Square, Henrietta would be tucked up in her bed. He wondered if she was sleeping. He wondered if she was thinking of him. He wondered what she was thinking of him.

Dammit all to hell and back!

It was too late, much too late to fool himself into thinking he didn't care. He did and it frightened him, all the more so because he suspected that *how* he cared, and how much, were quite different from the last time, with Julia. All his experience had taught him just how painful caring could be. He wouldn't go through that again. And, more importantly, he wouldn't let Henrietta go through it. He couldn't offer her happiness, that was not in his grasp, but he could make sure he did not make her more unhappy, even if it meant the ultimate sacrifice of giving her up.

For this really was the end. There was nowhere else to go. She had rejected what he could offer—he was not able to offer what she wanted. This was the end. Better a clean break, with the truth once and for all out in the open. He desperately needed her to understand. If he could not have anything else, at least there would be that.

Could he really bear it? Was he really going to tell her all those shameful, unsayable things, so long pent-up, lurking like rats in the dark corners of his mind, gnawing away at him day in, day out—*could* he? Even thinking about it made his gut wrench. But he had no option. A clean break with nothing left to fester. Perhaps then he could reconcile himself to life without her.

The ladies were breaking their fast next morning when a loud rap on the front door announced that a visitor had called at Berkeley Square. 'Really, who on earth can that be at such an ungodly hour?' Lady Gwendolyn asked, for it was far too early for morning callers.

She did not have to wait long for her curiosity to be satisfied. 'Lord Pentland is here, my lady, and requests an interview with Miss Markham,' her butler informed her.

Henrietta's coffee cup clattered into its delicate saucer, spilling the dregs on to the spotless white-linen cloth.

'We are not at home,' Lady Gwendolyn said firmly. 'Do sit back down, dear, and finish your meal.'

'But, Aunt Gwendolyn, I forgot to tell you.'

'Henrietta. I thought we had agreed last night that the subject was closed,' Lady Gwendolyn said, with a reproving look. 'Tell Lord Pentland we are most definitely not at home,' she said firmly to her waiting butler.

'You may tell me yourself. But then you quite patently *are* at home. Good morning, Lady Lattisbury-Hythe.' Rafe stood in the doorway, his hat in one hand, a riding crop in the other. 'Henrietta.' He bowed.

'Rafe! I mean, Lord Pentland. I mean—'

'What mean you by this unseemly interruption, my lord?' Lady Gwendolyn said in her haughtiest voice, reaching for her lorgnette.

'I have come to take your niece for a drive,' Rafe responded, quite unmoved by the fishy-eyed look he was receiving.

'My niece has no wish to go for a drive with you. In fact, my niece wishes to have nothing more to do with you under any circumstances.'

'I am sure you wish it were so,' Rafe said, pushing his way past the butler and entering the morning room, 'but the fact is that she has already made the engagement and I can assure you both it will prove most educational.'

'What arrangement? Henrietta, you would do well to heed my—'

But Henrietta was already pushing her chair back from the table. 'I am sorry, Aunt, but I must. I cannot—

you heard what Rafe—Lord Pentland said. Just this once…'

'If you are seen in his company in public, just this once may be enough to your sully your reputation for ever, especially after the exhibition you made of yourself at the dance last night,' Lady Gwendolyn said frankly. 'Henrietta! For heaven's sake, girl, if you must talk to the man, do so here in private. At least that way you will be safe from disapproving eyes. But I warn you, my lord,' she said, turning to Rafe, 'that the next time you come here uninvited I shall not hesitate to have you summarily shown off the premises, earl or no.'

'I assure you, my lady,' Rafe replied, 'I shall never again come here uninvited. I thank you for the offer of privacy, but I must decline. Henrietta, fetch your hat.'

He was looking quite distraught. Whatever he wanted to show her, it obviously meant a great deal to him. Henrietta planted a brief kiss on her aunt's cheek and left the room without further ado.

Seated beside Rafe in the phaeton ten minutes later, she was a mass of nerves. Clasping her hands in their pretty gloves, dyed emerald green to match her prom-enade dress and three-quarter pelisse, she was so intent on trying to calm herself after a sleepless night spent in fruitless speculation and woeful resolution that she did not register, until they crossed the river at Westminster Bridge, where they were headed.

Rafe drove in silence, a dark frown wreathing his features, giving him a saturnine look, taking a route that led them east of Lambeth towards the docks. Even when they could not see the river, obscured as it was by the huge warehouses that hugged its banks, its presence was mapped by the tall masts of the ships swaying against the gritty skyline. The streets were narrow and jammed full of traffic ferrying goods to and from the warehouses. Stevedores, sailors, draymen and port officials bustled about their business at top speed against a background of constant noise and chatter. The rich tang of spices, cinnamon and pepper, nutmeg and cloves, the ripe sweet smell of hogsheads of tobacco, the scent of perfumed tea from India—all wafted like a top-note on the breeze, overlaying the deeper base notes of muddy river water and dank streets overcrowded with horses and people.

People stared openly at Rafe's stylish equipage. It took Henrietta some time to notice that they were looking not in wonder, but in recognition. Hats were being tipped. Women were bobbing curtsies. A group of small ragged boys had accumulated behind them, running and jostling each other as they kept up. Beside her, Rafe lifted his whip in acknowledgement, occasionally called out a taciturn greeting. He showed a surprising knowledge of the warren of streets he navigated.

Not far from St Saviour's dock, itself not far from the notorious stews of Jacob's Island, which made Petticoat Lane look like Park Lane, he slowed the horses and made a sharp turn through a set of large, wrought-iron gates, the motley crew of urchins close behind them. The place looked like a town house, completely incongruous in its setting and obviously very newly built. With a spacious entrance fronted by four tall pillars, it had two identical wings, each of three stories, each with a set of long windows.

Rafe pulled the horses to a halt in the narrow court-yard and helped Henrietta down. Reaching into his pocket for a handful of pennies, he threw them at their entourage, to loud acclaim. 'Here, Frankie, take the horses round the back,' he said to the tallest of the boys.

'You know him?' Henrietta asked, wide-eyed.

Rafe shrugged.

'And you gave them money. You told me at St Paul's that—'

'These boys are not members of any gang. Yet.'

'How do you know?'

'I know their families.'

He could have laughed at her astonished expression, were he not so tense.

'St Nicholas's Lying-In Hospital,' Henrietta read on the brass plaque. 'Why on earth have you brought me here?'

'I wanted you to see it.'

She frowned, chewing on her lip. 'Are you one of the patrons, is that it? Is that how you came to know so much about those Bermondsey Boys you told me about?'

'I am one of the patrons. I suppose you could call me the founding member.'

'You mean you built it yourself?'

'Not with my own hands,' Rafe said with one of his enigmatic almost-smiles. 'And we do now have a growing number of sponsors these days. Not nearly enough, though. Caring for penniless mothers about to give birth to illegitimate children is not yet an acceptable good cause in polite society, as you know full well from your own charitable work,' he said grimly.

'The Poor House near our village does not allow illegitimate children to stay with their mothers,' Henrietta said sadly. 'They say that the sins of the mother would be visited on the child. It is one of the things that I cannot agree with Mama upon.'

'Well, here they are encouraged to stay together.'

'I can't believe you built this place.' Henrietta shook her head in utter amazement. 'It's so—so beautiful, peaceful, calm, even though it's surrounded by the bedlam out there.'

'It's here because this is where it's needed most. And it looks like this because we want people to come here. And it's left unmolested because the people who use it are also the local people, people with connections. They protect their own. Do you want to go in?'

She nodded. 'If you please.'

Rafe ushered her up to the main door and led her confidently through to a small room. 'This is Mrs Flowers, who is in charge of the nursing staff,' he said, introducing her to a sparrow-like woman dressed in grey kerseymere, who greeted Rafe with a beaming smile. 'You don't mind if I show Miss Markham round, do you?'

'Indeed, no, she is very welcome,' Mrs Flowers said, nodding in a friendly manner to Henrietta. 'We've five or six new arrivals since you were last here, my lord— we've been wondering where you'd got to. The new doctor has started and he's settling in nicely, you'll be pleased to know.'

'You have doctors. Goodness, that is unusual.'

'It is for lying-in, I know,' Mrs Flowers agreed, 'and, of course, if the mother prefers a midwife then that is what she has, but sadly our ladies are often ill as well as pregnant. It was my lord's idea, and a very good one at that. My lord here visits us nigh on every month,' she informed Henrietta, 'and always with some new notion for improving things. You'll see when he shows you round, always asking questions and making suggestions. Off you go, now, and take your time.'

As Henrietta followed Rafe from ward to day room to dining room to nursery, she was astonished by the reception he received. Women—girls, some of them—whether they were in an advanced state of pregnancy or clutching their newborn babes, greeted him not just with deference but with real affection. Rafe seemed quite at ease with them, chatting away about their existing children, enquiring about their husbands—which, to Henrietta's surprise, most of them seemed to have—and admiring the latest editions to their families. There was not a trace of the aloof and formidable earl. He seemed to have shed all reserve at the front door of the hospital. Here was yet another Rafe she did not recognise and Henrietta was enchanted. But it was the way he held the babies that was almost her undoing. Expertly supporting their wobbly little heads, he gazed into the unfocused blue eyes of each new-born with such an expression of tenderness that Henrietta felt the tears well.

'He's got a way with them,' a woman called Rose whispered to her, as she watched Rafe handing the newest of the babies back to its absurdly young mother. 'Don't throw them about like a sack of potatoes, the way my man does. You'll have nothing to worry about with him, love.'

'Oh, he's not my— We are not...' Henrietta protested.

'Get off, you're nuts about him, anyone can see that. Lucky you, he'll make gorgeous little ones. You just wait and see.'

Shaking her head, frantically sniffing back the tears, Henrietta asked for permission to hold Rose's daughter. Burying her nose in the delightful scent of the baby's neck, the notion of a child, her and Rafe's child, filled her for a brief moment with a surge of such yearning, she failed to see him looking at her, regret and sorrow darkening his eyes. By the time she looked up, he was on his feet, making his farewells, waiting patiently for her to rejoin him.

Back in the book room, taking tea with Mrs Flowers while Rafe attended to some business, Henrietta felt dazed. The woman could not enthuse enough about the support Rafe gave the hospital. 'He's a saint, in our eyes,' she said. 'It's not just money he gives, Miss Markham, but his time. He never fails to listen and he never judges. There's some of these lying-in places won't take unmarried women, never mind those who— well, let's say they're not exactly respectable. But here at St Nicholas's they know they won't be turned away. The most important thing is for us to do all we can to keep mother and babe together, no matter what the mother may be. And it works—mostly,' Mrs Flowers said proudly.

'Of course we have our failures,' she continued. 'Some women just can't cope. And some—well, some don't want to, and I don't just mean the people from round here, either. We might be in the heart of Bermondsey, but it's not so very far away from Mayfair. Some of the foundlings we find at the back door come swaddled in the finest linen, wrapped in blankets of the softest lamb's wool. We try to find them proper homes with proper families, our foundlings—his lordship has had several babes adopted by his estate workers. But sometimes we can't and then we have to send them on to the Foundling Hospital in Bloomsbury Fields. We don't like to do that, but—well, there's only so much you can do,' Mrs Flowers said sadly.

Henrietta recalled Rafe's words: *there are too many of them.* She had thought he was being callous, when he had been speaking from experience. Real experience. Far more real than her own pathetic attempts at making a difference. Touched beyond measure by what she had seen at St Nicholas's, she finally realised that what she had taken for Rafe's cynicism that day at St Paul's was actually simple realism. St Nicholas's was a ray of hope, but it was a very small one in the midst of a very dark existence.

What an idiot he must have thought her. When she remembered some of the things she'd said, she felt like a complete fool. Recalling her resolve that day in the stews of Petticoat Lane, to do more in future, she realised she could probably do no better than to consult Rafe on the subject. Then she remembered that, after today, she was not likely to see Rafe again.

'Well, now, I'd best be getting on.' Mrs Flowers bustled to her feet and shook Henrietta's hand. 'It was lovely to meet you, Miss Markham. I hope to see you again. I'll send his lordship up.'

'It's been wonderful. You should be so proud of your

hospital, Mrs Flowers. I've never seen anything quite so— Thank you.'

'Don't thank me. If it wasn't for his lordship there wouldn't be a hospital. He's a fine gentleman. One of the finest in England, if I'm any judge. But then you must already know that. Goodbye, Miss Markham.'

Mrs Flowers left in a swish of starched apron, which she had donned over her kerseymere dress. Alone, Henrietta sat on a straight-backed chair staring into space. Questions, as ever, swirled around her head. Why had he brought her here? How on earth was it related to what they had argued about last night? What did he mean, he did not deserve to be happy?

The door opened and Rafe strode in. 'You had tea?'

'Yes, thank you. Mrs Flowers was most kind. What Papa would call the salt of the earth.'

He was leaning against the small wooden mantel behind the desk. As ever, he was dressed extremely modishly. Dark blue coat with long tails. His neckcloth was intricately tied, a small diamond pin nestling in its snowy folds. His waistcoat was silver-and-dove-grey stripes. The tight-knit pantaloons which encased his legs were also dove grey. His boots were so glossy she could have seen her face in them if she had dared to look. His hair was blue-black, even glossier than his boots. And his face. His face was as it always was. There was a sheen to him of polished perfection. Yet underneath that sheen, so many flaws, so many contradictions and yet so many admirable qualities.

Who was he? Earl, knight errant, rake or philanthropist? The man she loved. Her heart squeezed painfully. She did love him, there was no doubt of that, despite all.

'Rafe, what you have done here, it's—words fail me. I feel so small, thinking of how ineffectual have been my attempts in comparison. You should be proud. I wish I could be part of something so wonderful. Really, truly, it's an admirable place.'

Rafe looked uncomfortable. 'You give me too much credit. I did not start St Nicholas's for philanthropic reasons. I'm not a do-gooder.'

'Like my parents, you mean? No, I know you're not. You're much more practical. Rafe, I wish—'

'Henrietta!'

She jumped.

'Henrietta, you're not listening. I didn't do this for altruistic reasons. At least not at first. I did it to atone.'

His fists were clenched. His shoulders were rigid. He was in the grip of some emotion more fearful than she had yet seen. 'What do you mean, atone?' she asked.

'I thought if I helped those women keep their babies, it would make me feel better. Atone in some small way. For the child I did not keep. Did not want.'

She had the awful sensation of standing on the edge of a steep staircase, knowing she was about to be pushed. She didn't want to know, but she had to ask. 'What child?'

'Mine. Mine and Julia's.'

'What happened to it?'

He couldn't say it, yet he had to say it. A clean break so that he could reconcile himself to their parting, he reminded himself. Last night, alone in his bedchamber, suffering from the after-effects of that ballroom confrontation, it had seemed possible, sensible even. Now, he wasn't so sure. Such a terrible admission—could he really make it? He needed to let her in, in order to let her go, but would the pain of it destroy him?

'Rafe? Rafe, what happened to it? The child.'

He braced himself. It was now or never. He could not face any more regrets. He took a jagged breath. 'I killed it.'

Henrietta's mouth fell open. She must have misheard. Surely she had misheard. 'You killed it?' Her voice was nothing more than a whisper.

'And Julia. I am responsible for her death, also.'

'You can't mean—no, Rafe, you *would* not—I don't believe you. You are not a murderer'

'As good as.'

The floor seemed to be moving. There was a whooshing noise like the sea in her ears. Rafe was still talking, but he sounded as if he was far away, behind a wall of glass. Henrietta could see his mouth moving, but she couldn't make out what he was saying. 'Wait. Stop. I can't—I'm sorry, I didn't…' She clutched her brow and took some deep breaths. This was important. Vitally important. Far too important for her to fall into a faint.

Rafe was looking at her with concern. 'Are you all right? Shall I fetch you some water?'

She waved him away. 'No. I'm all right. Please. Just tell me.'

He sat heavily down on the chair behind the desk upon which was a stack of leather-bound ledgers and picked up a quill. 'You remember—I told you that Julia and I resumed our marriage three years after we had separated?'

Henrietta nodded. 'You said it was for the sake of an heir.'

'It was such a mistake, that reunion, from start to finish. I knew it was wrong. I knew for a fact that I didn't love her, would never love her. But duty was such an ingrained habit, I didn't think through at all what bringing a child into the world would actually mean—any more than Julia did, I believe. When she told me she was pregnant...'

The pen nib bent as he stabbed it on the blotter. 'It was my fault. I shouldn't have taken her back. Julia was—she was—she knew, you see. It was obvious, I suppose, that I went to her bed only out of a sense of duty—no, that's not fair. I made no attempt to pretend and she— It was not her fault, it was just as bad for her, I presume. I'm sorry, I'm not explaining myself very well.'

'Rafe, you are explaining yourself. It's hard because it's a horribly painful thing. If you were more—' she broke off and shrugged '—then you would be feeling less. I know how hard it must be for you. I do know, I promise. I'm listening. Just take your time.'

He grimaced. 'I've never told anyone any of this before, but I needed you to— Anyway, Julia hadn't really forgiven me for our separation and she thought I hadn't forgiven her for being unfaithful. The truth is, I didn't care, which was worse, certainly more hurtful, though I didn't think about that at the time. I was using her to get what I wanted and she was using me. It was a recipe for disaster. We both knew it. I think we were both starting to recognise it, but it was too late by then. Julia was pregnant.'

Rafe drew a shaky breath, forcing himself to go on. Across from him, Henrietta sat perfectly still, her face chalk white. For once, he had no idea what she was thinking. 'The night she told me, I'll never forget it. I realised, you see, that I didn't want a child. Not Julia's child.' He dropped his head into his hands. 'I hadn't realised what it would mean,' he said. 'I was so bloody stupid, I'd thought about an having an heir, but I hadn't thought about having a baby. I hadn't thought about being a father. I had no idea. No bloody clue.'

'But, Rafe, today, with the babies in the nursery, you were so gentle with them—the expression on your face when you held them, you looked so moved. I thought— and Rose thought, too—what a perfect father you would make.'

He shook his head vehemently. 'No, you're wrong. You're quite wrong. I don't deserve such a precious gift. I had my chance and I destroyed it, I don't deserve another. I didn't realise back then how lucky I was. All I could think about was that I'd fail…between us, Julia and I would fail as parents. I was frightened I wouldn't be able to love it because Julia was its mother. I'd realised by then what I hadn't thought of before, that a child would bind us together. I didn't want to be tied to Julia.'

'Oh, Rafe, I wish you could have— Don't you see, what you were feeling is not so very unusual. Of course you were frightened, most new parents are, but once the baby was born…

'It wasn't born. My baby wasn't born. I told you, I killed it.'

'And I've told you, I can't believe you would do such a thing.'

'But I did, Henrietta. Julia had always been unstable,

but her pregnancy made her mood swings much more marked. She hated what the child was doing to her body. She didn't want it, any more than I did, but she was much more vocal on the subject. I thought it was just the old Julia, trying to manipulate me. I didn't realise she was so close to the edge. I thought her taunts and her petty accusations were just the same old games. I paid her no heed. I didn't want to. I didn't care. I was too racked by my own guilt. Too taken up by my own cares to see that Julia's fears were real. As our child grew inside her, she became more and more hostile. To me. To the baby. She kept threatening to rid herself of it, to take things— I had to have Mrs Peters watch her.'

'My God, Rafe, I can't believe—'

'Don't. Don't say anything. Just let me finish.' Rafe stared sightlessly down at the desk blotter, lost in the nightmare of his past. 'It was at Woodfield Manor. We were alone there but for the servants. Julia didn't want anyone to see her in what she called her bloated state. We were on the second floor, looking at the old nursery. Julia was in one of her moods. I hope it's a girl, she said. More likely it's a monster, sprung from your loins. On and on she went, until she'd worked herself up into such a rage. I've never seen the like, and still I didn't realise…'

He pushed his chair back and went over to the little window. With his back to her, he continued, his speech rushed now, words tumbling from him in his anxiety to have done with them. 'She said she wished she was dead. She said the agony of childbirth was too much for her to bear. She said it would kill her. She said she'd rather kill herself than bear it. She was always threatening to kill herself. I didn't think she meant it. I told her she could do as she wished. She went over to the window. I can still see it now. It seemed to happen so slowly, though it was all over in seconds. She threw the casement open—and then she jumped. She just jumped. So quickly, without a word, not even a sound as she fell—it was as if she had never been in the room. I didn't move. Not until I heard the cry from below. Molly Peters's husband it was who found her.'

He swayed and Henrietta jumped to her feet, staggering with the weight of him as he fell into her arms. 'I couldn't stop her, but I didn't try to,' Rafe said. 'I drove her to it. I didn't love her. I didn't try to make her happy. I didn't want her. I didn't want our baby. I killed her. I killed them both.'

'Rafe, oh God, Rafe. I can't believe—I had no idea you had been through such torments. Must still be going through them. It is awful. Awful. I can't begin to comprehend how awful.'

The scene he had so vividly described replayed over and over in Henrietta's head as she struggled with the enormity of Rafe's totally unexpected confession. She was aghast. Absolutely horrified. 'I just can't believe—God, what you must have gone through.'

'My suffering is deserved.'

'At least Julia's is over,' Henrietta whispered, more to herself than to Rafe, in an effort to make sense of what he had told her. 'Such a very unhappy person she sounds. She must have been a little deranged by her pregnancy. She would not have been responsible for her actions. Poor woman. Poor, poor little baby. Oh, Rafe, if only you'd had the opportunity, you would have loved the child, I know you would have. I could not doubt that, after seeing you today.'

Rafe grasped her by the shoulders, forcing himself to meet her eyes, caring not for the fact that his own were suspiciously bright. 'Henrietta, can't you see? Nothing I can do, no amount of babies and mothers saved, will make up for the child I lost. I thought they would. That's why I built this place. I thought it would help, but it didn't.'

He pushed her away. Henrietta slumped back down on her seat, tugging at the ribbons of her bonnet. Her head was aching. She had no idea what to say. Rafe's face was a blank—his confession had clearly flayed him clean of emotion. She shook her head, as if doing so would clear the fog of confusion that shrouded her mind. She had to try to make sense of things. She needed to, for both their sakes. 'But you have atoned,' she said slowly. 'You continue to atone. St Nicholas's is obviously making an enormous difference. Without it, I don't doubt any number of those babies would not have made it into the world.'

All true, but it wasn't the point. She needed to explain, because he quite obviously didn't understand it all himself. Guilt. That's what he was feeling. That's what drove him. Of course it was. So simple and yet so utterly complex. She felt like sobbing. Instead she forced herself to speak, though she had a horrible suspicion that the end of her speech would signal her own downfall.

'You're tearing yourself apart, Rafe.' Her voice was too much of a whisper. She swallowed. Throat dry. She coughed. 'Guilt. It's guilt. What happened is awful.

Horrible. I simply don't have the words. You are not blameless, but you are nowhere near as much at fault as you believe. Julia and the baby are dead, and nothing you can do will bring them back. Maybe there was nothing you could have done to prevent them suffering in the first place. I don't know, no one knows that, but I do know there is no point at all in continuing to torment yourself. You are allowing what happened to destroy you.'

Rafe made a bitter sound, like a demon laughing. 'I don't deserve anything else, Henrietta. I don't care about myself. What I'm trying to do is stop myself destroying you, too.'

The new twist in his logic threw her. 'Me?'

'I would make you miserable. I have given up the right to be happy. I've given up the right to love. I gave those things away when I killed my wife and child.' His voice cracked. 'I can't offer you those things, even if I wanted to, and you won't accept less—why should you? Now do you understand?'

Henrietta got to her feet, pushing her way past Rafe over to the window, where she pressed her forehead against the glass. Her skin was burning, though she felt freezing. The dread that had been lurking in the shadows of her traumatised mind began to edge its way towards centre stage. She wanted so desperately to help him. She wanted with all her heart to help him, but she could not surrender her soul to him, and that is what she would be doing if she gave in now, if she did not walk away. 'Your giving up the right to happiness is your true penance, isn't it?' Her voice seemed drained of all emotion. Already, she felt defeated, too tired to continue, though she knew she had to, must, or she would be lost. 'Is that what you are saying?'

Rafe nodded.

'Yes. Yes, I see it now.' And how much she wished she were blind, for what she saw was the end, the inevitable, inescapable conclusion she must reach. She spoke with the slow, weary precision of a judge delivering the death sentence. 'I wish with all my heart that I could ease the pain you must feel every day. I cannot imagine what it must be like. I wish you could see, Rafe, I truly wish that you could see that you are not wholly at fault, that there is a time for repenting and a time for taking what you have been given and making the best of it.' She paused for breath. It was painful. 'Do you really think this endless flaying of yourself serves any real purpose? Have you not acknowledged your faults, have you not changed? Is it not time that you forgave yourself?' Her voice was pleading now, though she knew she was advocating the impossible.

'How can I?'

He was too entrenched in his guilt, too far gone for her to reach. She could cast him the rope, but if he would not pull himself to safety, unless she released him, she, too, would drown. 'I can't tell you that,' Henrietta said with infinite sadness. 'I'm sorry. I wish with all my heart that I could but I can't, and so it seems then we must both be condemned to a lifetime of unhappiness.'

'What do you mean?'

'I thought you'd have realised by now,' she said wearily. 'I love you. I'm in love with you.' The words she had so longed to speak fell flat and empty, like her heart. 'I can't ever be happy without you, so you see, by punishing yourself you are punishing me.'

'Henrietta! Don't say that.'

'Don't worry, I won't say it again,' she said, unable to keep the trace of bitter hurt from her voice, 'I know perfectly well my love means nothing to you, but it's precious to me, and I won't let you destroy it.'

'That's not what I said. I meant— Henrietta, I meant— I just—'

'I'm sorry, I just can't take any more. I just can't. I wish I could help you. I wish you would help yourself. I wish that we wanted the same things. Oh God, Rafe, you have no idea how much I wish that, but I can't have what I want, and you can't give me what I want, and I can't live with what you can offer so—can't you see how hopeless it all is?' Her voice broke. She had no hope left. She was too empty even to feel the pain. Her limbs felt heavy, borne down with the dreadful things Rafe had told her. Her heart lay like a leaden weight in her chest. She jammed her bonnet on to her head. Tears burned behind her lids like acid. 'Please, just take me home.'

'Henrietta.' She looked defeated. He had never seen her look defeated before. He didn't want it to end like this. It didn't feel right. It didn't feel like the clean break he had planned. He didn't want—oh God, he didn't know what he wanted. But Henrietta was already opening the door, descending the stairs, clutching at the polished banister for support. Henrietta was walking away and there seemed to be nothing he could do to stop her. He had nothing left to say, after all. But it felt wrong, wrong, wrong.

* * *

The drive back, away from the docks, crossing the river by the new Waterloo Bridge, from a cityscape of oppressive squalor to opulent excess, had been accompanied by silence. At Berkeley Square, Henrietta got out of the phaeton without saying goodbye. She could not bear to look at him, lest she break down. She so desperately didn't want to break down. She made her way quickly to the sanctuary of her bedchamber, relieved to hear that Aunt Gwendolyn had gone out and would go straight on to dinner with Emily Cowper's gathering of Canningites.

She left word with her maid that she did not want to be disturbed until morning. Then she discarded her gown and crawled into bed in her undergarments. Burrowing her head under the pillow, she waited on the tears, but they would not fall. They seared her eyes and lids, but they would not fall. She was icy cold, shivering under the mound of blankets. She was bereft of words and thoughts. Emptied of emotion, she lay, listening to the clock ticking and her heart beating, though it felt like every beat signalled another small, excruciatingly painful, death.

Chapter Twelve

Rafe drove back to Mount Street, barely aware of having made the journey, narrowly avoiding numerous collisions along the way. Handing over the reins of his phaeton, he demanded of his bemused groom that a fresh horse be sent round immediately. Pacing the front steps, clutching his riding crop in one hand and his beaver hat in the other, his frown was forbiddingly deep. An acquaintance, on the brink of doffing his hat and passing the time of day, instead traversed to the other side of the street, averting his gaze. He had seen that look on Rafe St Alban's face once before and did not care to repeat the experience, nor witness the consequences. The crossing boy who habitually earned a sixpence from him chose to hide behind the pillar of the house next door. Careless of the fact that he was quite inappropriately dressed for riding, Rafe mounted, dismissing his groom curtly, urged the chestnut into a canter that would have been dangerous, were he not such an accomplished horseman, and made for Hyde Park.

It was relatively quiet at this time of day. Ignoring the prohibition, Rafe loosed his hold on the frisky horse and gave his mount free rein. The gallop took both their breaths away, as well as that of several outraged onlookers. Finally pulling up, both horse and man panting heavily, Rafe found he felt no better for it.

What the devil was wrong with him? What the devil had gone wrong? He'd wanted her to understand. She'd understood too well. This infuriating thought carried him round another circuit of the park, this time taken at something very slightly less than neck or nothing.

A clean break, he'd thought. But the break felt jagged, as if it would never heal. Not an ending, but something much bleaker. A black mood settled on Rafe, darker than any he had known for a long time. The future looked not grim, but impenetrable. The past equally foggy, clogged as it was now by Henrietta's insights. He felt as if she had taken a well-thumbed book and rewritten it.

Another circuit, at a slow canter this time, was completed before he turned back through the gates. He made his way back to Mount Street, his horse streaming with sweat. The problem with Henrietta—*one* of the problems with Henrietta—was that she never lied. Never.

Doubt, that most stealthy of creatures, had sidled into his mind, sowing the seeds of questions he didn't want to ask, let alone answer. Sitting in his favourite wingback chair in the ground-floor library, surrounded by the ancient tomes his ancestors had acquired with a view to populating the polished walnut shelves rather than their own minds, Rafe fought to reassemble the past in the image he had for so long held deep in his heart, but it was like trying to force the wrong pieces of a dissected puzzle back into place. Distorted. Mangled. A different picture was emerging.

Had he ever loved Julia? He'd thought so at the time, but now—no. Infatuated he might have been, but not in love. How could he be so sure? He didn't know, but he was.

His butler had set out a silver tray of decanters upon the desk. Rafe poured himself a small glass of Madeira, but set it aside after one sip. He needed to think and needed a clear head in order to do so. Guilt. Looking back to those early days of his marriage, he recognised its presence like a shadow. Guilt because he knew he did not love Julia enough. Guilt when he inevitably failed to make her happy.

Guilt, guilt and more guilt for his failure, and then his failing to care enough to try harder. It had not helped, his upbringing with its enormous sense of obligation. He had been raised to be the bearer of burdens. He felt guilty when Julia's unfaithfulness gave him the excuse he was looking for to separate. And he'd felt guilty enough about that to try again. Guilt it was that had driven him to the reconciliation, guilt fed this time by his grandmother, whose ceaseless sponsorship of the claims of the title to an heir he had allowed to sway him. And guilt every time he had forced himself to go to Julia's bed, going through the motions, the pretext of desire, making no attempt to sweeten the pill for her—his own petty punishment. And the ultimate guilt: his rejection of his own child. The two deaths that had resulted from that.

Guilt. Henrietta was right. It was destroying him.

Rafe picked up his Madeira glass, raised it to his mouth, stared at it uncomprehendingly and put it back down again. Henrietta. Such a ridiculous name and yet so very appropriate. She said it was time to forgive himself. Was she right about that, too?

He forced himself for the second time that day to replay the painful facts. Forced himself to ask the painful questions he had asked himself so many times, only this time, he tried to answer without the bias of guilt. He tried to answer them as Henrietta would want him to. As if she had reset his moral compass. *Was he wholly to blame? Could he have done this differently, or that? Had he cared more, or less, would it have changed things?*

He and Julia should never have married, but they had. Duty and circumstances and, yes, in the early days, affection and desire had conspired to join them together. Duty and circumstance had conspired to make them try that second fatal time. They were not faultless, but they were neither of them wholly to blame. Henrietta was right about that, too.

And the child? His child. Their child. Had it been born, would he really have rejected it? He recalled the countless little bundles—other people's bundles—he had held in his arms since founding St Nicholas's. Such helpless, utterly trusting, tiny little beings, smelling of milk and that distinctive baby smell. He allowed himself to remember the yearning, aching longing that enveloped him every time. The fierceness of his desire to keep them safe. The regret each time he handed them back to their mothers. The anxiety each time he watched mother and baby leave.

Relief so immense as to be palpable made him limp. He would not have rejected his own child. He might have wished it born under different circumstances, he might have continued to wish himself free of its mother, but he would not have rejected it. Henrietta was right about that, too. 'God dammit, of course she was!' Rafe exclaimed.

He smiled to himself, for he never used to talk to himself out loud, until he met Henrietta. Henrietta Markham, who had made him face up to some excruciatingly painful truths, who had not flinched from pointing out his wrongs, yet whose sympathy and empathy he never doubted. Henrietta Markham, who said she loved him.

Rafe sat bolt upright. Henrietta loved him. She was in love with him! Bloody hell, she was in love with him. She'd told him so and he'd been so damned caught up in everything else that he'd barely even registered it.

She loved him. Henrietta loved him. What a fool he had been not to see it before. Nothing else would have induced her to give herself to him. No wonder she had been so hurt by his offer. No wonder it was not enough, nor ever could be. Henrietta loved him. Being Henrietta, she would never, ever settle for anything less than everything.

And he? God, what a mull of it he had made. That damned stupid halfway-house proposition of his must have seemed contemptuous, as if he had thrown her love back in her face! 'Dammit, what a bloody, blind, damned fool I've been.' Rafe threw his Madeira glass across the room. It shattered with a satisfying crack on the claw foot of his desk, spraying the rug with wine.

All or nothing. All or nothing. He had chosen nothing and it felt fundamentally wrong. They were meant to be together. He could see that now, so clearly. Unbearably clearly. Just as he could see that he needed to do something about it, and urgently. Because—because…

'Dammit, because I love her!'

He loved her. *That* was why he was now so certain that he had never loved Julia. He loved Henrietta and it felt utterly different from anything he had ever felt before. He loved her. It was true. It must be true, because the bars of the cell in which he had deliberately imprisoned his heart had been suddenly flung open. All he had to do was to step forwards into the light and claim the prize. All he had to do was forgive himself. To stop paying penance, and start the process of redemption. Could he?

Rafe closed his eyes. He took each of his sins and held it up for inspection. Then he laid each down, saying a solemn farewell. The past was not gone, but already the scars were fading. He did not yet feel he deserved to be happy, but he did feel he deserved to try. Love. Love for Henrietta would be his redemption. From their love would grow happiness. A future worth inhabiting.

He wanted to start inhabiting it now. Galvanised by this thought into action, Rafe threw open the door of the library. If happiness really was within his grasp, he would reach out and take it. 'Now, without further ado,' he said to his startled footman.

'My lord?'

'My hat. My gloves,' Rafe said. 'Quickly, man, quickly.'

The items were handed over. Before Edward could pluck up the courage to point out to his master that he was expected to dine with the Dowager Countess in an hour and could not do so in pantaloons and a tailcoat, Rafe was out of the door, down the stairs and heading for Berkeley Square on foot.

It had taken him less than five minutes to reach Lady Gwendolyn's house. He rang the bell impatiently, pushed past her butler impatiently, demanded even more impatiently that Miss Markham be produced at once.

'Miss Markham has retired for the night, my lord,' the butler informed him. 'She gave us most strict instructions that she should not be disturbed. Lady Gwendolyn said—'

'Where is her ladyship?' Rafe demanded, forgetting all about his promise made earlier that day never to cross the threshold of Berkeley Square again uninvited. 'Fetch her, she will rouse Henrietta.'

'Lady Gwendolyn has gone to Lady Cowper's for dinner. I think Miss Markham has the migraine, she did not look at all well when she returned,' the butler said confidentially, though he was beginning to harbour a suspicion that Lord Pentland was the source of Miss Markham's illness.

'Then what I am about to tell her may affect the cure. Fetch her.'

'Lord Pentland…'

'Fetch her now, or I will fetch her myself. In fact, if you tell me where her bedchamber is…'

'My lord! Please, I beg of you, I cannot allow you to do that, her ladyship would have me summarily dismissed— I beseech you, if you will just wait in one of the salons I will endeavour to wake her.'

'Very well, see that you do. Tell her she has five minutes, or I'll come and get her myself.'

Scandalised and fascinated, Lady Gwendolyn's butler scurried up the stairs with Rafe at his heels. Showing his lordship, who had clearly gone quite mad, into a small but elegant withdrawing room, he continued to the second floor, there to tap tentatively on Miss Markham's bedchamber door.

Henrietta was still awake, still in shock, still unable to cry. She ignored the gentle knock on the door, but it came again, louder and more insistent this time. Clutching a wrapper around her, she dragged herself to the door and opened it tentatively.

'Beg pardon, miss,' the butler said, 'I know this is most irregular, but Lord Pentland is downstairs and absolutely insists on seeing you.'

'I can't see him, I won't.'

'Miss, I fear that if you do not—'

'If you do not, I will drag you out of your room myself,' Rafe said, making the butler, who had not heard his footsteps on the stairs, jump clean into the air.

'My lord, you should not—'

'Rafe! What are you doing here?'

'Henrietta, I need to talk to you. It is imperative that I talk to you.'

'No. I can't. There is nothing more left to say.'

'Henrietta…'

'My lord, if you would just…'

'Rafe, just go away.'

'Henrietta! I love you.'

It was hard to say who was more astounded by this declaration. Lady Gwendolyn's stately butler's jaw dropped in a most un-stately manner. Henrietta clutched at the doorknob, letting her hold on her wrapper go and revealing to both Rafe and the butler rather more of the satin and lace she wore next to her skin than either was prepared for.

Rafe himself was so astonished that he could for a moment think of nothing else to say after such momentous words, uttered in such completely mundane circumstances, though he recovered his poise more quickly than his audience.

'Now you know why my business with Miss Markham was so urgent. You can leave us alone and you would be doing me an enormous service if you would ensure our privacy is undisturbed,' he said to the butler. 'As you can imagine, there are a number of delicate matters that require further discussion.' He then prised Henrietta's hand free of the door handle. 'I think it would be safer to talk downstairs rather than in your chamber,' he said, leading her quickly past the gaping butler, back to the room on the first floor to which he had been originally shown.

'Rafe, I—'

'Sit down.'

'Rafe, I—'

'And listen.'

Henrietta sat down. She had no option, for her knees were shaking so much.

Rafe sat by her side and took her hand, rubbing it

between his to heat it. The elation that had carried him from Mount Street to here had deserted him. Now he was so nervous it felt as if a cloud of small butterflies were flapping their wings frantically inside his stomach. 'You were right,' he said finally.

'What about?'

'Everything?' His smile made a brief appearance. He swallowed hard. 'You were right. I've been hiding. I've been afraid.' Now he had started, it was getting easier. 'I've been hiding behind the terrible things that happened, allowing the pain and the guilt to blind me to the truth. I let guilt dictate how I behaved, who I was. I closed myself off lest I expose myself to hurt again. You were right. I've not been living, I've merely been existing, lurking in the shadows of life, holding it cheap. You were right about that, too, Henrietta.' His smile made another brief appearance. 'You see, I meant it. You were right about it all.'

'Oh.'

Rafe laughed. He picked up her hand and rubbed it against his cheek. 'Did you think I wasn't listening to you?'

'I thought you didn't want to,' she said frankly.

'I didn't, but in the end I had no option because there was something I wanted far more and until I faced up to the past I could never hope to have it.'

'What?'

'You.'

'Oh.'

'Henrietta, I know I'm not innocent of blame. I'm not as black as I've painted myself, but I'm no saint. I can't undo the wrongs I've done. I can't escape the fact that

I've done wrong, but I can do as you said. I can forgive myself.'

'Oh, Rafe, do you mean it?'

'Really and truly,' he said, his smile breaking through again. 'You've made me see that I can. Ever since I set eyes on you, you've been like a shaft of sunshine forcing its way through the clouds. Like a blinding ray of pure light coming through a door which is only slightly ajar. I knew what I felt for you was different, right from the start. But the very intensity of it frightened me. I felt exposed. Raw. Vulnerable.'

Her heart was thudding in a peculiar new way. Heavy beats that still left her breathless. She was afraid to hope. Like Rafe, she could see the light shining through the door, but he was still on the other side.

'I love you, Henrietta. I want to spend the rest of my life with you.' Rafe slipped on to the floor and knelt at her feet, clasping her hand between his. 'I love you, and I hope—I hope so very, very much—that you have it in your heart to forgive me for being such an idiot as not to recognise it before. Please, darling Henrietta, say it's not too late.'

'Oh, Rafe, of course it's not too late. I love you. I will always love you. How could you ever have doubted it?'

It was all he needed to hear. He swept her into his arms and kissed her. For the first time in his life, he kissed a lover's kiss, the kiss of a man who loves and is loved in return. Her mouth tasted all the sweeter. Her embrace felt infinitely more delightful. It was a kiss that was a promise of kisses to come, a kiss that lit up the world, forcing the cloud that had hung over him for so long to scud over the horizon and be for ever lost.

He got back down on to one knee. 'Henrietta, I most humbly ask you to do me the honour of becoming my wife. Darling, dearest, most enchanting and true Henrietta, marry me.'

'Oh, Rafe. Oh, Rafe. Do you mean it? Really? Truly?'

He pulled her towards him and kissed her lids. 'I mean it.' Her cheeks. 'Really.' Her upturned little nose. 'Truly.' He feathered kisses into the corners of her smiling mouth. 'I promise.' He rained kisses on to her brow. 'I love you. I love you, Henrietta Markham. I love you really and truly. I promise.'

She had toppled on to the floor beside him now. Their kisses were becoming feverish, their hands, anxious for the reassurance of the other's touch, plucking at clothes to reach skin. Henrietta's wrapper was cast to one side. 'Silk and lace,' Rafe murmured with a wolfish smile, burying his head between her breasts, where the lace edge of her chemise foamed over her flesh. His fingers were already undoing the laces of her stays. He pulled the chemise down to expose her nipples and, with a sigh of satisfaction, took one rosy pink bud into his mouth and sucked.

A jolt, like falling, ran between her nipples and her belly and her sex. Henrietta moaned deeply. Her head fell back to rest on the *chaise* on which she had been sitting only moments before. Rafe's mouth was doing the most delightful things. His fingers rolling her other nipple, tugging the most exquisitely intense shards of pleasure, sending waves of heat rolling and rippling through her. His coat and waistcoat lay discarded beside her wrapper. She slipped her hands under his shirt, tugging it free from his pantaloons. She could see the hard, solid length of his shaft clearly outlined. She stroked it through the tight-knit material, making him shudder, making herself shudder, too, in anticipation.

She wanted him now. She wanted him inside her now. Claiming her. Owning her. Possessing her. She wanted to feel skin on skin. Flesh inside flesh. Deep inside. Hard inside. Hot inside. 'Rafe,' she said urgently, tugging at his shirt. 'Rafe, please.'

He understood. Standing to disrobe quickly, without finesse, clothes landing incongruously on the furnishings of Lady Gwendolyn's salon, his shirt draped over a painted fire screen, his pantaloons wrapped around the delicately scrolled leg of a Hepplewhite pier table, though neither of them noticed. Wriggling out of her stays, her undergarments, Henrietta kept her eyes on Rafe. He was magnificent, naked. Her heart flip-flopped and stepped up to a higher rate as she stared with unashamed relish at the silken length of his manhood, nudging his belly. On her knees before him, she caressed it with her fingertips, then her tongue, the salty heat of him making her belly tighten, swelling and tensing the knot of arousal that burned between her thighs. She cupped him and he moaned again.

'Henrietta, I don't think I can wait much longer.'

'Rafe, I don't want you to.'

He pulled her to him. Kissed her deeply on the mouth. Pressed her hard against him, her breasts crushed to his chest, her thighs enveloping his erection. He kissed her again, then sank down on to the *chaise-longue*, pulling her down with him, on top of him, entering her with one long, swift, hard thrust that made them both gasp.

It was almost too much. Rafe felt himself tighten,

his shaft thicken, the prelude of the pulsing that would be his climax. Clutching on to the delightful curve of Henrietta's bottom, he held her still, breathing deep, resisting the overpowering urge to thrust up, waiting, breathing, holding her still, reaching down, between her dimpled thighs, to stroke the delicious wetness of her.

He stroked and Henrietta shuddered. She clenched her muscles around him, desperate for the thrusting friction that brought such delectable pleasure. Friction that his sliding, gliding fingers were rousing as they coaxed and then commanded the hard nub of her sex towards its climax. She could feel the rippling prelude. She tried to resist it, but it was too strong, a tide of feeling whipping her up, making her moan and arch; just when she thought she could bear it no longer, she climaxed, and into the ebb and flow of her orgasm Rafe gripped her waist and lifted her up, then let her fall, thrusting into her as she did, the force of her climaxing opening her for him.

She panted, picking up the rhythm, gripping his shoulders, lifting herself now, then encasing him, writhing on him as he thrust higher than before, and then again, and again, each lift and sheathing and thrust pulsing the purest of pleasure through her. With a moan that seemed to come from the depths of his being, he came, spurting his hot seed high inside her and telling her over and over that he loved her, loved her, loved her, gazing deep into her eyes, his face raw, ablaze with love, alight with the passion which that love fuelled. He kissed her again. She had never tasted such a kiss. It felt as if she were on the edge of the world. She had never kissed such a kiss, knowing that she loved and was loved. Would always be loved. For ever.

'Always,' Rafe said, reading her thoughts, stroking the wild curls that had become entangled with her lashes clear of her face, so that he could look into her eyes. Chocolate brown, striped with gold, glazed with love. 'I will love you always. I promise.'

'Darling Rafe, I believe you.'

'Darling Henrietta,' he said, looking over her shoulder at the chaos they had caused, 'you realise we are quite naked in your aunt's parlour and you have not yet formally agreed to be my wife. I had not thought you the type to prevaricate.'

Henrietta giggled. 'I think the fact that I am naked with you in my aunt's parlour is answer enough. Goodness, we didn't even lock the door.'

'I don't care about the door. Or the servants. Or even your aunt. Let me pose the question again. Henrietta Markham, will you marry me?'

She caught her breath as he smiled at her. His real smile. Somehow she knew she would be seeing a lot more of it in the future. 'Rafe St Alban, just try to stop me,' Henrietta replied.

Epilogue

It was not to be expected that Henrietta's parents would welcome their daughter's marriage to a notorious rake, no matter how well born or wealthy, without serious reservations. They had arrived in London, in response to the letter sent by Lady Gwendolyn when Henrietta had first arrived on her doorstep, to be greeted by this most unexpected and startling news. The explanation as to how this remarkable turn of events had come to pass, and so swiftly, necessitated their being appraised of the lurid tale of the Ipswich diamonds.

Mr Henry Markham, dressed habitually and entirely in brown clothes, which looked as if they dated, as indeed did their wearer, from some time in the middle of the previous century, was a tall man bent in the middle like a permanent question mark. His hair, a thick grey curtain through which his bald head rose like a brown-speckled egg, tangled with the folding legs of his brass eyeglasses, preventing them, when they slid down his nose—as they did at regular intervals—from actually quitting his face.

His wife was equally slim built, but there the resemblance ended. There was no doubt at all that Guinevere Markham had been, and still was, an extremely beautiful woman, with hair a rich Titian bronze, flawless skin, an equally flawless profile and perfectly arched brows under which eyes the same hue as her daughter's looked out at the world.

Guinevere's gaze was, however, not nearly as clear-sighted as her daughter's. Her perceptions for ever coloured by the loss of her innocence at the hands of a rake, she forbade Henrietta's marriage to a man who would, she claimed, weeping copious tears, break her innocent babe's heart.

Neither Henrietta's indignant protests, nor the publication of the forthcoming nuptials in the press, nor even the large emerald-and-diamond encrusted ring, which she wore upon the third finger of her left hand, had any effect on Mrs Markham. Her daughter, whose patience and loyalty was being tested beyond the limits, finally lost her temper and roundly informed Mama that she was three-and-twenty and therefore there was nothing Mama could do about it.

Into this heated exchange walked Lady Gwendolyn and out of this heated exchange emerged the truth of Guinevere's past.

'Which was rather a case of unrequited love than seduction,' Lady Gwendolyn frankly informed her niece, ignoring her sister's flapping denials. Guinevere, it seemed, was the one who did the pursuing. The gentleman in question was not interested in her declarations of love, any more than he was interested in her suggestion that they marry, since he was, in fact, already wed. 'Though to be fair,' Lady Gwendolyn said, 'the poor woman was more or less confined to their country estate by their brood of children.'

'I did not know, Gwen,' Guinevere protested faintly.

'Yes, you did, Gwinnie, for I told you myself,' Lady Gwendolyn said, 'but you were so set upon that blasted man that you weren't interested in listening.'

'He said he loved me.'

'No doubt he did, when you made it perfectly obvious that in return he could have you,' Lady Gwendolyn retorted.

'He said he would marry me.'

Lady Gwendolyn snorted. 'If he did, you knew very well it was a lie.' She eyed her sister through her lorgnette. 'All these years, I've kept my opinions to myself upon the subject, but I won't have you ruining Henrietta's chance of happiness with your foolishness.' She turned her attention back to her niece. 'The round tale is that your mother ran off with him, knowing full well that he had no honourable intentions at all. Our poor father brought her back, two nights after she left. As far as the world was concerned, of course, she was ruined. The fact that she went into a decline confirmed it, but the truth is that her decline was fuelled not by the loss of her innocence, but by the fact that he hadn't seduced her at all!'

With a soft sigh, Guinevere slumped into a faint on the floor. 'Leave her be,' Lady Gwendolyn said when Henrietta made to rush to her mother's aid. 'She always could faint at will. Your mother was not seduced, Hen-

rietta, she was rejected. That is why she went to live in
the country—of her own free will, I may add. Why she
married your poor father, I don't know. I suspect he fell
hook, line and sinker for her tragic tale and played the
knight errant. We all have a weakness for that. Whatever the reason, I trust you will not spoil his illusions.
The breach between us was Gwinnie's fault, you know.
She preferred to fabricate her own version of events and
didn't want me putting her straight. It's been so long
since anyone forced her to confront the truth, I expect
she doesn't know what it is any more.'

The revelations astounded Henrietta, but when she
confided them to her future husband, he laughed, and
confounded her by admitting that he'd always had his
suspicions about the truth of her mother's past. He did
not make the connection between Mrs Markham and his
dead first wife, but he did not have to. Henrietta made
it for herself and, for once, decided to say nothing more
upon the subject.

Mrs Markham was forced to resign herself to Henrietta's marriage. Her husband was rather more enthusiastic. Mr Markham, a kindly man with good intentions,
even if they were somewhat pedantic, had dedicated
his last few years to creating a map of penury. This,
he informed Rafe, would ensure that in future philanthropic efforts could be guided to the most appropriate
and most deserving of the poor. His future son-in-law
was rather impressed by this and saw merit in it, to
Henrietta's surprise. Mr Markham, in his turn, unim-
pressed by the generous settlements and title to which
his daughter was about to accede, was so affected by his

visit to St Nicholas's that he decided he could overlook Rafe's reputation. A mere five days after his permission for the union was initially sought, it was finally granted.

The wedding took place at the end of June and was hailed as the event of the Season. Everyone who was anyone attended the nuptials. Not to have received one of the gold-edged invitations was to be a social pariah. Lady Helen Ipswich was one such. Though not surprised, it did not make her pain at missing the society event of the year any less acute.

With her niece safely betrothed, Lady Gwendolyn had succumbed to the temptation of letting just the tiniest titbits of the stolen emeralds' story fall upon the ears of a select few. Helen Ipswich was shunned, not only in the best of circles, but in the worst—though to be fair, none of this was Rafe's doing. By the time Rafe was dressing to walk his bride up the aisle of St James's, Helen Ipswich had closed up her London house, packed her sons off to school and retired to the Continent where, as Lady Gwendolyn happily informed her sister, to whom she had been reconciled during the complex and costly process of providing Henrietta with a trousseau, Helen Ipswich would find herself quite at home among the loose morals of the French court.

At the ceremony, the ladies wept, the gentlemen harrumphed into their kerchiefs, Lucas Hamilton, in tribute to the solemnity of the occasion, remained almost sober, and all agreed that the proceedings were most touching, the bridegroom most handsome and the bride herself really rather charming. Though he had insisted on the biggest, most extravagant affair that could be arranged in the shortest amount of time, it could not be said that Rafe noticed, for he had eyes only for Henrietta. As she walked down the short aisle of St James's Church on her father's arm, his heart really did feel as if it were swelling in his chest with love. The sun could not shine brighter than the smile she gave him as he took her hand in his, nor could the stars compete with the look in her eyes when he made his vows and placed the ring upon her finger.

The passionate kiss they exchanged, shocking some of the congregation, filling others with longing and some with unabashed jealousy, sealed their vows. The wedding breakfast, the orange blossom, the champagne and the toasts—all were a blur as they sat together, hands clasped tight under the table, waiting for the time when they could be alone.

Later, the newly-weds made love slowly, disrobing each other item by item, unable to take their eyes from each other, the slow build from overture to crescendo lifting them together to a new plane upon which they began their married life.

They lived for most of the year in Woodfield Manor, their happiness filling the place with noise and joyous laughter, turning the once-sombre house into a home once more. 'It had become a mausoleum this place,' Mrs Peters said, a tear in her eyes, 'and look at it now. Filled with life, just as it should be.'

The cries of their adored first-born had added a new joy, yet another layer to their happiness, which, Rafe declared on the morning of their son's first birthday, could surely not increase further.

Henrietta, lying naked, propped on her side in their huge bed, smiled languorously at her husband. 'You say that at the start of every day,' she said, 'and at the end of every day you change your mind.'

Rafe rolled her on top of him. The crush of her soft curves had an achingly familiar effect. His erection strained between her thighs. 'I know. Isn't it amazing?' he said, kissing the corners of her smiling, infinitely kissable mouth. He could feel her heating, her sex dampening, her nipples hardening. 'Darling Henrietta, there is one way of ensuring that I shall say the same at the end of this day, too.' He wanted to be inside her. He rolled her over, taking one of her rosy nipples into his mouth and sucking hard, at the same time reaching down, between, inside, stroking with unerring precision, making her gasp and arch against the solid heft of his shaft.

'Rafe…'

'Henrietta, I can never get enough of you, you know that.'

'I know,' she said with a deep chuckle. 'And in a month or so, everyone else will know, too.'

'What do you mean?' Her eyes were shining, chocolate and gold. Her mouth was ripe. Like her body. 'Henrietta, do you mean…?'

She nodded. 'Are you pleased?'

'Pleased!' Rafe kissed her tenderly. 'I don't think I could be any happier. I didn't think it was possible to be any happier. I love you so much, my own, lovely, darling wife.' He kissed her softly rounded belly, then he kissed her mouth again.

Henrietta wrapped her arms around her husband. 'Show me how much,' she said, arching up against him. 'With pleasure,' he said. And he did.

* * * * *

HISTORICAL

Where Love is Timeless™

HARLEQUIN® HISTORICAL

COMING NEXT MONTH
AVAILABLE MAY 22, 2012

WEDDINGS UNDER A WESTERN SKY
Elizabeth Lane, Kate Welsh and Lisa Plumley
(Western)

MARRIAGE OF MERCY
Carla Kelly
(Regency)

UNBUTTONING MISS HARDWICK
Deb Marlowe
(Regency)

MY FAIR CONCUBINE
Jeannie Lin
(Tang Dynasty)

REQUEST YOUR FREE BOOKS!

 HARLEQUIN® HISTORICAL:
Where love is timeless

2 FREE NOVELS PLUS 2 **FREE GIFTS!**

YES! Please send me 2 FREE Harlequin® Historical novels and my 2 FREE gifts (gifts are worth about $10). After receiving them, if I don't wish to receive any more books, I can return the shipping statement marked "cancel." If I don't cancel, I will receive 6 brand-new novels every month and be billed just $5.19 per book in the U.S. or $5.74 per book in Canada. That's a savings of at least 17% off the cover price! It's quite a bargain! Shipping and handling is just 50¢ per book in the U.S. and 75¢ per book in Canada.* I understand that accepting the 2 free books and gifts places me under no obligation to buy anything. I can always return a shipment and cancel at any time. Even if I never buy another book, the two free books and gifts are mine to keep forever.

246/349 HDN FEQQ

Name _____ (PLEASE PRINT)

Address _____ Apt. #

City _____ State/Prov. _____ Zip/Postal Code

Signature (if under 18, a parent or guardian must sign)

Mail to the **Reader Service:**
IN U.S.A.: P.O. Box 1867, Buffalo, NY 14240-1867
IN CANADA: P.O. Box 609, Fort Erie, Ontario L2A 5X3

Not valid for current subscribers to Harlequin Historical books.

**Want to try two free books from another line?
Call 1-800-873-8635 or visit www.ReaderService.com.**

* Terms and prices subject to change without notice. Prices do not include applicable taxes. Sales tax applicable in N.Y. Canadian residents will be charged applicable taxes. Offer not valid in Quebec. This offer is limited to one order per household. All orders subject to credit approval. Credit or debit balances in a customer's account(s) may be offset by any other outstanding balance owed by or to the customer. Please allow 4 to 6 weeks for delivery. Offer available while quantities last.

Your Privacy—The Reader Service is committed to protecting your privacy. Our Privacy Policy is available online at www.ReaderService.com or upon request from the Reader Service.

We make a portion of our mailing list available to reputable third parties that offer products we believe may interest you. If you prefer that we not exchange your name with third parties, or if you wish to clarify or modify your communication preferences, please visit us at www.ReaderService.com/consumerschoice or write to us at Reader Service Preference Service, P.O. Box 9062, Buffalo, NY 14269. Include your complete name and address.